I0563115

Copyright Page

Published by: Osoria Asibor
Winnipeg, Manitoba
ISBN: 978-1-998308-11-8

This book is a work of nonfiction. The names, characters, businesses, organizations, places, events, and incidents are either the product of the author's imagination or used in a fictitious manner. Any resemblance to actual persons, living or dead, or actual events is purely coincidental.

Cover design by: Osoria Asibor
Printed in Canada
For permissions or more information, contact:
Osoria Asibor
standardwordz@gmail.com

Disclaimer: The information provided in this book is for educational and informational purposes only. The content is not intended to be a substitute for professional advice, diagnosis, or treatment. Always seek the advice of your physician, therapist, or other qualified health provider with any questions you may have regarding a medical condition or relationship issue. Never disregard professional advice or delay in seeking it because of something you have read in this book.

Dedication: This book is dedicated to all those who seek wisdom, love, and guidance in their relationships. May this work help you build stronger, healthier, and more fulfilling connections.

Acknowledgement

I would like to express my deepest gratitude to everyone who has supported me throughout the creation of this book. Your encouragement, prayers, and guidance have been invaluable.

First and foremost, I thank God for giving me the strength, wisdom, and inspiration to write this book. His love and guidance have been my constant source of motivation.

To my family, thank you for your unwavering support and love. Your patience and understanding have been my anchor during this journey. I am especially grateful to my spouse for being my rock and my greatest cheerleader.

I extend my heartfelt thanks to my friends and colleagues who provided feedback, encouragement, and constructive criticism. Your insights have greatly enriched this book and helped me present a more comprehensive and balanced perspective.

A special thank you to my church community for their spiritual support and for being a source of inspiration in my life. Your prayers and fellowship have been a blessing.

I also wish to acknowledge the readers of my previous works. Your feedback and support have been instrumental in shaping my writing journey. Your engagement and encouragement have kept me motivated to continue sharing my thoughts and insights.

Lastly, thank you to all the professionals who have helped me along the way, including editors, designers, and publishers. Your expertise and dedication have been essential in bringing this book to life.

To everyone who has been a part of this journey, whether mentioned here or not, I am deeply grateful. Your support has made this book possible, and I pray that it serves as a valuable resource for all who seek to build healthy, fulfilling, and God-honoring relationships.

Thank you.
Osoria Asibor
standardwordz@gmail.com

Purpose of the Book
Guarding Your Heart: A Biblical Perspective

Marriage is a sacred covenant, ordained by God as a union between a man and a woman. As Christians, we understand that entering into this covenant is a significant decision that impacts not only our earthly lives but also our spiritual journey. The Bible teaches us in Proverbs 4:23, "Above all else, guard your heart, for everything you do flows from it." This book aims to help you guard your heart by recognizing the red flags that may indicate potential problems in a future marriage.

The Importance of Discernment

Discernment is a gift from God that allows us to make wise decisions. In Philippians 1:9-10, Paul prays, "And this is my prayer: that your love may abound more and more in knowledge and depth of insight, so that you may be able to discern what is best and may be pure and blameless for the day of Christ." This book seeks to equip you with the knowledge and insight necessary to discern potential red flags in a relationship, ensuring that your decision to marry is made with wisdom and clarity.

Building a Strong Foundation

A strong and godly marriage is built on a solid foundation of love, trust, and mutual respect. Ephesians 5:25-33 outlines the roles and responsibilities of husbands and wives, emphasizing the need for love, respect, and self-sacrifice. By identifying and addressing red flags before marriage, you can lay the groundwork for a healthy and thriving relationship that honors God.

Avoiding Heartache and Pain

The Bible warns us about the consequences of making unwise decisions. Proverbs 22:3 says, "The prudent see danger and take refuge, but the simple keep going and pay the penalty." Recognizing red flags early on can help you avoid the heartache and pain that often result from marrying someone who is not right for you. This book aims to protect you from such outcomes by highlighting potential warning signs.

Preparing for a Godly Marriage

Ultimately, the goal of this book is to prepare you for a godly marriage that reflects Christ's love for the Church. Colossians 3:14 reminds us, "And over all these virtues put on love, which binds them all together in perfect unity." By paying attention to red flags and seeking God's guidance, you can enter into a marriage that glorifies Him and brings joy and fulfillment to both partners.

Why Recognizing Red Flags Matters

Protecting Your Spiritual Well-Being
Recognizing red flags in a potential marriage partner is crucial for protecting your spiritual well-being. The Bible warns us about being unequally yoked with unbelievers (2 Corinthians 6:14), as such relationships can lead us away from our faith and into compromising situations. By identifying red flags early, you can ensure that your future spouse will support and strengthen your relationship with God, rather than hinder it.

Maintaining a God-Honoring Relationship
Marriage is intended to reflect the relationship between Christ and the Church (Ephesians 5:25-27). When red flags are ignored, the foundation of your relationship can be compromised, leading to dysfunction and discord. Proverbs 31:10-12 describes a virtuous spouse who brings good and not harm. By recognizing red flags, you can pursue a relationship that honors God and embodies His principles of love, respect, and mutual support.

Avoiding Emotional and Physical Harm
Ignoring red flags can lead to emotional and physical harm. Proverbs 27:12 states, "The prudent see danger and take refuge, but the simple keep going and pay the penalty." Red flags such as abusive behavior, lack of self-control, and manipulation can result in significant pain and suffering. Recognizing these signs early on allows you to take protective measures and seek a relationship that is safe and nurturing.

Ensuring Long-Term Compatibility
Amos 3:3 asks, "Do two walk together unless they have agreed to do so?" Long-term compatibility is essential for a healthy marriage.

Differences in values, life goals, and communication styles can lead to constant conflict and dissatisfaction. By identifying red flags that signal incompatibility, you can make informed decisions about whether a relationship is sustainable and fulfilling in the long run.

Fostering a Peaceful and Joyful Union

Proverbs 21:9 says, "Better to live on a corner of the roof than share a house with a quarrelsome wife." This principle applies to both spouses and highlights the importance of peace and harmony in marriage. Recognizing red flags helps you avoid entering a marriage marked by constant strife and unhappiness. Instead, you can seek a partner who contributes to a joyful and peaceful union.

Making Wise and Godly Decisions

The Bible emphasizes the importance of wisdom in making life choices. Proverbs 3:5-6 encourages us to trust in the Lord and not rely on our own understanding. Recognizing red flags is part of seeking God's wisdom and guidance in the decision to marry. By being vigilant and discerning, you can make choices that align with God's will and lead to a blessed and successful marriage.

In summary, recognizing red flags matters because it safeguards your spiritual health, ensures a God-honoring relationship, protects you from harm, guarantees compatibility, promotes peace and joy, and helps you make wise decisions. As you navigate the path to marriage, trust in God's wisdom and seek His guidance in identifying and addressing potential warning signs.

How to Use This Book

A Step-by-Step Guide
This book is designed to be a practical and spiritual guide for identifying red flags in a potential marriage partner. Each chapter focuses on a specific area of concern, providing biblical references and practical advice to help you discern potential issues. Here's how to get the most out of this book:

Read Prayerfully
Begin each reading session with prayer, asking God for wisdom and discernment. James 1:5 says, "If any of you lacks wisdom, you should ask God, who gives generously to all without finding fault, and it will be given to you." Approach each chapter with an open heart and mind, seeking God's guidance as you evaluate your relationship.

Reflect on Biblical Insights
Each red flag is accompanied by relevant biblical references to help you understand why it is important from a Christian perspective. Take time to read and reflect on these scriptures, considering how they apply to your relationship. Psalm 119:105 reminds us, "Your word is a lamp for my feet, a light on my path." Let the Bible illuminate your understanding as you navigate this important decision.

Evaluate Your Relationship
As you read through each chapter, use the practical advice and questions provided to evaluate your relationship. Be honest with yourself and with God about what you observe. Proverbs 27:19 states, "As water reflects the face, so one's life reflects the heart." Your relationship should reflect the love and grace of God.

Seek Godly Counsel

Proverbs 15:22 says, "Plans fail for lack of counsel, but with many advisers they succeed." Don't hesitate to seek advice from trusted Christian friends, family members, or mentors as you work through this book. They can provide valuable insights and support as you discern potential red flags.

Journal Your Thoughts

Keep a journal to record your thoughts, feelings, and observations as you progress through the book. Writing down your reflections can help you process your thoughts and see patterns that may not be immediately apparent. Proverbs 16:3 encourages us to "Commit to the Lord whatever you do, and he will establish your plans."

Pray for Guidance

Throughout this journey, continually pray for God's guidance. Philippians 4:6-7 advises, "Do not be anxious about anything, but in every situation, by prayer and petition, with thanksgiving, present your requests to God. And the peace of God, which transcends all understanding, will guard your hearts and your minds in Christ Jesus." Trust that God will lead you to make the right decision.

Discuss with Your Partner

If you are in a relationship, consider discussing the red flags and insights with your partner. Open and honest communication is essential for a healthy relationship. Ephesians 4:15 encourages us to "speak the truth in love." Use this book as a tool to foster meaningful conversations and address any concerns together.

Make Informed Decisions

After working through the book, take time to reflect on what you have learned and seek God's will for your future. Proverbs 3:5-6 reminds us to "Trust in the Lord with all your heart and lean not on your own understanding; in all your ways submit to him, and he will make your paths straight." Use the insights gained to make informed and godly decisions about your relationship.

By following these steps, you can use this book effectively to recognize red flags and ensure that your path to marriage is guided by wisdom, discernment, and faith.

Table of Contents

Chapter 1: Personality and Character Traits

1. Dishonesty
Understanding Dishonesty

Dishonesty is a fundamental red flag that can severely undermine a relationship. The Bible repeatedly emphasizes the importance of truthfulness. Proverbs 12:22 says, "The Lord detests lying lips, but he delights in people who are trustworthy." Dishonesty, whether in small matters or significant issues, erodes trust and creates a foundation of deceit.

Biblical Perspective on Honesty

God calls us to be people of integrity. Ephesians 4:25 instructs, "Therefore each of you must put off falsehood and speak truthfully to your neighbor, for we are all members of one body." In a marriage, where partners are meant to be one flesh (Genesis 2:24), honesty is crucial for unity and mutual trust.

Identifying Dishonesty

Dishonesty can manifest in various ways, including:

- **Lies:** Whether they are small white lies or significant fabrications, lies break down trust.

- **Deception:** Intentionally misleading or withholding important information is a form of dishonesty.

- **Inconsistencies:** Frequent changes in stories or explanations can indicate a lack of truthfulness.

- **Secretive Behavior:** Being overly secretive or hiding aspects of their life from you.

Consequences of Dishonesty

The repercussions of dishonesty are far-reaching. Proverbs 19:9 warns, "A false witness will not go unpunished, and whoever pours out lies will perish." In the context of marriage, dishonesty can lead to:

- **Loss of Trust:** Trust is the bedrock of any relationship. Once broken, it can be challenging to rebuild.
- **Emotional Pain:** Discovering deceit can cause significant emotional distress and insecurity.

- **Conflict:** Lies and deception often lead to arguments and misunderstandings.

- **Instability:** A relationship built on dishonesty is inherently unstable and prone to failure.

Addressing Dishonesty

If you notice signs of dishonesty in your partner, it is essential to address it promptly and biblically:

- **Open Communication:** Have an honest conversation about your concerns. Ephesians 4:15 encourages us to "speak the truth in love."

- **Seek Counsel:** Proverbs 11:14 states, "Where there is no guidance, a people falls, but in an abundance of counselors there is safety." Seek advice from trusted Christian mentors or counselors.

- **Pray for Wisdom:** James 1:5 promises, "If any of you lacks wisdom, you should ask God, who gives generously to all without finding fault, and it will be given to you." Pray for wisdom and discernment in handling the situation.

Reflection Questions

1. Have you noticed any patterns of dishonesty in your partner's behavior?
2. How has dishonesty affected your relationship thus far?
3. Are you able to have open and honest conversations with your partner about important issues?

4. What steps can you take to address dishonesty in a godly manner?

Conclusion

Dishonesty is a serious red flag that should not be ignored. By being vigilant and seeking God's guidance, you can discern whether your partner's dishonesty is a pattern that indicates deeper character issues. Remember, a successful and godly marriage is built on the foundation of trust and truthfulness. Proverbs 12:19 reminds us, "Truthful lips endure forever, but a lying tongue lasts only a moment." Strive for a relationship grounded in honesty and integrity, reflecting the truth and love of Christ.

2. Lack of Empathy
Understanding Empathy

Empathy is the ability to understand and share the feelings of others. It is a crucial trait for a healthy and loving relationship. The Bible teaches us to be compassionate and empathetic toward one another. Romans 12:15 encourages us to "Rejoice with those who rejoice; mourn with those who mourn." A lack of empathy can lead to a disconnect in relationships, making it difficult to build a strong, emotional bond.

Biblical Perspective on Empathy

Empathy is rooted in love and compassion. Ephesians 4:32 urges, "Be kind and compassionate to one another, forgiving each other, just as in Christ God forgave you." Jesus exemplified empathy throughout His ministry, showing compassion to the sick, the poor, and the marginalized. As followers of Christ, we are called to emulate His example in our relationships.

Identifying Lack of Empathy

Signs of a lack of empathy in a partner include:

- **Indifference to Your Feelings:** They seem uninterested or unconcerned about your emotions and experiences.

- **Inability to Comfort:** They struggle to provide comfort or support when you are going through a tough time.

- **Self-Centeredness:** They focus primarily on their own needs and desires, often at the expense of yours.

- **Dismissiveness:** They dismiss or belittle your feelings and experiences.

- **Inability to Apologize:** They rarely acknowledge their mistakes or show remorse for hurting you.

Consequences of Lack of Empathy

A lack of empathy can have detrimental effects on a relationship:

- **Emotional Disconnect:** Without empathy, partners may feel misunderstood and isolated.

- **Increased Conflict:** Misunderstandings and insensitivity can lead to frequent arguments.

- **Unmet Emotional Needs:** One or both partners may feel their emotional needs are not being met, leading to dissatisfaction.

- **Erosion of Trust:** A lack of empathy can erode trust and intimacy, which are essential for a healthy marriage.

Addressing Lack of Empathy

If you notice a lack of empathy in your partner, consider the following steps:

- **Communicate Your Needs:** Express how their behavior affects you. Ephesians 4:15 encourages us to "speak the truth in love."

- **Encourage Empathy Development:** Suggest ways to develop empathy, such as active listening and considering others' perspectives.

- **Seek Professional Help:** Counseling can help individuals develop empathy and improve relationship dynamics.

- **Pray for Transformation:** Ask God to work in your partner's heart. Ezekiel 36:26 promises, "I will give you a new heart and put a new spirit in you; I will remove from you your heart of stone and give you a heart of flesh."

Reflection Questions

1. How does your partner respond when you express your emotions or concerns?
2. Have you felt understood and supported in your relationship?
3. What steps can you take to encourage empathy in your relationship?
4. How has a lack of empathy affected your emotional connection with your partner?

Conclusion

Empathy is a vital component of a loving and supportive relationship. Without it, partners may struggle to connect and understand each other. Recognizing and addressing a lack of empathy is essential for building a marriage that reflects Christ's love and compassion. Colossians 3:12 reminds us, "Therefore, as God's chosen people, holy and dearly loved, clothe yourselves with compassion, kindness, humility, gentleness, and patience." Strive to cultivate these qualities in your relationship, seeking God's guidance and grace every step of the way.

3. Arrogance
Understanding Arrogance

Arrogance is an inflated sense of self-importance and a lack of humility. The Bible repeatedly warns against pride and arrogance, emphasizing the value of humility. Proverbs 16:18 cautions, "Pride goes before destruction, a haughty spirit before a fall." Arrogance can lead to numerous issues in a relationship, including a lack of respect and understanding.

Biblical Perspective on Humility

The Bible encourages humility as a virtue that honors God and fosters healthy relationships. Philippians 2:3-4 instructs, "Do nothing out of selfish ambition or vain conceit. Rather, in humility value others above yourselves, not looking to your own interests but each of you to the interests of the others." Arrogance is the antithesis of this teaching, making it a significant red flag.

Identifying Arrogance

Signs of arrogance in a partner include:

- **Dismissiveness:** They often dismiss your opinions and feelings as unimportant or inferior.

- **Self-Centeredness:** They frequently talk about themselves and their achievements, showing little interest in others.

- **Resistance to Feedback:** They are unwilling to accept constructive criticism or acknowledge their mistakes.

- **Belittling Behavior:** They may belittle or demean others to feel superior.

- **Sense of Entitlement:** They believe they deserve special treatment or privileges over others.

Consequences of Arrogance

Arrogance can have several negative effects on a relationship:

- **Lack of Mutual Respect:** Arrogance undermines the mutual respect necessary for a healthy relationship.

- **Conflict and Tension:** Arrogant behavior can lead to frequent arguments and tension.

- **Emotional Distance:** Arrogance creates emotional distance, as one partner feels undervalued and unheard.

- **Erosion of Trust:** A lack of humility and acknowledgment of mistakes can erode trust over time.

Addressing Arrogance

If you observe arrogance in your partner, consider these steps:

- **Open Communication:** Address the behavior directly and respectfully. Proverbs 27:5 says, "Better is open rebuke than hidden love."

- **Encourage Humility:** Encourage practices that foster humility, such as gratitude and serving others.

- **Model Humility:** Demonstrate humility in your own actions and interactions. 1 Peter 5:5 reminds us, "Clothe yourselves with humility toward one another, because, 'God opposes the proud but shows favor to the humble.'"

- **Seek Counseling:** Professional counseling can help address underlying issues of arrogance and promote healthier behavior.

- **Pray for Change:** Pray for your partner's heart to be transformed by God's grace. James 4:10 urges, "Humble yourselves before the Lord, and he will lift you up."

Reflection Questions
1. How does your partner respond to feedback or criticism?
2. Have you felt respected and valued in your relationship?
3. What behaviors indicate arrogance in your partner?
4. How can you encourage and model humility in your relationship?

Conclusion
Arrogance is a destructive trait that can severely impact the health and happiness of a relationship. Recognizing and addressing arrogance is essential for building a marriage based on mutual respect, humility, and love. As Christians, we are called to emulate the humility of Christ, who "humbled himself by becoming obedient to death—even death on a cross!" (Philippians 2:8). Strive to cultivate humility in your relationship, seeking God's wisdom and guidance as you navigate this important journey.

4. Jealousy and Possessiveness
Understanding Jealousy and Possessiveness

Jealousy and possessiveness are signs of insecurity and a lack of trust. These traits can create a controlling and suffocating environment, hindering the growth of a healthy relationship. The Bible warns against jealousy, as seen in James 3:16, "For where you have envy and selfish ambition, there you find disorder and every evil practice."

Biblical Perspective on Trust and Freedom

A godly relationship is built on trust and mutual respect. 1 Corinthians 13:4-5 reminds us that "Love is patient, love is kind. It does not envy, it does not boast, it is not proud. It does not dishonor others, it is not self-seeking, it is not easily angered, it keeps no record of wrongs." True love fosters an environment where both partners feel secure and free.

Identifying Jealousy and Possessiveness

Signs of jealousy and possessiveness in a partner include:

- **Constant Monitoring:** They frequently check on you, wanting to know your whereabouts and activities at all times.

- **Unfounded Accusations:** They often accuse you of being unfaithful or dishonest without any evidence.

- **Isolation:** They try to isolate you from friends and family, limiting your interactions with others.

- **Controlling Behavior:** They dictate what you can wear, who you can talk to, and where you can go.

- **Overreaction to Attention:** They become excessively upset if you receive attention from others, even in innocent situations.

Consequences of Jealousy and Possessiveness

These traits can lead to various negative outcomes in a relationship:

- **Erosion of Trust:** Constant suspicion and accusations can destroy the foundation of trust.

- **Loss of Independence:** One partner may feel trapped and unable to live freely, leading to resentment.

- **Emotional Distress:** Jealous and possessive behavior can cause significant emotional strain and anxiety.

- **Relationship Breakdown:** Over time, these issues can lead to frequent conflicts and, ultimately, the breakdown of the relationship.

Addressing Jealousy and Possessiveness

If you notice jealousy and possessiveness in your partner, take these steps:

- **Open Communication:** Discuss your concerns openly and honestly. Galatians 6:1 encourages us to restore others gently if they are caught in wrongdoing.

- **Set Boundaries:** Establish clear boundaries and ensure they are respected. Proverbs 25:28 states, "Like a city whose walls are broken through is a person who lacks self-control."

- **Encourage Trust:** Work together to build trust and security in the relationship.

- **Seek Professional Help:** Counseling can help address underlying insecurities and promote healthier behavior.

- **Pray for Healing:** Pray for God's intervention and healing in your partner's heart. Psalm 34:17 says, "The righteous cry out, and the Lord hears them; he delivers them from all their troubles."

Reflection Questions
1. How does your partner react when you spend time with others?
2. Do you feel free to maintain relationships with friends and family?
3. What specific behaviors indicate jealousy and possessiveness in your partner?
4. How can you work together to build trust and respect in your relationship?

Conclusion
Jealousy and possessiveness are harmful traits that can undermine the health and stability of a relationship. Recognizing these red flags and addressing them is crucial for fostering a relationship based on trust, freedom, and mutual respect. Ephesians 4:2 encourages us to "Be completely humble and gentle; be patient, bearing with one another in love." Strive to cultivate a loving and trusting environment in your relationship, seeking God's guidance and wisdom along the way.

5. Anger Management Issues

Understanding Anger Management Issues
Anger is a natural human emotion, but how it is managed can significantly impact a relationship. Uncontrolled anger can lead to destructive behavior, causing harm to oneself and others. The Bible warns about the dangers of uncontrolled anger in Proverbs 29:11, "Fools give full vent to their rage, but the wise bring calm in the end." Recognizing anger management issues early can prevent future conflicts and emotional distress.

Biblical Perspective on Anger
The Bible provides guidance on how to handle anger in a way that honors God. Ephesians 4:26-27 advises, "In your anger do not sin: Do not let the sun go down while you are still angry, and do not give the devil a foothold." This passage underscores the importance of addressing anger promptly and constructively to prevent it from causing harm.

Identifying Anger Management Issues
Signs of anger management issues in a partner include:
- **Frequent Outbursts:** They often lose their temper over minor issues.

- **Verbal or Physical Aggression:** Their anger manifests in yelling, insults, or even physical violence.

- **Holding Grudges:** They struggle to forgive and frequently bring up past offenses.

- **Blaming Others:** They tend to blame others for their anger, refusing to take responsibility.

- **Unresolved Conflict:** They have difficulty resolving conflicts calmly and constructively.

Consequences of Anger Management Issues

Uncontrolled anger can have severe consequences for a relationship:

- **Emotional Harm:** Frequent outbursts can cause significant emotional pain and fear.

- **Erosion of Trust:** Verbal and physical aggression can destroy trust and safety in the relationship.

- **Constant Conflict:** Persistent anger issues lead to ongoing conflicts and a toxic environment.

- **Physical Harm:** In extreme cases, uncontrolled anger can result in physical violence, posing serious risks to safety.

Addressing Anger Management Issues

If you observe anger management issues in your partner, consider these steps:

- **Encourage Open Dialogue:** Talk about your concerns and how their anger affects the relationship. James 1:19 advises, "Everyone should be quick to listen, slow to speak and slow to become angry."

- **Promote Healthy Outlets:** Encourage activities and practices that help manage anger, such as exercise, prayer, and relaxation techniques.

- **Set Clear Boundaries:** Establish boundaries regarding acceptable behavior during conflicts.

- **Seek Professional Help:** Counseling or anger management programs can provide strategies for handling anger constructively.

- **Pray for Transformation:** Pray for God to work in your partner's heart, bringing peace and self-control. Philippians 4:6-7 encourages, "Do not be anxious about anything, but in every situation, by prayer and petition, with thanksgiving, present your requests to God. And the peace of God, which transcends all understanding, will guard your hearts and your minds in Christ Jesus."

Reflection Questions
1. How does your partner typically react to frustration or stress?
2. Have you felt unsafe or emotionally harmed by your partner's anger?
3. What specific behaviors indicate a struggle with anger management in your partner?
4. How can you support your partner in developing healthier ways to manage anger?

Conclusion
Anger management issues are a significant red flag that can undermine the foundation of a loving and respectful relationship. Recognizing and addressing these issues is crucial for building a healthy and godly marriage. Colossians 3:8 urges, "But now you must also rid yourselves of all such things as these: anger, rage, malice, slander, and filthy language from your lips." Strive to cultivate a relationship marked by peace, patience, and understanding, seeking God's guidance and grace in overcoming challenges.

6. Lack of Responsibility

Understanding Lack of Responsibility
A lack of responsibility manifests in various ways, such as failing to meet obligations, avoiding accountability, and neglecting important duties. The Bible emphasizes the importance of responsibility and diligence in our daily lives. Colossians 3:23-24 states, "Whatever you do, work at it with all your heart, as working for the Lord, not for human masters, since you know that you will receive an inheritance from the Lord as a reward. It is the Lord Christ you are serving." A responsible partner contributes to a stable and fulfilling relationship.

Biblical Perspective on Responsibility
Responsibility is a key aspect of Christian living. 1 Timothy 5:8 highlights the importance of providing and caring for one's family: "Anyone who does not provide for their relatives, and especially for their own household, has denied the faith and is worse than an unbeliever." This verse underscores the significance of responsibility in maintaining a healthy and God-honoring household.

Identifying Lack of Responsibility
Signs of a lack of responsibility in a partner include:
- **Avoidance of Duties:** They frequently neglect their responsibilities, both small and large.

- **Blame Shifting:** They often blame others for their own mistakes or failures.

- **Irresponsible Behavior:** They engage in reckless or negligent activities without considering the consequences.

- **Financial Irresponsibility:** They manage finances poorly, leading to debt and financial instability.

- **Inconsistency:** They fail to follow through on commitments and promises.

Consequences of Lack of Responsibility

A lack of responsibility can lead to various negative outcomes in a relationship:

- **Unstable Environment:** Irresponsible behavior creates instability and unpredictability in the relationship.

- **Increased Stress:** Constantly managing the fallout from a partner's irresponsibility can lead to significant stress and frustration.

- **Erosion of Trust:** Failure to fulfill commitments erodes trust and reliability.

- **Financial Strain:** Poor financial management can result in debt and economic hardship.

- **Emotional Toll:** Continually covering for an irresponsible partner can cause emotional exhaustion and resentment.

Addressing Lack of Responsibility

If you notice a lack of responsibility in your partner, consider these steps:

- **Communicate Clearly:** Discuss your concerns and the impact of their behavior on the relationship. Proverbs 27:17 says, "As iron sharpens iron, so one person sharpens another."

- **Set Expectations:** Establish clear expectations and consequences for fulfilling responsibilities.

- **Encourage Growth:** Support your partner in developing better habits and taking ownership of their actions.

- **Seek Accountability:** Encourage them to seek accountability from trusted friends, mentors, or a counselor.

- **Pray for Change:** Pray for God's intervention and transformation in their heart. Philippians 2:13 assures us, "For it is God who works in you to will and to act in order to fulfill his good purpose."

Reflection Questions
1. How does your partner handle their daily responsibilities and commitments?
2. Have you felt burdened by having to manage the consequences of their irresponsibility?
3. What specific behaviors indicate a lack of responsibility in your partner?
4. How can you encourage and support your partner in becoming more responsible?

Conclusion
A lack of responsibility is a significant red flag that can jeopardize the health and stability of a relationship. Recognizing and addressing this issue is essential for building a solid foundation for marriage. As Christians, we are called to be diligent and accountable in all aspects of our lives. Proverbs 12:24 reminds us, "Diligent hands will rule, but laziness ends in forced labor." Strive to cultivate responsibility and accountability in your relationship, seeking God's wisdom and strength as you navigate this important journey.

7. Unreliability
Understanding Unreliability

Unreliability is a trait where an individual frequently fails to fulfill promises, commitments, and responsibilities. This characteristic can significantly disrupt a relationship, causing frustration and mistrust. The Bible emphasizes the importance of reliability and faithfulness. Proverbs 25:19 warns, "Like a broken tooth or a lame foot is reliance on the unfaithful in a time of trouble." A reliable partner is crucial for building a stable and dependable relationship.

Biblical Perspective on Reliability

Reliability reflects integrity and faithfulness, qualities highly valued in the Bible. Matthew 5:37 encourages us to be trustworthy in our words and actions: "All you need to say is simply 'Yes' or 'No'; anything beyond this comes from the evil one." Being reliable means being true to your word and dependable in your actions.

Identifying Unreliability

Signs of unreliability in a partner include:

- **Broken Promises:** Frequently failing to keep promises and commitments.

- **Inconsistency:** Being inconsistent in behavior, making it hard to predict their actions.

- **Tardiness:** Regularly being late or missing appointments and important events.

- **Forgetfulness:** Often forgetting important dates, tasks, or responsibilities.

- **Excuses:** Constantly making excuses for failing to fulfill obligations.

Consequences of Unreliability

Unreliability can lead to several negative outcomes in a relationship:

- **Erosion of Trust:** Consistent failure to keep promises undermines trust.

- **Increased Frustration:** Dealing with an unreliable partner can cause significant frustration and disappointment.

- **Emotional Insecurity:** Unreliability can create feelings of insecurity and uncertainty in the relationship.

- **Lack of Progress:** Important plans and goals may be hindered by an unreliable partner's failure to follow through.

- **Strained Communication:** Frequent failures and excuses can lead to communication breakdowns and conflicts.

Addressing Unreliability

If you observe unreliability in your partner, consider these steps:

- **Open Communication:** Discuss the impact of their unreliability on the relationship. Ephesians 4:15 advises us to "speak the truth in love."

- **Set Clear Expectations:** Establish clear expectations for reliability and follow-through on commitments.

- **Encourage Accountability:** Encourage your partner to seek accountability from trusted friends or mentors.

- **Support Improvement:** Help your partner develop better habits and strategies for staying organized and committed.

- **Pray for Change:** Pray for God to work in their heart, fostering reliability and faithfulness. Psalm 37:5 encourages us, "Commit your way to the Lord; trust in him and he will do this."

Reflection Questions
1. How does your partner's unreliability affect your trust and security in the relationship?
2. Have you had open conversations about the importance of reliability and commitment?
3. What specific behaviors indicate unreliability in your partner?
4. How can you support your partner in becoming more reliable and dependable?

Conclusion
Unreliability is a significant red flag that can undermine the foundation of trust and stability in a relationship. Recognizing and addressing this issue is crucial for building a healthy and dependable marriage. As Christians, we are called to be reliable and faithful in our commitments. Proverbs 20:6 reminds us, "Many claim to have unfailing love, but a faithful person who can find?" Strive to cultivate reliability and faithfulness in your relationship, seeking God's guidance and strength as you navigate this important journey.

8. Manipulative Behavior

Understanding Manipulative Behavior

Manipulative behavior involves influencing or controlling others to one's advantage, often through deceptive or underhanded tactics. This can severely undermine trust and respect in a relationship. The Bible condemns deceit and manipulation, as seen in Proverbs 12:22, "The Lord detests lying lips, but he delights in people who are trustworthy." Recognizing manipulative behavior early is crucial to safeguarding the integrity of your relationship.

Biblical Perspective on Integrity

God calls us to live with integrity and honesty. Proverbs 10:9 states, "Whoever walks in integrity walks securely, but whoever takes crooked paths will be found out." A relationship built on manipulation lacks the foundation of honesty and transparency that God desires for us. True love, as described in 1 Corinthians 13:6, "does not delight in evil but rejoices with the truth."

Identifying Manipulative Behavior

Signs of manipulative behavior in a partner include:

- **Emotional Manipulation:** Using guilt, fear, or flattery to influence your decisions.

- **Deceptive Tactics:** Frequently lying or withholding information to control outcomes.

- **Gaslighting:** Making you doubt your own perceptions and reality.

- **Playing the Victim:** Constantly portraying themselves as the victim to gain sympathy and control.

- **Overstepping Boundaries:** Ignoring or disrespecting your personal boundaries to get what they want.

Consequences of Manipulative Behavior
Manipulative behavior can have numerous detrimental effects on a relationship:

- **Erosion of Trust:** Manipulation undermines trust, making it difficult to believe in the partner's sincerity.

- **Emotional Damage:** Constant manipulation can lead to emotional distress and confusion.

- **Imbalanced Power Dynamics:** Manipulation creates an unhealthy imbalance of power in the relationship.

- **Resentment and Bitterness:** Being manipulated can lead to feelings of resentment and bitterness over time.

- **Loss of Self-Esteem:** Constant manipulation can erode your self-esteem and sense of self-worth.

Addressing Manipulative Behavior
If you observe manipulative behavior in your partner, take these steps:

- **Open and Honest Communication:** Discuss your observations and feelings directly and honestly. Ephesians 4:25 advises, "Therefore each of you must put off falsehood and speak truthfully to your neighbor, for we are all members of one body."

- **Set Firm Boundaries:** Establish and enforce clear boundaries to protect yourself from manipulation.

- **Seek External Support:** Engage the help of trusted friends, family, or a counselor to provide perspective and support.

- **Encourage Transparency:** Promote open and honest communication in the relationship.

- **Pray for Change:** Pray for God's intervention in transforming your partner's heart and fostering honesty. Psalm 51:10 says, "Create in me a pure heart, O God, and renew a steadfast spirit within me."

Reflection Questions

1. How does your partner's manipulative behavior affect your trust and emotional well-being?
2. Have you discussed the impact of their behavior on the relationship?
3. What specific actions indicate manipulation in your partner?
4. How can you establish and maintain healthy boundaries to prevent manipulation?

Conclusion

Manipulative behavior is a significant red flag that can severely damage the foundation of a healthy relationship. Recognizing and addressing this issue is essential for building a marriage based on trust, respect, and honesty. As Christians, we are called to walk in integrity and truth. Proverbs 11:3 reminds us, "The integrity of the upright guides them, but the unfaithful are destroyed by their duplicity." Strive to cultivate honesty and transparency in your relationship, seeking God's guidance and strength as you navigate this important journey.

9. Self-Centeredness

Understanding Self-Centeredness
Self-centeredness is characterized by a focus on one's own needs and desires to the exclusion of others. This trait can hinder the development of a loving and mutually supportive relationship. The Bible calls us to consider others and to serve one another in love. Philippians 2:3-4 instructs, "Do nothing out of selfish ambition or vain conceit. Rather, in humility value others above yourselves, not looking to your own interests but each of you to the interests of the others."

Biblical Perspective on Selflessness
Jesus modeled selflessness throughout His ministry. Mark 10:45 says, "For even the Son of Man did not come to be served, but to serve, and to give his life as a ransom for many." As followers of Christ, we are called to emulate His example of humility and service. A self-centered partner, however, may struggle to prioritize the well-being of the relationship.

Identifying Self-Centeredness
Signs of self-centeredness in a partner include:
- **Lack of Consideration:** Rarely taking your feelings or needs into account.

- **Dominating Conversations:** Frequently steering conversations back to themselves.

- **Reluctance to Compromise:** Unwilling to make sacrifices or compromises for the benefit of the relationship.

- **Attention-Seeking:** Constantly seeking validation and attention from others.

- **Neglect of Responsibilities:** Failing to fulfill responsibilities that require considering others' needs.

Consequences of Self-Centeredness

Self-centeredness can have several negative effects on a relationship:

- **Emotional Distance:** A self-centered partner can create emotional distance by neglecting your needs.

- **Frequent Conflict:** Constantly prioritizing their own needs can lead to frequent arguments and resentment.

- **Imbalanced Relationship:** An imbalance of give-and-take can result in one partner feeling undervalued and unsupported.

- **Lack of Intimacy:** True intimacy requires mutual consideration and understanding, which is hindered by self-centered behavior.

- **Reduced Trust:** Over time, self-centered behavior can erode trust and the sense of partnership.

Addressing Self-Centeredness

If you observe self-centeredness in your partner, consider these steps:

- **Open Communication:** Discuss your observations and feelings honestly and respectfully. Proverbs 27:5 says, "Better is open rebuke than hidden love."

- **Encourage Empathy:** Help your partner understand the importance of considering others' needs and feelings.

- **Model Selflessness:** Demonstrate selflessness in your own actions, serving as a positive example. Galatians 5:13 encourages us, "Serve one another humbly in love."

- **Set Boundaries:** Establish clear boundaries to ensure your needs and feelings are respected.

- **Pray for Transformation:** Pray for God to work in your partner's heart, fostering humility and selflessness. Romans 12:2 advises, "Do not conform to the pattern of this world, but be transformed by the renewing of your mind."

Reflection Questions
1. How does your partner's self-centered behavior affect your emotional well-being?
2. Have you discussed the impact of their behavior on the relationship?
3. What specific actions indicate self-centeredness in your partner?
4. How can you encourage and model selflessness in your relationship?

Conclusion
Self-centeredness is a significant red flag that can undermine the health and happiness of a relationship. Recognizing and addressing this issue is crucial for building a marriage based on mutual respect, love, and selflessness. As Christians, we are called to consider others and to serve one another in love. Philippians 2:5 reminds us, "In your relationships with one another, have the same mindset as Christ Jesus." Strive to cultivate selflessness and humility in your relationship, seeking God's guidance and strength as you navigate this important journey.

10. Inability to Forgive

Understanding the Inability to Forgive

Forgiveness is a fundamental aspect of any healthy relationship, particularly in marriage. The inability to forgive can lead to prolonged conflicts and resentment, preventing a relationship from moving forward. The Bible places a strong emphasis on the power and necessity of forgiveness. Ephesians 4:31-32 says, "Let all bitterness and wrath and anger and clamor and slander be put away from you, along with all malice. Be kind to one another, tenderhearted, forgiving one another, as God in Christ forgave you."

Biblical Perspective on Forgiveness

Forgiveness is not just a recommendation in Christian life; it is a command that reflects the character of God. Matthew 6:15 warns, "But if you do not forgive others their sins, your Father will not forgive your sins." This underscores the importance of forgiveness as a reflection of our own forgiveness by God through Christ.

Identifying an Inability to Forgive

Signs of an inability to forgive in a partner may include:

- **Holding Grudges:** Persistently holding onto anger and resentment from past conflicts.

- **Bringing Up Past Issues:** Frequently bringing up past mistakes in current disagreements.

- **Persistent Bitterness:** Displaying ongoing bitterness and negativity towards others who have wronged them.

- **Resistance to Reconciliation:** Showing reluctance or refusal to reconcile after conflicts, even when the other party has apologized.

- **Emotional Withdrawal:** Withdrawing affection or communication as a form of punishment.

Consequences of an Inability to Forgive
The refusal to forgive can severely impact a relationship:
- **Erosion of Trust and Intimacy:** Persistent grudges can erode trust and intimacy, making it difficult to maintain a close bond.

- **Cycle of Conflict:** An inability to forgive can perpetuate a cycle of conflict, where old issues resurface continually.

- **Emotional Distance:** Holding onto past hurts can create an emotional barrier that hinders deeper connection.

- **Stress and Unhappiness:** Constantly reliving past wrongs contributes to ongoing stress and unhappiness in the relationship.

- **Spiritual Stagnation:** From a Christian perspective, an unwillingness to forgive can also hinder spiritual growth and fellowship with God.

Addressing an Inability to Forgive
If you recognize an inability to forgive in your partner, consider these approaches:
- **Encourage Open Dialogue:** Discuss the importance of forgiveness and how holding onto past hurts affects the relationship. Proverbs 17:9 highlights, "Whoever would foster love covers over an offense, but whoever repeats the matter separates close friends."

- **Model Forgiveness:** Demonstrate forgiveness in your own actions by letting go of grievances and showing grace.

- **Seek Pastoral or Professional Help:** Sometimes, the roots of unforgiveness are deep and may require pastoral counseling or professional therapy to address.

- **Pray Together:** Pray for God's help in softening hearts and enabling forgiveness. Matthew 18:19-20 encourages praying together for agreement and healing.

- **Set Boundaries and Expectations:** Discuss the need for forgiveness as an ongoing commitment in your relationship.

Reflection Questions
1. How does your partner handle offenses or mistakes made by you or others?
2. Have unresolved issues affected your relationship's growth and happiness?
3. What steps can you take together to cultivate a spirit of forgiveness?
4. How can you personally model forgiveness in your relationship?

Conclusion

An inability to forgive is a significant obstacle in any relationship, especially in marriage. It can prevent the relationship from healing and growing. Addressing this issue is crucial for maintaining a loving and healthy relationship, built on the biblical principles of forgiveness and grace. As you work through these challenges, remember the promise in Colossians 3:13, "Bear with each other and forgive one another if any of you has a grievance against someone. Forgive as the Lord forgave you." Strive to embody this command in your life and relationship, seeking God's strength and wisdom.

Chapter 2: Communication Issues

11. Poor Listening Skills

Understanding Poor Listening Skills
Effective communication is a cornerstone of any successful relationship, and listening is a critical component of communication. Poor listening skills can lead to misunderstandings, conflicts, and feelings of being undervalued. The Bible emphasizes the importance of listening as part of wise communication. James 1:19 advises, "My dear brothers and sisters, take note of this: Everyone should be quick to listen, slow to speak and slow to become angry."

Biblical Perspective on Listening
Listening is an act of love and humility. Proverbs 18:13 states, "To answer before listening — that is folly and shame." This scripture highlights the importance of truly hearing and understanding others before responding. Jesus Himself exemplified attentive listening, showing compassion and understanding to those who sought His counsel.

Identifying Poor Listening Skills
Signs of poor listening skills in a partner include:
- **Interrupting:** Frequently interrupting you while you speak.

- **Distraction:** Appearing distracted or uninterested during conversations.

- **Selective Hearing:** Only listening to parts of the conversation that interest them or support their views.

- **Lack of Engagement:** Failing to respond appropriately to what you have said, indicating they weren't fully listening.

- **Forgetting Details:** Frequently forgetting important details or points you've discussed.

Consequences of Poor Listening Skills

Poor listening skills can have several negative impacts on a relationship:

- **Misunderstandings:** Frequent miscommunications can lead to misunderstandings and conflicts.

- **Feeling Undervalued:** Consistently feeling unheard can make one feel undervalued and unimportant.

- **Emotional Distance:** Lack of attentive listening can create emotional distance between partners.

- **Ineffective Problem Solving:** Without effective listening, resolving conflicts and making decisions together becomes challenging.

- **Resentment:** Over time, poor listening can breed resentment and frustration.

Addressing Poor Listening Skills

If you notice poor listening skills in your partner, consider these steps:

- **Communicate Your Needs:** Express the importance of being heard and how their listening habits affect you. Proverbs 25:12 states, "Like an earring of gold or an ornament of fine gold is the rebuke of a wise judge to a listening ear."

- **Model Good Listening:** Demonstrate active listening in your interactions. Reflect on what your partner says and respond thoughtfully.

- **Set Aside Distractions:** Encourage both of you to minimize distractions (like phones and TV) during important conversations.

- **Practice Reflective Listening:** Repeat back what your partner has said to ensure understanding and show that you are listening.

- **Pray for Improved Communication:** Pray together for God's help in improving your communication skills. Psalm 141:3 says, "Set a guard over my mouth, Lord; keep watch over the door of my lips."

Reflection Questions

1. How do you feel when your partner does not listen attentively to you?
2. What specific behaviors indicate poor listening skills in your partner?
3. How can you foster better listening habits in your relationship?
4. What steps can you both take to ensure more focused and engaged conversations?

Conclusion

Poor listening skills are a significant communication issue that can hinder the growth and intimacy of a relationship. Addressing this issue is crucial for building a marriage that honors God and reflects mutual respect and understanding. As Christians, we are called to listen and understand each other deeply. Proverbs 19:20 reminds us, "Listen to advice and accept discipline, and at the end you will be counted among the wise." Strive to cultivate attentive and compassionate listening in your relationship, seeking God's guidance and grace as you grow together.

12. Frequent Interruptions

Understanding Frequent Interruptions
Frequent interruptions during conversations can signify a lack of respect and consideration for the other person's thoughts and feelings. This behavior disrupts the flow of communication, leading to misunderstandings and frustration. The Bible emphasizes the value of listening and patience in communication. Proverbs 18:2 says, "Fools find no pleasure in understanding but delight in airing their own opinions."

Biblical Perspective on Respectful Communication
Respectful communication involves allowing others to speak without interruption and giving full attention to their words. James 1:19 advises, "My dear brothers and sisters, take note of this: Everyone should be quick to listen, slow to speak and slow to become angry." This verse highlights the importance of being attentive and patient in our interactions with others.

Identifying Frequent Interruptions
Signs of frequent interruptions in a partner include:
- **Cutting Off Mid-Sentence:** Frequently cutting you off before you finish speaking.

- **Changing the Subject:** Interrupting to change the topic to something they want to discuss.

- **Correcting:** Constantly correcting you or providing unsolicited advice before you finish your point.

- **Monopolizing Conversations:** Dominating the conversation by interrupting and not allowing you to express your thoughts fully.

- **Showing Impatience:** Displaying impatience or irritation when you speak for an extended period.

Consequences of Frequent Interruptions

Frequent interruptions can have several negative effects on a relationship:

- **Miscommunication:** Interruptions can lead to incomplete or misunderstood messages.

- **Frustration and Resentment:** Feeling constantly interrupted can cause frustration and resentment.

- **Reduced Intimacy:** Effective communication is key to intimacy; frequent interruptions hinder meaningful conversations.

- **Feeling Undervalued:** Consistently being interrupted can make one feel that their thoughts and feelings are not valued.

- **Conflict Escalation:** Interruptions during disagreements can escalate conflicts rather than resolve them.

Addressing Frequent Interruptions

If you notice frequent interruptions in your partner, consider these steps:

- **Discuss the Issue:** Share how interruptions affect your communication and relationship. Ephesians 4:15 encourages us to "speak the truth in love."

- **Set Ground Rules:** Agree on conversation rules, such as allowing each person to finish speaking before the other responds.

- **Practice Active Listening:** Encourage both partners to practice active listening, which involves fully focusing on the speaker without planning a response.

- **Use Non-Verbal Cues:** Develop non-verbal signals to gently remind each other to avoid interrupting.

- **Pray for Patience:** Pray together for patience and the ability to communicate respectfully. Colossians 4:6 says, "Let your conversation be always full of grace, seasoned with salt, so that you may know how to answer everyone."

Reflection Questions

1. How do frequent interruptions affect your ability to communicate effectively with your partner?
2. Have you discussed the impact of this behavior on your relationship?
3. What specific actions indicate a tendency to interrupt in your partner?
4. How can you both work together to ensure more respectful and uninterrupted conversations?

Conclusion

Frequent interruptions are a significant communication issue that can undermine the quality of interactions and the overall health of a relationship. Addressing this issue is crucial for fostering a respectful and understanding marriage. As Christians, we are called to listen attentively and speak wisely. Proverbs 18:13 reminds us, "To answer before listening — that is folly and shame." Strive to cultivate patience and respect in your communication, seeking God's guidance and grace as you grow together.

13. Refusal to Compromise

Understanding Refusal to Compromise

Compromise is essential in any healthy relationship, allowing both partners to find mutually acceptable solutions to disagreements. A refusal to compromise indicates rigidity and a lack of willingness to consider the other person's perspective. The Bible teaches us the importance of humility and putting others before ourselves. Philippians 2:3-4 says, "Do nothing out of selfish ambition or vain conceit. Rather, in humility value others above yourselves, not looking to your own interests but each of you to the interests of the others."

Biblical Perspective on Compromise and Unity

Compromise is rooted in love and mutual respect, which are fundamental to Christian relationships. Ephesians 4:2-3 encourages us to "Be completely humble and gentle; be patient, bearing with one another in love. Make every effort to keep the unity of the Spirit through the bond of peace." Compromise helps maintain unity and peace in relationships.

Identifying Refusal to Compromise

Signs of a refusal to compromise in a partner include:

- **Inflexibility:** Insisting on having things their way without considering alternatives.

- **Stubbornness:** Refusing to change their stance even when presented with reasonable arguments.

- **Dominance:** Trying to control decisions and outcomes to suit their preferences.

- **Dismissiveness:** Ignoring or belittling your opinions and suggestions.

- **Conflict Avoidance:** Avoiding discussions that require compromise, leading to unresolved issues.

Consequences of Refusal to Compromise

A refusal to compromise can have several negative impacts on a relationship:

- **Increased Conflict:** Inflexibility can lead to frequent arguments and unresolved disputes.

- **Emotional Distance:** Feeling unheard and unvalued can create emotional distance between partners.

- **Resentment:** One partner may feel resentful if their needs and desires are consistently overlooked.

- **Imbalanced Relationship:** A lack of compromise can create an imbalance of power and control in the relationship.

- **Erosion of Trust:** Constant inflexibility can erode trust and mutual respect over time.

Addressing Refusal to Compromise

If you notice a refusal to compromise in your partner, consider these steps:

- **Communicate the Importance:** Discuss the importance of compromise and how it benefits the relationship. Ephesians 4:15 advises us to "speak the truth in love."

- **Model Compromise:** Demonstrate a willingness to compromise in your own actions, showing its positive impact on the relationship.

- **Seek Common Ground:** Focus on finding common ground and mutually beneficial solutions.

- **Encourage Empathy:** Help your partner understand your perspective and the value of considering both sides.

- **Pray for Unity:** Pray together for unity and a spirit of cooperation. Colossians 3:14 says, "And over all these virtues put on love, which binds them all together in perfect unity."

Reflection Questions

1. How does your partner's refusal to compromise affect your relationship and decision-making?
2. Have you discussed the impact of this behavior on your relationship?
3. What specific actions indicate a refusal to compromise in your partner?
4. How can you both work together to develop a more flexible and cooperative approach?

Conclusion

A refusal to compromise is a significant communication issue that can hinder the growth and harmony of a relationship. Addressing this issue is crucial for fostering a loving and respectful marriage. As Christians, we are called to value others and seek unity in our relationships. Romans 12:10 reminds us, "Be devoted to one another in love. Honor one another above yourselves." Strive to cultivate a spirit of compromise and cooperation in your relationship, seeking God's guidance and grace as you grow together.

14. Defensive Responses

Understanding Defensive Responses
Defensive responses occur when a person reacts to feedback or criticism with hostility, denial, or deflection instead of openness and reflection. This behavior can hinder productive communication and problem-solving in a relationship. The Bible encourages humility and openness to correction. Proverbs 15:31-32 says, "Whoever heeds life-giving correction will be at home among the wise. Those who disregard discipline despise themselves, but the one who heeds correction gains understanding."

Biblical Perspective on Humility and Correction
Being open to correction and avoiding defensive reactions is essential for personal and relational growth. James 1:19 advises, "My dear brothers and sisters, take note of this: Everyone should be quick to listen, slow to speak and slow to become angry." This scripture emphasizes the importance of being receptive and calm when receiving feedback.

Identifying Defensive Responses
Signs of defensive responses in a partner include:
- **Denial:** Refusing to acknowledge any wrongdoing or fault.

- **Blaming:** Shifting the blame to others instead of taking responsibility.

- **Minimizing:** Downplaying the significance of the issue being discussed.

- **Counterattacking:** Responding to criticism with criticism or hostility.

- **Avoidance:** Evading the conversation altogether or shutting down emotionally.

Consequences of Defensive Responses

Defensive responses can have several negative effects on a relationship:

- **Stifled Communication:** Productive conversations and conflict resolution become difficult.

- **Increased Conflict:** Defensive behavior often escalates conflicts rather than resolving them.

- **Emotional Distance:** A lack of openness can create emotional barriers between partners.

- **Resentment:** Persistent defensiveness can lead to feelings of frustration and resentment.

- **Lack of Growth:** Without addressing issues constructively, personal and relational growth is hindered.

Addressing Defensive Responses

If you notice defensive responses in your partner, consider these steps:

- **Create a Safe Environment:** Foster an atmosphere of safety and trust where both partners feel comfortable discussing sensitive issues. Proverbs 15:1 says, "A gentle answer turns away wrath, but a harsh word stirs up anger."

- **Use "I" Statements:** Frame feedback using "I" statements to express your feelings without sounding accusatory. For example, "I feel hurt when..." instead of "You always..."

- **Stay Calm and Patient:** Respond to defensiveness with patience and calmness. Avoid escalating the situation with anger or frustration.

- **Encourage Self-Reflection:** Gently encourage your partner to reflect on their reactions and consider the feedback being given.

- **Pray for Openness:** Pray together for humility and openness to correction. Proverbs 12:1 reminds us, "Whoever loves discipline loves knowledge, but whoever hates correction is stupid."

Reflection Questions
1. How do defensive responses from your partner affect your communication and relationship?
2. Have you discussed the impact of this behavior on your ability to resolve conflicts?
3. What specific actions indicate defensiveness in your partner?
4. How can you both work together to create a more open and receptive communication environment?

Conclusion
Defensive responses are a significant communication issue that can impede the growth and harmony of a relationship. Addressing this issue is essential for fostering a loving and respectful marriage. As Christians, we are called to be humble and open to correction. Proverbs 9:8-9 advises, "Do not rebuke mockers or they will hate you; rebuke the wise and they will love you. Instruct the wise and they will be wiser still; teach the righteous and they will add to their learning." Strive to cultivate an environment of openness and humility in your relationship, seeking God's guidance and grace as you grow together.

15. Constant Criticism

Understanding Constant Criticism
Constant criticism involves frequently pointing out a partner's faults or shortcomings in a way that is harsh and unconstructive. This behavior can be damaging to self-esteem and can create a negative atmosphere in the relationship. The Bible instructs us to speak words that build up rather than tear down. Ephesians 4:29 says, "Do not let any unwholesome talk come out of your mouths, but only what is helpful for building others up according to their needs, that it may benefit those who listen."

Biblical Perspective on Encouragement and Kindness
Christians are called to encourage one another and to be kind and compassionate. Colossians 3:12-13 urges, "Therefore, as God's chosen people, holy and dearly loved, clothe yourselves with compassion, kindness, humility, gentleness and patience. Bear with each other and forgive one another if any of you has a grievance against someone." Criticism should be replaced with constructive feedback given in a spirit of love and support.

Identifying Constant Criticism
Signs of constant criticism in a partner include:
- **Frequent Negative Comments:** Regularly making negative remarks about your actions, decisions, or character.

- **Focusing on Faults:** Highlighting your flaws more often than your strengths or positive qualities.

- **Harsh Language:** Using harsh or demeaning language when pointing out mistakes.

- **Lack of Positive Feedback:** Rarely offering praise or encouragement.

- **Public Criticism:** Criticizing you in front of others, leading to embarrassment and humiliation.

Consequences of Constant Criticism

Constant criticism can have several negative effects on a relationship:

- **Erosion of Self-Esteem:** Regular criticism can damage self-esteem and self-worth.

- **Emotional Distance:** Feeling constantly criticized can lead to emotional withdrawal and distance.

- **Increased Conflict:** Persistent negativity can lead to frequent arguments and tension.

- **Loss of Intimacy:** Criticism can create a barrier to emotional and physical intimacy.

- **Resentment:** Over time, constant criticism can breed resentment and bitterness.

Addressing Constant Criticism

If you experience constant criticism from your partner, consider these steps:

- **Communicate Your Feelings:** Share how the constant criticism affects you emotionally and relationally. Proverbs 15:4 says, "The soothing tongue is a tree of life, but a perverse tongue crushes the spirit."

- **Seek Constructive Feedback:** Encourage your partner to offer feedback in a constructive and supportive manner.

- **Set Boundaries:** Establish clear boundaries regarding acceptable ways of giving and receiving feedback.

- **Model Positive Communication:** Demonstrate how to give positive feedback and constructive criticism in a loving way.

- **Pray for Transformation:** Pray together for a heart change and the ability to speak words that build up rather than tear down. Psalm 19:14 encourages, "May these words of my mouth and this meditation of my heart be pleasing in your sight, Lord, my Rock and my Redeemer."

Reflection Questions

1. How does constant criticism from your partner affect your self-esteem and emotional well-being?
2. Have you discussed the impact of this behavior on your relationship?
3. What specific actions indicate constant criticism in your partner?
4. How can you both work together to create a more positive and supportive communication environment?

Conclusion

Constant criticism is a significant communication issue that can undermine the health and happiness of a relationship. Addressing this issue is crucial for fostering a loving and respectful marriage. As Christians, we are called to speak words of encouragement and kindness. Proverbs 16:24 reminds us, "Gracious words are a honeycomb, sweet to the soul and healing to the bones." Strive to cultivate a spirit of encouragement and positivity in your relationship, seeking God's guidance and grace as you grow together.

16. Silent Treatment

Understanding the Silent Treatment
The silent treatment involves deliberately ignoring or refusing to communicate with a partner as a form of punishment or control. This behavior can be deeply hurtful and damaging to the relationship. The Bible emphasizes the importance of resolving conflicts and maintaining open lines of communication. Matthew 5:23-24 says, "Therefore, if you are offering your gift at the altar and there remember that your brother or sister has something against you, leave your gift there in front of the altar. First go and be reconciled to them; then come and offer your gift."

Biblical Perspective on Communication and Reconciliation
Effective communication and reconciliation are vital to maintaining a healthy relationship. Ephesians 4:26-27 advises, "In your anger do not sin: Do not let the sun go down while you are still angry, and do not give the devil a foothold." This scripture highlights the importance of addressing conflicts promptly and not allowing anger to fester.

Identifying the Silent Treatment
Signs of the silent treatment in a partner include:
- **Refusal to Speak:** Deliberately ignoring you or refusing to engage in conversation.

- **Emotional Withdrawal:** Withdrawing affection and communication as a means of control or punishment.

- **Avoidance:** Avoiding eye contact, physical presence, or any form of interaction.

- **Prolonged Silence:** Extending the silent treatment for an unreasonable period, often to manipulate or control the situation.

- **Passive-Aggressive Behavior:** Using silence to express anger or disapproval without directly addressing the issue.

Consequences of the Silent Treatment

The silent treatment can have several negative effects on a relationship:

- **Emotional Pain:** Feeling ignored and unloved can cause significant emotional distress.

- **Erosion of Trust:** Using silence as a weapon undermines trust and respect in the relationship.

- **Increased Conflict:** Unresolved issues can escalate into larger conflicts over time.

- **Communication Breakdown:** The silent treatment disrupts healthy communication and problem-solving.

- **Resentment:** Persistent use of the silent treatment can lead to feelings of resentment and bitterness.

Addressing the Silent Treatment

If you experience the silent treatment from your partner, consider these steps:

- **Address the Behavior:** Communicate how the silent treatment affects you and the relationship. Proverbs 25:11 says, "A word fitly spoken is like apples of gold in settings of silver."

- **Encourage Open Dialogue:** Promote open and honest communication to resolve conflicts. Encourage your partner to express their feelings verbally rather than through silence.

- **Set Boundaries:** Establish clear boundaries about acceptable ways to handle disagreements and conflicts.

- **Seek Reconciliation:** Work towards reconciliation and healing after conflicts. Colossians 3:13 reminds us, "Bear with each other and forgive one another if any of you has a grievance against someone. Forgive as the Lord forgave you."

- **Pray for Healing:** Pray together for healing and the ability to communicate effectively. James 5:16 encourages, "Therefore confess your sins to each other and pray for each other so that you may be healed. The prayer of a righteous person is powerful and effective."

Reflection Questions

1. How does the silent treatment from your partner affect your emotional well-being and the relationship?
2. Have you discussed the impact of this behavior on your ability to resolve conflicts?
3. What specific actions indicate the use of the silent treatment in your partner?
4. How can you both work together to foster open and honest communication?

Conclusion

The silent treatment is a significant communication issue that can undermine the health and happiness of a relationship. Addressing this issue is crucial for fostering a loving and respectful marriage. As Christians, we are called to resolve conflicts and communicate openly. Proverbs 15:1 reminds us, "A gentle answer turns away wrath, but a harsh word stirs up anger." Strive to cultivate an environment of open and honest communication in your relationship, seeking God's guidance and grace as you grow together.

17. Avoidance of Important Discussions

Understanding Avoidance of Important Discussions
Avoiding important discussions involves steering clear of conversations that are crucial to the health and future of the relationship. This behavior can lead to unresolved issues and misunderstandings. The Bible encourages open and honest communication, as seen in Proverbs 27:5, "Better is open rebuke than hidden love." Facing important discussions head-on is essential for a strong and transparent relationship.

Biblical Perspective on Honest Communication
The Bible emphasizes the importance of truthfulness and addressing issues directly. Ephesians 4:25 states, "Therefore each of you must put off falsehood and speak truthfully to your neighbor, for we are all members of one body." Honest communication fosters trust and understanding, helping couples to navigate challenges together.

Identifying Avoidance of Important Discussions
Signs of avoidance in a partner include:
- **Changing the Subject:** Frequently diverting conversations away from important topics.

- **Excuses:** Making excuses to delay or avoid discussions about serious matters.

- **Deflection:** Shifting the focus to unrelated issues to avoid the main topic.

- **Silence:** Responding with silence or minimal input when important discussions arise.

- **Disinterest:** Showing a lack of interest or engagement in conversations about the future, finances, family, or other significant areas.

Consequences of Avoidance of Important Discussions

Avoiding important discussions can have several negative impacts on a relationship:

- **Unresolved Issues:** Key problems remain unresolved, leading to ongoing tension.

- **Misunderstandings:** Lack of clear communication can result in misunderstandings and false assumptions.

- **Emotional Distance:** Avoidance creates emotional barriers and hinders intimacy.

- **Lack of Progress:** Failure to address important topics can stall the growth and progress of the relationship.

- **Frustration and Resentment:** One partner may feel frustrated and resentful if their concerns are consistently ignored.

Addressing Avoidance of Important Discussions

If you notice avoidance of important discussions in your partner, consider these steps:

- **Express the Importance:** Communicate the significance of having these discussions for the health of the relationship. Proverbs 18:13 reminds us, "To answer before listening — that is folly and shame."

- **Create a Safe Space:** Foster an environment where both partners feel safe and comfortable discussing sensitive topics.

- **Schedule Discussions:** Set aside specific times to address important issues, ensuring that both partners are prepared and focused.

- **Encourage Honesty:** Promote a culture of honesty and openness, where both partners feel heard and valued.

- **Pray for Guidance:** Pray together for the courage and wisdom to face important discussions. Philippians 4:6-7 advises, "Do not be anxious about anything, but in every situation, by prayer and petition, with thanksgiving, present your requests to God. And the peace of God, which transcends all understanding, will guard your hearts and your minds in Christ Jesus."

Reflection Questions
1. How does avoiding important discussions affect your relationship and communication?
2. Have you discussed the impact of this behavior on your ability to resolve conflicts and plan for the future?
3. What specific actions indicate avoidance of important discussions in your partner?
4. How can you both work together to ensure that important topics are addressed openly and honestly?

Conclusion
Avoidance of important discussions is a significant communication issue that can undermine the stability and growth of a relationship. Addressing this issue is crucial for fostering a loving and transparent marriage. As Christians, we are called to communicate openly and truthfully. Proverbs 24:26 reminds us, "An honest answer is like a kiss on the lips." Strive to cultivate a relationship where important discussions are approached with honesty and courage, seeking God's guidance and grace as you grow together.

18. Passive-Aggressive Behavior
Understanding Passive-Aggressive Behavior

Passive-aggressive behavior involves expressing negative feelings indirectly rather than openly addressing them. This can manifest as sarcasm, backhanded compliments, procrastination, or intentional inefficiency. The Bible encourages direct and honest communication, as seen in Proverbs 10:18, "Whoever conceals hatred with lying lips and spreads slander is a fool." Addressing passive-aggressive behavior is essential for maintaining transparency and trust in a relationship.

Biblical Perspective on Honest and Direct Communication

The Bible teaches the importance of speaking the truth in love. Ephesians 4:15 instructs, "Instead, speaking the truth in love, we will grow to become in every respect the mature body of him who is the head, that is, Christ." Honest and direct communication helps build a healthy and mature relationship.

Identifying Passive-Aggressive Behavior

Signs of passive-aggressive behavior in a partner include:

- **Sarcasm:** Using sarcastic remarks to express displeasure or criticism indirectly.

- **Procrastination:** Delaying tasks or responsibilities as a way of expressing resistance.

- **Silent Treatment:** Withholding communication to express anger or dissatisfaction.

- **Backhanded Compliments:** Giving compliments that are actually disguised criticisms.

- **Intentional Inefficiency:** Deliberately performing tasks poorly to avoid future requests.

Consequences of Passive-Aggressive Behavior

Passive-aggressive behavior can have several negative effects on a relationship:

- **Miscommunication:** Indirect expression of feelings can lead to misunderstandings and confusion.

- **Increased Frustration:** The underlying issues remain unresolved, causing ongoing frustration.

- **Emotional Distance:** Passive-aggressive behavior creates emotional barriers and hinders intimacy.

- **Erosion of Trust:** Consistently dealing with indirect negativity can erode trust and respect.

- **Escalation of Conflict:** Unaddressed passive-aggressive behavior can escalate into larger conflicts over time.

Addressing Passive-Aggressive Behavior

If you notice passive-aggressive behavior in your partner, consider these steps:

- **Communicate Clearly:** Address the behavior directly and express how it affects you and the relationship. Proverbs 27:5 says, "Better is open rebuke than hidden love."

- **Encourage Open Expression:** Encourage your partner to express their feelings and concerns openly and directly.

- **Model Direct Communication:** Demonstrate direct and honest communication in your interactions.

- **Seek Understanding:** Try to understand the underlying causes of the passive-aggressive behavior and address them together.

- **Pray for Change:** Pray together for the ability to communicate openly and address issues directly. James 5:16 encourages, "Therefore confess your sins to each other and pray for each other so that you may be healed. The prayer of a righteous person is powerful and effective."

Reflection Questions
1. How does passive-aggressive behavior from your partner affect your emotional well-being and the relationship?
2. Have you discussed the impact of this behavior on your ability to communicate effectively?
3. What specific actions indicate passive-aggressive behavior in your partner?
4. How can you both work together to promote direct and honest communication?

Conclusion
Passive-aggressive behavior is a significant communication issue that can undermine the health and happiness of a relationship. Addressing this issue is crucial for fostering a loving and transparent marriage. As Christians, we are called to communicate openly and honestly. Proverbs 15:4 reminds us, "The soothing tongue is a tree of life, but a perverse tongue crushes the spirit." Strive to cultivate a relationship where feelings and concerns are expressed directly and lovingly, seeking God's guidance and grace as you grow together.

19. Lack of Open Communication

Understanding Lack of Open Communication

Open communication is essential for building trust, resolving conflicts, and fostering intimacy in a relationship. A lack of open communication can lead to misunderstandings, resentment, and emotional distance. The Bible encourages us to communicate honestly and openly. Proverbs 15:1 says, "A gentle answer turns away wrath, but a harsh word stirs up anger." Transparency in communication is vital for maintaining a healthy and strong relationship.

Biblical Perspective on Open Communication

The Bible highlights the importance of honest and open communication. Ephesians 4:25 instructs, "Therefore each of you must put off falsehood and speak truthfully to your neighbor, for we are all members of one body." This scripture emphasizes the need for truthfulness and openness in our interactions with others.

Identifying Lack of Open Communication

Signs of a lack of open communication in a partner include:

- **Avoiding Difficult Conversations:** Steering clear of discussions about important or sensitive topics.

- **Withholding Information:** Failing to share important details or keeping secrets.

- **Minimal Sharing:** Providing only brief or vague responses to questions or discussions.

- **Emotional Guarding:** Refusing to express feelings or thoughts openly.

- **Unresponsiveness:** Not engaging or showing interest in meaningful conversations.

Consequences of Lack of Open Communication

A lack of open communication can have several negative effects on a relationship:

- **Misunderstandings:** Important information may be misunderstood or overlooked.

- **Emotional Distance:** Without open communication, partners may feel disconnected and distant.

- **Resentment:** Unresolved issues and unexpressed feelings can lead to resentment over time.

- **Erosion of Trust:** Keeping secrets or withholding information can undermine trust.

- **Increased Conflict:** Poor communication can lead to frequent conflicts and frustration.

Addressing Lack of Open Communication

If you notice a lack of open communication in your partner, consider these steps:

- **Encourage Honest Dialogue:** Foster an environment where both partners feel safe to share their thoughts and feelings. Proverbs 24:26 says, "An honest answer is like a kiss on the lips."

- **Ask Open-Ended Questions:** Encourage your partner to elaborate on their thoughts and feelings by asking open-ended questions.

- **Be Vulnerable:** Share your own thoughts and feelings openly, setting an example of honest communication.

- **Listen Actively:** Show genuine interest and attentiveness when your partner speaks. James 1:19 advises, "Everyone should be quick to listen, slow to speak and slow to become angry."

- **Pray for Openness:** Pray together for the courage and willingness to communicate openly. Colossians 4:6 encourages, "Let your conversation be always full of grace, seasoned with salt, so that you may know how to answer everyone."

Reflection Questions
1. How does a lack of open communication affect your relationship and emotional connection?
2. Have you discussed the impact of this behavior on your ability to resolve conflicts and understand each other?
3. What specific actions indicate a lack of open communication in your partner?
4. How can you both work together to promote more open and honest communication?

Conclusion
A lack of open communication is a significant issue that can undermine the health and stability of a relationship. Addressing this issue is crucial for fostering a loving and transparent marriage. As Christians, we are called to communicate openly and truthfully. Proverbs 12:18 reminds us, "The words of the reckless pierce like swords, but the tongue of the wise brings healing." Strive to cultivate a relationship where open communication is encouraged and valued, seeking God's guidance and grace as you grow together.

20. Inconsistent Communication

Understanding Inconsistent Communication
Inconsistent communication refers to a lack of regular and reliable interaction, where a partner's communication habits are unpredictable or erratic. This inconsistency can create confusion, misunderstandings, and a sense of instability in the relationship. The Bible emphasizes the importance of faithfulness and reliability in our words and actions. Proverbs 25:19 says, "Like a broken tooth or a lame foot is reliance on the unfaithful in a time of trouble." Consistent communication is key to building trust and understanding.

Biblical Perspective on Consistent Communication
The Bible teaches us to be consistent and faithful in our interactions. Matthew 5:37 encourages us, "All you need to say is simply 'Yes' or 'No'; anything beyond this comes from the evil one." This verse underscores the importance of being straightforward and dependable in our communication.

Identifying Inconsistent Communication
Signs of inconsistent communication in a partner include:
- **Irregular Contact:** Sporadic and unpredictable communication patterns.

- **Unreliable Responses:** Sometimes responding promptly, other times delaying responses without explanation.

- **Mixed Messages:** Sending contradictory messages that create confusion.

- **Frequent Cancellations:** Often canceling plans or not following through on commitments.

- **Emotional Unpredictability:** Being emotionally available at times and distant at others.

Consequences of Inconsistent Communication

Inconsistent communication can have several negative effects on a relationship:

- **Confusion:** Unpredictable communication patterns can lead to confusion and misunderstandings.

- **Emotional Instability:** Inconsistency can create a sense of instability and uncertainty in the relationship.

- **Lack of Trust:** Unreliable communication can undermine trust and reliability.

- **Increased Conflict:** Erratic communication can lead to frustration and frequent conflicts.

- **Emotional Distance:** Partners may feel emotionally distant and disconnected.

Addressing Inconsistent Communication

If you notice inconsistent communication in your partner, consider these steps:

- **Discuss the Issue:** Share your feelings about the inconsistency and its impact on the relationship. Ephesians 4:15 encourages us to "speak the truth in love."

- **Set Expectations:** Establish clear expectations for regular and reliable communication.

- **Encourage Reliability:** Encourage your partner to be more consistent and dependable in their interactions.

- **Be a Role Model:** Demonstrate consistent and reliable communication in your own behavior.

- **Pray for Stability:** Pray together for stability and reliability in your communication. Colossians 3:17 advises, "And whatever you do, whether in word or deed, do it all in the name of the Lord Jesus, giving thanks to God the Father through him."

Reflection Questions

1. How does inconsistent communication from your partner affect your emotional well-being and the relationship?
2. Have you discussed the impact of this behavior on your ability to trust and understand each other?
3. What specific actions indicate inconsistent communication in your partner?
4. How can you both work together to promote more consistent and reliable communication?

Conclusion

Inconsistent communication is a significant issue that can undermine the health and stability of a relationship. Addressing this issue is crucial for fostering a loving and reliable marriage. As Christians, we are called to be faithful and dependable in our words and actions. Proverbs 15:23 reminds us, "A person finds joy in giving an apt reply — and how good is a timely word!" Strive to cultivate a relationship where consistent communication is encouraged and valued, seeking God's guidance and grace as you grow together.

Chapter 3: Financial Red Flags

21. Irresponsible Spending
Understanding Irresponsible Spending

Irresponsible spending involves making purchases that are unnecessary, excessive, or beyond one's financial means. This behavior can lead to financial instability and stress within a relationship. The Bible emphasizes the importance of wise financial stewardship. Proverbs 21:20 says, "The wise store up choice food and olive oil, but fools gulp theirs down." Being prudent with finances is essential for maintaining a healthy and stable relationship.

Biblical Perspective on Financial Stewardship

The Bible teaches us to manage our resources wisely and to avoid wastefulness. Proverbs 13:11 advises, "Dishonest money dwindles away, but whoever gathers money little by little makes it grow." Responsible financial management is a reflection of good stewardship and aligns with biblical principles.

Identifying Irresponsible Spending

Signs of irresponsible spending in a partner include:

- **Frequent Impulse Purchases:** Regularly making spontaneous and unnecessary purchases.

- **Accumulating Debt:** Frequently using credit cards or loans to fund a lifestyle beyond their means.

- **Lack of Budgeting:** Failing to plan or adhere to a budget.

- **Ignoring Financial Goals:** Disregarding agreed-upon financial goals and priorities.

- **Hiding Purchases:** Concealing purchases or financial transactions from you.

Consequences of Irresponsible Spending

Irresponsible spending can have several negative impacts on a relationship:

- **Financial Instability:** Excessive spending can lead to debt and financial hardship.

- **Stress and Anxiety:** Financial problems can cause significant stress and anxiety for both partners.

- **Trust Issues:** Hiding purchases or accumulating debt can undermine trust.

- **Conflict:** Disagreements over money can lead to frequent arguments and tension.

- **Delayed Goals:** Irresponsible spending can hinder the ability to achieve long-term financial goals, such as buying a home or saving for retirement.

Addressing Irresponsible Spending

If you notice irresponsible spending in your partner, consider these steps:

- **Discuss Financial Goals:** Have an open conversation about your financial goals and how you can work together to achieve them. Proverbs 15:22 says, "Plans fail for lack of counsel, but with many advisers they succeed."

- **Create a Budget:** Work together to create a budget that reflects your priorities and helps manage spending.

- **Monitor Spending:** Keep track of expenses to identify areas where spending can be reduced.

- **Encourage Accountability:** Hold each other accountable for sticking to the budget and making wise financial decisions.

- **Pray for Wisdom:** Pray together for wisdom and self-control in managing finances. James 1:5 encourages, "If any of you lacks wisdom, you should ask God, who gives generously to all without finding fault, and it will be given to you."

Reflection Questions
1. How does irresponsible spending affect your financial stability and relationship?
2. Have you discussed the impact of this behavior on your ability to achieve financial goals?
3. What specific actions indicate irresponsible spending in your partner?
4. How can you both work together to promote responsible financial management?

Conclusion
Irresponsible spending is a significant financial red flag that can undermine the health and stability of a relationship. Addressing this issue is crucial for fostering a financially sound and trusting marriage. As Christians, we are called to be wise stewards of the resources God has entrusted to us. Luke 16:10 reminds us, "Whoever can be trusted with very little can also be trusted with much, and whoever is dishonest with very little will also be dishonest with much." Strive to cultivate responsible financial habits in your relationship, seeking God's guidance and wisdom as you manage your finances together.

22. Significant Debt

Understanding Significant Debt
Significant debt refers to a large amount of money owed to creditors, which can be a major financial burden. This can include credit card debt, personal loans, student loans, and other forms of borrowing. While some debt may be unavoidable, especially for major expenses like education or a home, excessive and unmanaged debt can signal financial irresponsibility. The Bible warns against the dangers of debt. Proverbs 22:7 says, "The rich rule over the poor, and the borrower is slave to the lender."

Biblical Perspective on Debt
The Bible encourages us to live within our means and avoid unnecessary debt. Romans 13:8 advises, "Let no debt remain outstanding, except the continuing debt to love one another, for whoever loves others has fulfilled the law." Managing debt wisely is a part of good financial stewardship.

Identifying Significant Debt
Signs of significant debt in a partner include:
- **Multiple Credit Accounts:** Having numerous credit cards or loans with high balances.

- **Missed Payments:** Frequently missing payment due dates or making late payments.

- **Debt Over Income:** Debt that significantly exceeds their annual income.

- **Debt Hiding:** Hiding or being secretive about debt amounts and obligations.

- **No Repayment Plan:** Lacking a clear plan to repay debt or reduce debt load.

Consequences of Significant Debt

Significant debt can have several negative effects on a relationship:

- **Financial Stress:** The burden of debt can cause significant stress and anxiety.

- **Trust Issues:** Secrecy or dishonesty about debt can undermine trust.

- **Delayed Financial Goals:** High debt can delay achieving important financial milestones such as buying a home, saving for retirement, or starting a family.

- **Increased Conflict:** Financial problems are a common source of conflict in relationships.

- **Limited Financial Freedom:** High debt repayments can limit your ability to make choices about your lifestyle and future.

Addressing Significant Debt

If your partner has significant debt, consider these steps:

- **Open Discussion:** Have an honest conversation about the debt and its impact on your future together. Proverbs 11:14 says, "For lack of guidance a nation falls, but victory is won through many advisers."

- **Create a Debt Repayment Plan:** Work together to develop a realistic plan to pay down the debt.

- **Budgeting:** Establish a budget to manage expenses and avoid accumulating more debt.

- **Seek Professional Advice:** Consider consulting a financial advisor or credit counselor for assistance.

- **Pray for Wisdom and Discipline:** Pray together for wisdom and discipline in managing debt. Proverbs 3:9-10 encourages, "Honor the Lord with your wealth, with the firstfruits of all your crops; then your barns will be filled to overflowing, and your vats will brim over with new wine."

Reflection Questions
1. How does significant debt affect your financial stability and relationship?
2. Have you discussed the impact of this debt on your future financial goals?
3. What steps can you take together to reduce and manage debt effectively?
4. How can you support each other in creating and sticking to a debt repayment plan?

Conclusion
Significant debt is a major financial red flag that can impact the health and stability of a relationship. Addressing this issue is crucial for fostering a financially sound and trusting marriage. As Christians, we are called to be wise stewards of the resources God has entrusted to us. Proverbs 22:26-27 warns, "Do not be one who shakes hands in pledge or puts up security for debts; if you lack the means to pay, your very bed will be snatched from under you." Strive to manage debt responsibly and work together to achieve financial freedom, seeking God's guidance and wisdom as you navigate financial challenges together.

23. Lack of Financial Planning

Understanding Lack of Financial Planning
Financial planning involves setting financial goals, creating budgets, and developing strategies to achieve these goals. A lack of financial planning can lead to poor money management, unpreparedness for emergencies, and an inability to reach long-term financial objectives. The Bible emphasizes the importance of planning and stewardship. Proverbs 21:5 says, "The plans of the diligent lead to profit as surely as haste leads to poverty."

Biblical Perspective on Financial Planning
The Bible encourages us to be wise stewards of our resources and to plan for the future. Luke 14:28-30 illustrates this principle: "Suppose one of you wants to build a tower. Won't you first sit down and estimate the cost to see if you have enough money to complete it? For if you lay the foundation and are not able to finish it, everyone who sees it will ridicule you, saying, 'This person began to build and wasn't able to finish.'" Effective financial planning is essential for a stable and prosperous life.

Identifying Lack of Financial Planning
Signs of a lack of financial planning in a partner include:
- **No Budget:** Failing to create or adhere to a budget for managing income and expenses.
- **Impulse Spending:** Making financial decisions on a whim without considering long-term effects.
- **No Savings:** Lacking savings for emergencies, retirement, or future goals.
- **Debt Mismanagement:** Having debt but no clear plan to pay it off.
- **Financial Disorganization:** Keeping finances in disarray, with no clear understanding of income, expenses, or financial health.

Consequences of Lack of Financial Planning

A lack of financial planning can have several negative impacts on a relationship:

- **Financial Instability:** Without planning, managing unexpected expenses or emergencies becomes challenging.

- **Stress and Anxiety:** Financial uncertainty can cause significant stress and anxiety.

- **Delayed Goals:** Long-term financial goals, such as buying a home or saving for retirement, may be unattainable.

- **Increased Conflict:** Financial disorganization and stress can lead to frequent arguments.

- **Dependence:** Poor planning can lead to financial dependence on others or credit.

Addressing Lack of Financial Planning

If you notice a lack of financial planning in your partner, consider these steps:

- **Discuss the Importance:** Have an open conversation about the importance of financial planning for your future together. Proverbs 16:3 advises, "Commit to the Lord whatever you do, and he will establish your plans."

- **Create a Budget:** Work together to develop a realistic budget that aligns with your financial goals.

- **Set Financial Goals:** Establish short-term and long-term financial goals and create a plan to achieve them.

- **Encourage Savings:** Make saving a priority to build an emergency fund and plan for the future.

- **Seek Professional Advice:** Consider consulting a financial advisor to help create a comprehensive financial plan.

- **Pray for Wisdom:** Pray together for wisdom and guidance in managing your finances. James 1:5 encourages, "If any of you lacks wisdom, you should ask God, who gives generously to all without finding fault, and it will be given to you."

Reflection Questions
1. How does a lack of financial planning affect your financial stability and relationship?
2. Have you discussed the impact of this behavior on your ability to achieve financial goals?
3. What steps can you take together to promote effective financial planning?
4. How can you support each other in developing and sticking to a financial plan?

Conclusion
A lack of financial planning is a significant financial red flag that can undermine the health and stability of a relationship. Addressing this issue is crucial for fostering a financially sound and trusting marriage. As Christians, we are called to be wise stewards of the resources God has entrusted to us. Proverbs 24:27 advises, "Put your outdoor work in order and get your fields ready; after that, build your house." Strive to manage your finances responsibly and work together to achieve financial stability and success, seeking God's guidance and wisdom as you plan for your future.

24. Secretive About Finances
Understanding Secrecy About Finances

Being secretive about finances involves hiding financial information, decisions, or transactions from a partner. This behavior can undermine trust and transparency in a relationship. The Bible emphasizes the importance of honesty and openness. Proverbs 11:1 says, "The Lord detests dishonest scales, but accurate weights find favor with him." Transparency in financial matters is essential for building a healthy and trusting relationship.

Biblical Perspective on Honesty and Transparency

The Bible teaches us to live in the light, which includes being honest and transparent with one another. Ephesians 4:25 states, "Therefore each of you must put off falsehood and speak truthfully to your neighbor, for we are all members of one body." In a relationship, financial transparency is crucial for unity and trust.

Identifying Secrecy About Finances

Signs of secrecy about finances in a partner include:

- **Hiding Transactions:** Concealing purchases, bank statements, or financial documents.

- **Unexplained Withdrawals:** Making withdrawals or transfers without explanation.

- **Avoiding Financial Discussions:** Reluctance to discuss financial matters or share information.

- **Secret Accounts:** Maintaining undisclosed bank accounts or credit cards.

- **Defensive Responses:** Reacting defensively when asked about financial matters.

Consequences of Secrecy About Finances

Secrecy about finances can have several negative impacts on a relationship:

- **Erosion of Trust:** Hiding financial information undermines trust and honesty.

- **Financial Discrepancies:** Secretive behavior can lead to financial discrepancies and misunderstandings.

- **Increased Conflict:** Discovering hidden financial matters can lead to significant conflict and resentment.

- **Financial Instability:** Unmanaged or hidden financial issues can cause instability and stress.

- **Emotional Distance:** Secrecy can create emotional distance and hinder intimacy.

Addressing Secrecy About Finances

If you notice secrecy about finances in your partner, consider these steps:

- **Open Communication:** Discuss the importance of financial transparency and how secrecy affects the relationship. Proverbs 27:5 says, "Better is open rebuke than hidden love."

- **Encourage Openness:** Foster an environment where both partners feel safe to share financial information openly.

- **Set Financial Goals Together:** Work together to set financial goals and create a plan for managing finances.

- **Share Financial Responsibilities:** Ensure both partners are involved in financial decisions and management.

- **Pray for Honesty and Unity:** Pray together for honesty and unity in managing finances. Colossians 3:9-10 encourages, "Do not lie to each other, since you have taken off your old self with its practices and have put on the new self, which is being renewed in knowledge in the image of its Creator."

Reflection Questions

1. How does secrecy about finances affect your trust and emotional well-being in the relationship?
2. Have you discussed the impact of this behavior on your ability to manage finances together?
3. What specific actions indicate secrecy about finances in your partner?
4. How can you both work together to promote financial transparency and honesty?

Conclusion

Secrecy about finances is a significant financial red flag that can undermine the trust and stability of a relationship. Addressing this issue is crucial for fostering a financially sound and trusting marriage. As Christians, we are called to live in the light and be transparent with one another. 1 John 1:7 reminds us, "But if we walk in the light, as he is in the light, we have fellowship with one another, and the blood of Jesus, his Son, purifies us from all sin." Strive to cultivate honesty and transparency in your financial matters, seeking God's guidance and wisdom as you manage your finances together.

25. Frequent Borrowing
Understanding Frequent Borrowing

Frequent borrowing involves consistently taking out loans or borrowing money to cover expenses. This can indicate financial mismanagement or living beyond one's means. The Bible advises against accumulating unnecessary debt. Proverbs 22:7 states, "The rich rule over the poor, and the borrower is slave to the lender." Frequent borrowing can lead to financial bondage and stress.

Biblical Perspective on Borrowing

The Bible encourages living within our means and being good stewards of our resources. Romans 13:8 says, "Let no debt remain outstanding, except the continuing debt to love one another, for whoever loves others has fulfilled the law." Avoiding excessive borrowing aligns with biblical principles of financial stewardship.

Identifying Frequent Borrowing

Signs of frequent borrowing in a partner include:

- **Regularly Taking Loans:** Continuously applying for new loans or credit lines.

- **Reliance on Credit Cards:** Using credit cards to cover everyday expenses.

- **Borrowing from Friends/Family:** Frequently asking friends or family for financial help.

- **High Debt-to-Income Ratio:** Having a large portion of income dedicated to debt repayment.

- **Inability to Save:** Struggling to save money due to constant debt obligations.

Consequences of Frequent Borrowing

Frequent borrowing can have several negative effects on a relationship:

- **Financial Instability:** Continuous borrowing can lead to significant financial instability and stress.

- **Increased Debt:** Accumulating debt can become overwhelming and difficult to manage.

- **Strain on Relationships:** Borrowing from friends and family can strain those relationships.

- **Delayed Goals:** Constant debt repayment can delay achieving financial goals.

- **Trust Issues:** Borrowing without discussing with a partner can undermine trust.

Addressing Frequent Borrowing

If you notice frequent borrowing in your partner, consider these steps:

- **Discuss Financial Habits:** Have an open conversation about borrowing habits and their impact on your future. Proverbs 15:22 says, "Plans fail for lack of counsel, but with many advisers they succeed."

- **Create a Repayment Plan:** Develop a plan to pay off existing debts and avoid taking on new ones.

- **Budgeting:** Establish a budget to manage expenses and reduce the need for borrowing.

- **Encourage Financial Education:** Suggest learning more about financial management together.

- **Pray for Wisdom:** Pray together for wisdom and discipline in managing finances. James 1:5 advises, "If any of you lacks wisdom, you should ask God, who gives generously to all without finding fault, and it will be given to you."

Reflection Questions

1. How does frequent borrowing affect your financial stability and relationship?
2. Have you discussed the impact of this behavior on your financial future?
3. What steps can you take together to reduce the need for borrowing?
4. How can you support each other in developing better financial habits?

Conclusion

Frequent borrowing is a significant financial red flag that can undermine the health and stability of a relationship. Addressing this issue is crucial for fostering a financially sound and trusting marriage. As Christians, we are called to be wise stewards of the resources God has entrusted to us. Proverbs 22:26-27 warns, "Do not be one who shakes hands in pledge or puts up security for debts; if you lack the means to pay, your very bed will be snatched from under you." Strive to manage your finances responsibly, seeking God's guidance and wisdom as you work together towards financial stability.

26. Financial Dependence
Understanding Financial Dependence

Financial dependence occurs when one partner relies heavily on the other for financial support, often without contributing to the household income or managing finances responsibly. While some level of financial interdependence is normal in relationships, complete dependence can create an imbalance. The Bible encourages diligence and responsibility. 2 Thessalonians 3:10 says, "For even when we were with you, we gave you this rule: 'The one who is unwilling to work shall not eat.'"

Biblical Perspective on Responsibility

The Bible teaches the importance of working diligently and providing for oneself and one's family. Proverbs 12:11 says, "Those who work their land will have abundant food, but those who chase fantasies have no sense." Taking responsibility for financial contributions is part of good stewardship.

Identifying Financial Dependence

Signs of financial dependence in a partner include:

- **Lack of Employment:** Not seeking employment or contributing to household income.
- **Reliance on Partner's Income:** Depending entirely on the partner's earnings for all expenses.
- **Avoiding Financial Responsibilities:** Refusing to participate in budgeting or financial planning.
- **No Effort to Improve:** Showing no interest in gaining skills or education to improve employment prospects.
- **Expecting Financial Support:** Expecting the partner to cover all financial needs without contributing.

Consequences of Financial Dependence

Financial dependence can have several negative effects on a relationship:

- **Financial Strain:** One partner bearing all financial responsibilities can cause strain and stress.
- **Resentment:** The working partner may feel resentful or burdened by the imbalance.

- **Power Imbalance:** Financial dependence can create a power imbalance in the relationship.
- **Delayed Goals:** The inability to contribute financially can delay achieving mutual goals.
- **Erosion of Self-Worth:** The dependent partner may struggle with self-esteem and a sense of purpose.

Addressing Financial Dependence

If you notice financial dependence in your partner, consider these steps:

- **Open Dialogue:** Discuss the importance of financial contribution and how dependence affects the relationship. Proverbs 13:11 says, "Dishonest money dwindles away, but whoever gathers money little by little makes it grow."
- **Set Financial Goals:** Establish shared financial goals and a plan for achieving them together.
- **Encourage Employment:** Support your partner in finding employment or gaining skills for better job opportunities.
- **Share Financial Responsibilities:** Divide financial responsibilities to promote a sense of partnership and mutual contribution.
- **Pray for Guidance:** Pray together for wisdom and opportunities to improve your financial situation. Philippians 4:19 reassures, "And my God will meet all your needs according to the riches of his glory in Christ Jesus."

Reflection Questions

1. How does financial dependence affect your relationship and financial stability?
2. Have you discussed the impact of this behavior on your mutual financial goals?
3. What steps can you take together to promote financial independence and contribution?
4. How can you support each other in achieving a balanced financial partnership?

Conclusion

Financial dependence is a significant financial red flag that can impact the health and balance of a relationship. Addressing this issue is crucial for fostering a financially sound and mutually supportive marriage. As Christians, we are called to be diligent and responsible in our financial stewardship. Proverbs 14:23 reminds us, "All hard work brings a profit, but mere talk leads only to poverty." Strive to cultivate a balanced and responsible approach to financial management, seeking God's guidance and wisdom as you work together towards financial independence and stability.

27. Disregard for Budgeting

Understanding Disregard for Budgeting
Disregard for budgeting means neglecting to create or follow a financial plan that manages income and expenses. This behavior can lead to financial chaos and stress. The Bible emphasizes the importance of prudent financial management. Proverbs 21:5 says, "The plans of the diligent lead to profit as surely as haste leads to poverty." Budgeting helps ensure that resources are used wisely and responsibly.

Biblical Perspective on Financial Stewardship
The Bible encourages careful planning and stewardship of resources. Luke 14:28-30 highlights the importance of planning: "Suppose one of you wants to build a tower. Won't you first sit down and estimate the cost to see if you have enough money to complete it?" Budgeting aligns with biblical principles of planning and stewardship.

Identifying Disregard for Budgeting
Signs of disregard for budgeting in a partner include:
- **Overspending:** Regularly spending more than their income.

- **Lack of Planning:** No attempt to track or plan finances.

- **Impulse Purchases:** Frequent, unplanned spending.

- **Debt Accumulation:** Increasing debt due to unmanaged spending.

- **Ignoring Financial Goals:** Disregarding agreed-upon financial objectives.

Consequences of Disregard for Budgeting

Disregard for budgeting can have several negative impacts:

- **Financial Instability:** Lack of planning can lead to financial crises.

- **Increased Debt:** Uncontrolled spending can result in significant debt.

- **Stress and Anxiety:** Financial uncertainty can cause ongoing stress.

- **Conflict:** Disagreements over money management can lead to conflicts.

- **Delayed Goals:** Financial goals such as saving for a home or retirement may be unachievable.

Addressing Disregard for Budgeting

To address disregard for budgeting, consider these steps:

- **Discuss the Importance:** Explain how budgeting benefits your financial health. Proverbs 16:3 says, "Commit to the Lord whatever you do, and he will establish your plans."

- **Create a Budget Together:** Develop a realistic budget that aligns with your financial goals.

- **Track Expenses:** Monitor spending to ensure adherence to the budget.

- **Set Financial Goals:** Establish short-term and long-term financial goals.

- **Pray for Discipline:** Pray together for discipline in financial management. James 1:5 encourages, "If any of you lacks wisdom, you should ask God, who gives generously to all without finding fault, and it will be given to you."

Reflection Questions

1. How does disregard for budgeting affect your financial stability and relationship?
2. Have you discussed the impact of this behavior on your financial goals?
3. What steps can you take together to promote effective budgeting?
4. How can you support each other in maintaining financial discipline?

Conclusion

Disregard for budgeting is a significant financial red flag. Addressing this issue is crucial for fostering financial stability and trust. As Christians, we are called to be wise stewards of our resources. Proverbs 13:11 says, "Dishonest money dwindles away, but whoever gathers money little by little makes it grow." Strive to manage your finances responsibly, seeking God's guidance and wisdom.

28. Inconsistent Employment

Understanding Inconsistent Employment

Inconsistent employment refers to a pattern of unstable or irregular work history. This can lead to financial uncertainty and stress. The Bible emphasizes the value of diligent work. Proverbs 12:11 says, "Those who work their land will have abundant food, but those who chase fantasies have no sense." Steady employment is important for financial stability and planning.

Biblical Perspective on Work

The Bible encourages diligent and consistent work. Colossians 3:23 advises, "Whatever you do, work at it with all your heart, as working for the Lord, not for human masters." Consistent employment aligns with biblical principles of hard work and responsibility.

Identifying Inconsistent Employment

Signs of inconsistent employment in a partner include:

- **Frequent Job Changes:** Regularly changing jobs without a stable career path.

- **Periods of Unemployment:** Long or frequent periods of unemployment without effort to find stable work.

- **Lack of Commitment:** Showing little commitment to jobs or career development.

- **Financial Dependence:** Relying on others for financial support due to lack of stable income.

- **No Long-Term Goals:** Absence of long-term career or employment goals.

Consequences of Inconsistent Employment
Inconsistent employment can have several negative impacts:

- **Financial Instability:** Irregular income can lead to financial difficulties.

- **Stress and Anxiety:** Uncertainty about financial future can cause stress.

- **Increased Debt:** Irregular income can lead to debt accumulation.

- **Conflict:** Financial instability can cause conflicts in relationships.

- **Delayed Goals:** Inconsistent employment can delay achieving financial and personal goals.

Addressing Inconsistent Employment
To address inconsistent employment, consider these steps:

- **Discuss Career Goals:** Talk about the importance of stable employment and career planning. Proverbs 15:22 says, "Plans fail for lack of counsel, but with many advisers they succeed."

- **Encourage Career Development:** Support your partner in pursuing education or training for stable employment.

- **Create a Job Search Plan:** Develop a plan to find and maintain stable employment.

- **Budgeting for Uncertainty:** Create a budget that accounts for periods of unemployment.

- **Pray for Guidance:** Pray together for guidance and opportunities. Philippians 4:19 reassures, "And my God will meet all your needs according to the riches of his glory in Christ Jesus."

Reflection Questions

1. How does inconsistent employment affect your financial stability and relationship?
2. Have you discussed the impact of this behavior on your future goals?
3. What steps can you take together to promote stable employment?
4. How can you support each other in achieving career and financial stability?

Conclusion

Inconsistent employment is a significant financial red flag. Addressing this issue is crucial for fostering financial stability and trust. As Christians, we are called to work diligently and responsibly. Proverbs 10:4 says, "Lazy hands make for poverty, but diligent hands bring wealth." Strive to maintain steady employment and responsible financial management, seeking God's guidance and wisdom.

29. Unwillingness to Discuss Financial Goals

Understanding Unwillingness to Discuss Financial Goals
An unwillingness to discuss financial goals can indicate a lack of transparency and shared vision in a relationship. Financial planning is crucial for achieving mutual goals and ensuring financial stability. The Bible emphasizes the importance of planning and unity. Amos 3:3 says, "Do two walk together unless they have agreed to do so?"

Biblical Perspective on Planning Together
The Bible encourages us to work together in unity and agreement. Proverbs 16:3 advises, "Commit to the Lord whatever you do, and he will establish your plans." Discussing and agreeing on financial goals is essential for a harmonious and prosperous relationship.

Identifying Unwillingness to Discuss Financial Goals
Signs of unwillingness to discuss financial goals in a partner include:
- **Avoidance:** Avoiding conversations about financial planning and goals.

- **Dismissiveness:** Dismissing the importance of setting financial goals.

- **Defensiveness:** Becoming defensive or hostile when financial goals are brought up.

- **Lack of Interest:** Showing little or no interest in financial planning.

- **Secretive Behavior:** Keeping personal financial plans and goals hidden.

Consequences of Unwillingness to Discuss Financial Goals

Unwillingness to discuss financial goals can have several negative impacts on a relationship:

- **Lack of Direction:** Without clear goals, financial planning and progress are hindered.

- **Financial Instability:** Inability to plan for future expenses can lead to financial instability.

- **Conflict:** Disagreements about money can lead to frequent arguments.

- **Delayed Goals:** Mutual financial goals, such as buying a home or saving for retirement, may be delayed or unachievable.

- **Erosion of Trust:** Lack of transparency and cooperation can erode trust.

Addressing Unwillingness to Discuss Financial Goals

If your partner is unwilling to discuss financial goals, consider these steps:

- **Communicate the Importance:** Explain how setting and discussing financial goals benefits your future together. Proverbs 15:22 says, "Plans fail for lack of counsel, but with many advisers they succeed."

- **Create a Safe Space:** Foster an environment where both partners feel comfortable discussing finances.

- **Set Mutual Goals:** Work together to establish short-term and long-term financial goals.

- **Seek Professional Advice:** Consider consulting a financial advisor to facilitate goal-setting.

- **Pray for Unity:** Pray together for unity and cooperation in financial planning. James 1:5 encourages, "If any of you lacks wisdom, you should ask God, who gives generously to all without finding fault, and it will be given to you."

Reflection Questions

1. How does an unwillingness to discuss financial goals affect your relationship and financial stability?
2. Have you discussed the impact of this behavior on your future plans?
3. What steps can you take together to promote open discussions about financial goals?
4. How can you support each other in achieving your financial objectives?

Conclusion

Unwillingness to discuss financial goals is a significant financial red flag. Addressing this issue is crucial for fostering a financially sound and cooperative marriage. As Christians, we are called to work together in unity and transparency. Proverbs 24:3-4 reminds us, "By wisdom a house is built, and through understanding it is established; through knowledge its rooms are filled with rare and beautiful treasures." Strive to discuss and set financial goals together, seeking God's guidance and wisdom.

30. Financial Manipulation
Understanding Financial Manipulation

Financial manipulation involves using money or financial control to exert power over a partner. This behavior can create an unhealthy power dynamic and undermine trust and equality in a relationship. The Bible warns against manipulation and promotes fairness and integrity. Proverbs 11:1 says, "The Lord detests dishonest scales, but accurate weights find favor with him."

Biblical Perspective on Fairness and Integrity

The Bible encourages fairness and integrity in all dealings, including financial matters. Proverbs 16:11 states, "Honest scales and balances belong to the Lord; all the weights in the bag are of his making." Financial integrity is essential for a just and equitable relationship.

Identifying Financial Manipulation

Signs of financial manipulation in a partner include:

- **Control of Finances:** Controlling all financial resources and decisions.

- **Withholding Money:** Withholding money to punish or control.

- **Secret Accounts:** Maintaining secret accounts or financial dealings.

- **Using Money as Leverage:** Using financial support as leverage in arguments or decisions.

- **Intimidation:** Using financial threats or intimidation to influence behavior.

Consequences of Financial Manipulation
Financial manipulation can have several negative impacts on a relationship:

- **Power Imbalance:** Creating an unhealthy power dynamic and dependency.

- **Erosion of Trust:** Undermining trust and mutual respect.

- **Financial Insecurity:** Causing financial insecurity and stress for the manipulated partner.

- **Emotional Distress:** Leading to emotional distress and feelings of powerlessness.

- **Conflict:** Increasing the likelihood of conflict and resentment.

Addressing Financial Manipulation
If you notice financial manipulation in your partner, consider these steps:

- **Communicate Clearly:** Address the behavior directly and express how it affects you. Ephesians 4:15 advises, "Instead, speaking the truth in love, we will grow to become in every respect the mature body of him who is the head, that is, Christ."

- **Seek Fairness:** Advocate for fair and equal financial decision-making.

- **Establish Boundaries:** Set clear boundaries to prevent financial control and manipulation.

- **Seek Counseling:** Consider professional counseling to address underlying issues.

- **Pray for Integrity:** Pray together for integrity and fairness in your financial dealings. Micah 6:8 reminds us, "He has shown you, O mortal, what is good. And what does the Lord require of you? To act justly and to love mercy and to walk humbly with your God."

Reflection Questions

1. How does financial manipulation affect your emotional well-being and relationship?
2. Have you discussed the impact of this behavior on your trust and mutual respect?
3. What steps can you take together to ensure fair and equitable financial management?
4. How can you support each other in maintaining financial integrity?

Conclusion

Financial manipulation is a significant financial red flag that can undermine the health and equality of a relationship. Addressing this issue is crucial for fostering a just and trusting marriage. As Christians, we are called to act with integrity and fairness. Proverbs 21:3 says, "To do what is right and just is more acceptable to the Lord than sacrifice." Strive to manage your finances with honesty and fairness, seeking God's guidance and wisdom as you work together towards financial integrity.

Chapter 4: Relationship Dynamics

31. Controlling Behavior

Understanding Controlling Behavior
Controlling behavior involves one partner trying to dominate or manipulate the other's actions, decisions, and interactions. This can manifest through excessive monitoring, making unilateral decisions, or limiting the other person's autonomy. The Bible warns against such behavior, emphasizing mutual respect and freedom. Galatians 5:13 says, "You, my brothers and sisters, were called to be free. But do not use your freedom to indulge the flesh; rather, serve one another humbly in love."

Biblical Perspective on Respect and Freedom
The Bible encourages relationships built on mutual respect, love, and freedom. Ephesians 5:21 states, "Submit to one another out of reverence for Christ." A healthy relationship should promote mutual submission and respect, rather than control and domination.

Identifying Controlling Behavior
Signs of controlling behavior in a partner include:

- **Excessive Monitoring:** Constantly checking on your whereabouts, activities, and communications.

- **Isolation:** Trying to isolate you from family and friends.

- **Decision-Making:** Making important decisions without consulting you.

- **Jealousy:** Displaying irrational jealousy and possessiveness.

- **Criticism:** Criticizing your choices, appearance, or actions to undermine your confidence.

Consequences of Controlling Behavior

Controlling behavior can have several negative impacts on a relationship:

- **Erosion of Trust:** Control undermines trust and mutual respect.

- **Loss of Autonomy:** The controlled partner may feel a loss of independence and self-worth.

- **Emotional Distress:** Controlling behavior can lead to significant emotional distress and anxiety.

- **Increased Conflict:** Power struggles and resentment can result in frequent conflicts.

- **Isolation:** The controlled partner may become isolated from supportive relationships.

Addressing Controlling Behavior

If you notice controlling behavior in your partner, consider these steps:

- **Communicate Boundaries:** Clearly communicate your boundaries and the need for mutual respect. Proverbs 25:28 says, "Like a city whose walls are broken through is a person who lacks self-control."

- **Seek Support:** Engage with trusted friends, family, or counselors for support and perspective.

- **Encourage Equality:** Promote a relationship dynamic based on equality and mutual decision-making.

- **Establish Independence:** Maintain your own interests, friendships, and activities to preserve your independence.

- **Pray for Change:** Pray together for humility and respect in your relationship. Colossians 3:14 advises, "And over all these virtues put on love, which binds them all together in perfect unity."

Reflection Questions

1. How does controlling behavior affect your emotional well-being and sense of autonomy?
2. Have you discussed the impact of this behavior on your relationship?
3. What steps can you take together to promote mutual respect and equality?
4. How can you support each other in maintaining healthy boundaries?

Conclusion

Controlling behavior is a significant relationship red flag that can undermine the health and equality of a partnership. Addressing this issue is crucial for fostering a loving and respectful marriage. As Christians, we are called to honor and respect each other. 1 Peter 3:8 reminds us, "Finally, all of you, be like-minded, be sympathetic, love one another, be compassionate and humble." Strive to cultivate a relationship based on mutual respect, seeking God's guidance and wisdom as you navigate these challenges.

32. Isolation from Family and Friends

Understanding Isolation from Family and Friends
Isolation from family and friends involves one partner attempting to cut off or limit the other's interactions with their social network. This can be a tactic to exert control and create dependency. The Bible emphasizes the importance of community and relationships. Ecclesiastes 4:9-10 says, "Two are better than one, because they have a good return for their labor: If either of them falls down, one can help the other up."

Biblical Perspective on Community
The Bible highlights the value of community and supportive relationships. Hebrews 10:24-25 encourages us, "And let us consider how we may spur one another on toward love and good deeds, not giving up meeting together, as some are in the habit of doing, but encouraging one another — and all the more as you see the Day approaching." Healthy relationships should foster connections, not isolate.

Identifying Isolation from Family and Friends
Signs of isolation from family and friends in a partner include:
- **Discouraging Visits:** Discouraging or preventing visits to or from family and friends.

- **Negative Influence:** Speaking negatively about your loved ones to create a divide.

- **Monitoring Communication:** Monitoring or restricting your phone calls, messages, or social media interactions.

- **Creating Dependency:** Encouraging dependency on the partner for emotional and social needs.

- **Undermining Relationships:** Undermining your relationships with others through manipulation or lies.

Consequences of Isolation from Family and Friends

Isolation from family and friends can have several negative impacts on a relationship:

- **Loss of Support System:** Cutting off supportive relationships can leave one feeling isolated and unsupported.

- **Emotional Distress:** Isolation can lead to feelings of loneliness and depression.

- **Dependency:** Creating an unhealthy dependency on the controlling partner.

- **Resentment:** The isolated partner may feel resentful and trapped.
- **Reduced Perspective:** Lack of external perspectives can skew one's view of the relationship.

Addressing Isolation from Family and Friends

If you notice isolation from family and friends in your partner, consider these steps:

- **Maintain Connections:** Actively maintain your relationships with family and friends. Proverbs 17:17 says, "A friend loves at all times, and a brother is born for a time of adversity."

- **Communicate Boundaries:** Clearly communicate your need to maintain these relationships and set firm boundaries.

- **Seek Support:** Engage with trusted friends, family, or counselors for support and perspective.

- **Encourage Social Interaction:** Promote social interactions and inclusivity within your relationship.

- **Pray for Community:** Pray together for healthy relationships and community support. Romans 12:10 encourages, "Be devoted to one another in love. Honor one another above yourselves."

Reflection Questions
1. How does isolation from family and friends affect your emotional well-being and social support?
2. Have you discussed the impact of this behavior on your relationship?
3. What steps can you take together to maintain healthy connections with others?
4. How can you support each other in fostering inclusive and supportive relationships?

Conclusion
Isolation from family and friends is a significant relationship red flag that can undermine the health and supportiveness of a partnership. Addressing this issue is crucial for fostering a loving and inclusive marriage. As Christians, we are called to value and maintain our relationships with others. Proverbs 27:17 reminds us, "As iron sharpens iron, so one person sharpens another." Strive to cultivate a relationship that supports and encourages connections with family and friends, seeking God's guidance and wisdom.

33. Lack of Respect

Understanding Lack of Respect
Lack of respect in a relationship can manifest as dismissive behavior, belittling comments, or disregarding a partner's feelings and opinions. Respect is foundational to any healthy relationship. The Bible teaches us to honor one another. Romans 12:10 says, "Be devoted to one another in love. Honor one another above yourselves."

Biblical Perspective on Respect
The Bible emphasizes mutual respect and honor. Ephesians 5:21 instructs, "Submit to one another out of reverence for Christ." Respect involves valuing each other's perspectives, treating each other with kindness, and honoring each other's dignity.

Identifying Lack of Respect
Signs of a lack of respect in a partner include:
- **Dismissive Attitude:** Ignoring or belittling your opinions and feelings.

- **Criticism and Insults:** Regularly criticizing or insulting you.

- **Interruptions:** Frequently interrupting you when you speak.

- **Ignoring Boundaries:** Disregarding your personal boundaries and limits.

- **Contempt:** Displaying contemptuous behavior, such as eye-rolling or sarcasm.

Consequences of Lack of Respect

Lack of respect can have several negative impacts on a relationship:

- **Erosion of Trust:** Disrespect undermines trust and mutual regard.

- **Emotional Hurt:** Feeling disrespected can lead to emotional pain and resentment.

- **Conflict:** Disrespect often leads to frequent arguments and tension.

- **Low Self-Esteem:** Constant disrespect can erode self-esteem and self-worth.

- **Relationship Breakdown:** Persistent lack of respect can ultimately lead to the breakdown of the relationship.

Addressing Lack of Respect

If you notice a lack of respect in your partner, consider these steps:

- **Communicate Clearly:** Discuss how their behavior affects you and the relationship. Proverbs 15:1 says, "A gentle answer turns away wrath, but a harsh word stirs up anger."

- **Set Boundaries:** Establish clear boundaries and expectations for respectful behavior.

- **Model Respect:** Demonstrate respectful behavior in your interactions.

- **Seek Counseling:** Consider professional counseling to address underlying issues and improve communication.

- **Pray for Change:** Pray together for mutual respect and understanding. Colossians 3:12-14 encourages, "Therefore, as God's chosen people, holy and dearly loved, clothe yourselves with compassion, kindness, humility, gentleness and patience. Bear with each other and forgive one another if any of you has a grievance against someone. Forgive as the Lord forgave you. And over all these virtues put on love, which binds them all together in perfect unity."

Reflection Questions

1. How does a lack of respect affect your emotional well-being and relationship?
2. Have you discussed the impact of this behavior on your mutual trust and understanding?
3. What steps can you take together to promote respect and kindness in your relationship?
4. How can you support each other in maintaining a respectful and loving relationship?

Conclusion

Lack of respect is a significant relationship red flag that can undermine the health and harmony of a partnership. Addressing this issue is crucial for fostering a loving and respectful marriage. As Christians, we are called to honor and respect each other. Philippians 2:3-4 reminds us, "Do nothing out of selfish ambition or vain conceit. Rather, in humility value others above yourselves, not looking to your own interests but each of you to the interests of the others." Strive to cultivate a relationship based on mutual respect and love, seeking God's guidance and wisdom as you grow together.

34. Infidelity

Understanding Infidelity
Infidelity involves betraying a partner's trust by engaging in a romantic or sexual relationship with someone else. This breach of trust can have devastating effects on a relationship. The Bible clearly condemns adultery. Exodus 20:14 states, "You shall not commit adultery."

Biblical Perspective on Faithfulness
The Bible calls for faithfulness and purity in relationships. Hebrews 13:4 says, "Marriage should be honored by all, and the marriage bed kept pure, for God will judge the adulterer and all the sexually immoral." Faithfulness is crucial for maintaining trust and integrity in a relationship.

Identifying Infidelity
Signs of infidelity in a partner include:
- **Secretive Behavior:** Hiding phone calls, messages, or activities.

- **Emotional Distance:** Becoming emotionally distant or withdrawn.

- **Changes in Routine:** Unexplained changes in schedule or routine.

- **Increased Defensiveness:** Becoming defensive or accusatory when questioned about behavior.

- **Physical Evidence:** Finding physical evidence of infidelity, such as unfamiliar items or messages.

Consequences of Infidelity

Infidelity can have several devastating impacts on a relationship:

- **Betrayal of Trust:** Infidelity severely undermines trust and security.

- **Emotional Pain:** The betrayed partner may experience deep emotional pain and trauma.

- **Conflict:** Infidelity often leads to intense conflict and arguments.

- **Self-Esteem Issues:** The betrayed partner may struggle with self-esteem and feelings of inadequacy.

- **Relationship Breakdown:** Infidelity can lead to the breakdown of the relationship, including separation or divorce.

Addressing Infidelity

If infidelity has occurred in your relationship, consider these steps:

- **Seek Counseling:** Professional counseling can help address the underlying issues and work towards healing.

- **Communicate Openly:** Have honest and open discussions about the impact of the infidelity and your feelings. Ephesians 4:25 encourages, "Therefore each of you must put off falsehood and speak truthfully to your neighbor, for we are all members of one body."

- **Set Boundaries:** Establish clear boundaries to rebuild trust and prevent future occurrences.

- **Forgiveness and Healing:** Work towards forgiveness and healing, if both partners are committed to repairing the relationship. Colossians 3:13 advises, "Bear with each other and forgive one another if any of you has a grievance against someone. Forgive as the Lord forgave you."

- **Pray for Restoration:** Pray together for God's guidance and strength to restore your relationship. Psalm 51:10 says, "Create in me a pure heart, O God, and renew a steadfast spirit within me."

Reflection Questions
1. How does infidelity affect your emotional well-being and trust in the relationship?
2. Have you discussed the impact of this behavior on your future together?
3. What steps can you take together to rebuild trust and restore your relationship?
4. How can you support each other in healing from the effects of infidelity?

Conclusion
Infidelity is a significant relationship red flag that can have devastating effects on a partnership. Addressing this issue is crucial for fostering a loving and faithful marriage. As Christians, we are called to be faithful and honor our commitments. Proverbs 5:18-19 encourages, "May your fountain be blessed, and may you rejoice in the wife of your youth. A loving doe, a graceful deer — may her breasts satisfy you always, may you ever be intoxicated with her love." Strive to cultivate faithfulness and integrity in your relationship, seeking God's guidance and wisdom as you work towards healing and restoration.

35. Lack of Support for Your Goals

Understanding Lack of Support for Your Goals

A partner who lacks support for your goals may dismiss or belittle your aspirations, fail to encourage you, or show indifference towards your ambitions. Support from a partner is essential for personal growth and mutual fulfillment. The Bible encourages us to build each other up. 1 Thessalonians 5:11 says, "Therefore encourage one another and build each other up, just as in fact you are doing."

Biblical Perspective on Support

The Bible emphasizes the importance of mutual encouragement and support in relationships. Ecclesiastes 4:9-10 states, "Two are better than one, because they have a good return for their labor: If either of them falls down, one can help the other up. But pity anyone who falls and has no one to help them up." Supporting each other's goals is vital for a healthy and thriving relationship.

Identifying Lack of Support

Signs of lack of support for your goals in a partner include:

- **Dismissiveness:** Dismissing or belittling your aspirations and dreams.

- **Indifference:** Showing indifference or lack of interest in your goals.

- **Criticism:** Criticizing your ambitions or efforts to achieve them.

- **Undermining Efforts:** Actively undermining or sabotaging your attempts to reach your goals.

- **Lack of Encouragement:** Failing to provide encouragement or assistance when needed.

Consequences of Lack of Support

Lack of support for your goals can have several negative impacts on a relationship:

- **Emotional Hurt:** Feeling unsupported can lead to emotional pain and resentment.

- **Stifled Growth:** Lack of support can hinder personal and professional growth.

- **Conflict:** Disagreements and conflicts may arise over the lack of support.

- **Decreased Motivation:** Feeling unsupported can decrease motivation to pursue goals.

- **Erosion of Trust:** A lack of support can undermine trust and mutual respect.

Addressing Lack of Support

If you notice a lack of support for your goals in your partner, consider these steps:

- **Communicate Your Needs:** Discuss how their support impacts your goals and well-being. Ephesians 4:15 encourages, "Instead, speaking the truth in love, we will grow to become in every respect the mature body of him who is the head, that is, Christ."

- **Seek Understanding:** Help your partner understand the importance of your goals and how they contribute to your fulfillment.

- **Encourage Mutual Support:** Promote a culture of mutual support and encouragement in your relationship.

- **Set Shared Goals:** Work together to set and support each other's goals.

- **Pray for Encouragement:** Pray together for the ability to encourage and support one another. Hebrews 10:24-25 advises, "And let us consider how we may spur one another on toward love and good deeds, not giving up meeting together, as some are in the habit of doing, but encouraging one another — and all the more as you see the Day approaching."

Reflection Questions
1. How does a lack of support for your goals affect your emotional well-being and motivation?
2. Have you discussed the impact of this behavior on your relationship?
3. What steps can you take together to promote mutual support and encouragement?
4. How can you support each other in achieving your individual and shared goals?

Conclusion
Lack of support for your goals is a significant relationship red flag that can undermine personal growth and mutual fulfillment. Addressing this issue is crucial for fostering a supportive and encouraging marriage. As Christians, we are called to build each other up and encourage one another. Romans 12:10 reminds us, "Be devoted to one another in love. Honor one another above yourselves." Strive to cultivate a relationship where mutual support and encouragement are foundational, seeking God's guidance and wisdom.

36. Constant Blaming

Understanding Constant Blaming
Constant blaming involves one partner consistently assigning fault to the other for problems and issues, often without taking responsibility for their own actions. This behavior can create a toxic and hostile environment. The Bible calls us to humility and accountability. Matthew 7:3-5 says, "Why do you look at the speck of sawdust in your brother's eye and pay no attention to the plank in your own eye? How can you say to your brother, 'Let me take the speck out of your eye,' when all the time there is a plank in your own eye? You hypocrite, first take the plank out of your own eye, and then you will see clearly to remove the speck from your brother's eye."

Biblical Perspective on Accountability
The Bible teaches the importance of self-reflection and taking responsibility for our actions. Galatians 6:5 states, "For each one should carry their own load." A healthy relationship involves both partners acknowledging their own contributions to problems and working together to find solutions.

Identifying Constant Blaming
Signs of constant blaming in a partner include:
- **Frequent Accusations:** Regularly accusing you of causing problems or issues.

- **Lack of Accountability:** Refusing to take responsibility for their own actions or mistakes.

- **Defensiveness:** Becoming defensive when confronted about their behavior.

- **Emotional Manipulation:** Using blame to manipulate or control your actions.

- **Avoidance of Solutions:** Focusing on assigning blame rather than finding solutions.

Consequences of Constant Blaming

Constant blaming can have several negative impacts on a relationship:

- **Erosion of Trust:** Blame undermines trust and mutual respect.

- **Emotional Hurt:** Feeling constantly blamed can lead to emotional pain and resentment.

- **Conflict:** Blame often leads to frequent arguments and tension.

- **Low Self-Esteem:** Constant blame can erode self-esteem and self-worth.

- **Relationship Breakdown:** Persistent blaming can ultimately lead to the breakdown of the relationship.

Addressing Constant Blaming

If you notice constant blaming in your partner, consider these steps:

- **Communicate Clearly:** Discuss how their behavior affects you and the relationship. Proverbs 15:1 advises, "A gentle answer turns away wrath, but a harsh word stirs up anger."

- **Encourage Accountability:** Promote a culture of accountability and self-reflection in your relationship.

- **Seek Solutions Together:** Focus on finding solutions together rather than assigning blame.

- **Set Boundaries:** Establish clear boundaries to prevent emotional manipulation and blame.

- **Pray for Change:** Pray together for humility and a spirit of cooperation. Colossians 3:13 encourages, "Bear with each other and forgive one another if any of you has a grievance against someone. Forgive as the Lord forgave you."

Reflection Questions

1. How does constant blaming affect your emotional well-being and relationship?

2. Have you discussed the impact of this behavior on your mutual trust and respect?

3. What steps can you take together to promote accountability and cooperation?

4. How can you support each other in maintaining a positive and constructive relationship?

Conclusion

Constant blaming is a significant relationship red flag that can undermine the health and harmony of a partnership. Addressing this issue is crucial for fostering a loving and respectful marriage. As Christians, we are called to practice humility and accountability. James 5:16 advises, "Therefore confess your sins to each other and pray for each other so that you may be healed. The prayer of a righteous person is powerful and effective." Strive to cultivate a relationship based on mutual respect and cooperation, seeking God's guidance and wisdom as you grow together.

37. Gaslighting

Understanding Gaslighting
Gaslighting is a form of psychological manipulation where one partner makes the other question their reality, memory, or perceptions. This behavior can be deeply damaging, leading to confusion, anxiety, and a loss of self-trust. The Bible calls us to speak the truth in love. Ephesians 4:25 says, "Therefore each of you must put off falsehood and speak truthfully to your neighbor, for we are all members of one body."

Biblical Perspective on Truthfulness
The Bible emphasizes the importance of honesty and truthfulness in all relationships. John 8:32 states, "Then you will know the truth, and the truth will set you free." A healthy relationship is built on honesty, integrity, and mutual trust.

Identifying Gaslighting
Signs of gaslighting in a partner include:
- **Denying Reality:** Consistently denying things they have said or done, making you doubt your memory.

- **Blaming You:** Shifting blame onto you for their actions or mistakes.

- **Minimizing Your Feelings:** Telling you that your feelings are irrational or exaggerated.

- **Manipulating Facts:** Twisting facts or retelling events to cast doubt on your perception.

- **Isolation:** Encouraging you to doubt your perceptions and rely solely on them for the "truth."

Consequences of Gaslighting

Gaslighting can have several severe impacts on a relationship:

- **Loss of Trust:** Undermines trust and mutual respect.

- **Emotional Distress:** Causes significant emotional pain, anxiety, and confusion.

- **Erosion of Self-Esteem:** Leads to a loss of self-confidence and trust in one's judgment.

- **Isolation:** Can result in emotional and social isolation as the victim doubts their reality.

- **Control:** Enables the gaslighter to exert control and power over the victim.

Addressing Gaslighting

If you notice gaslighting in your partner, consider these steps:

- **Document Incidents:** Keep a record of events and conversations to maintain clarity.

- **Seek Support:** Engage with trusted friends, family, or a counselor for support and perspective.

- **Set Boundaries:** Establish clear boundaries to protect yourself from manipulation.

- **Communicate Clearly:** Address the behavior directly and express how it affects you. Proverbs 12:22 says, "The Lord detests lying lips, but he delights in people who are trustworthy."

- **Pray for Strength:** Pray for strength, wisdom, and discernment. Psalm 25:4-5 encourages, "Show me your ways, Lord, teach me your paths. Guide me in your truth and teach me, for you are God my Savior, and my hope is in you all day long."

Reflection Questions

1. How does gaslighting affect your emotional well-being and self-perception?

2. Have you discussed the impact of this behavior on your trust and mutual respect?

3. What steps can you take to protect yourself and seek support?

4. How can you work towards restoring honesty and integrity in your relationship?

Conclusion

Gaslighting is a significant relationship red flag that can deeply damage trust and emotional well-being. Addressing this issue is crucial for fostering a loving and respectful marriage. As Christians, we are called to live in truth and integrity. Proverbs 3:3-4 advises, "Let love and faithfulness never leave you; bind them around your neck, write them on the tablet of your heart. Then you will win favor and a good name in the sight of God and man." Strive to cultivate a relationship based on honesty and mutual respect, seeking God's guidance and wisdom.

38. Unequal Partnership
Understanding Unequal Partnership
An unequal partnership occurs when one partner consistently dominates or controls the relationship, leading to an imbalance in decision-making, responsibilities, and contributions. This dynamic can create resentment and undermine the mutual respect needed for a healthy relationship. The Bible emphasizes mutual submission and partnership. Ephesians 5:21 states, "Submit to one another out of reverence for Christ."

Biblical Perspective on Equality
The Bible teaches that relationships should be based on mutual respect and equality. Galatians 3:28 says, "There is neither Jew nor Gentile, neither slave nor free, nor is there male and female, for you are all one in Christ Jesus." A healthy partnership involves shared responsibilities and respect for each other's contributions.

Identifying Unequal Partnership
Signs of an unequal partnership in a relationship include:

- **Dominating Decision-Making:** One partner makes most or all of the decisions.

- **Unequal Responsibilities:** One partner bears the majority of responsibilities, whether financial, household, or emotional.

- **Lack of Contribution:** One partner does not contribute fairly to the relationship.

- **Disregarding Opinions:** One partner's opinions and preferences are consistently ignored.

- **Power Imbalance:** A clear imbalance of power and control in the relationship.

Consequences of Unequal Partnership

An unequal partnership can have several negative impacts on a relationship:

- **Resentment:** The less dominant partner may feel resentful and undervalued.

- **Emotional Strain:** Bearing unequal responsibilities can lead to stress and burnout.

- **Conflict:** Power imbalances often result in frequent conflicts and arguments.

- **Erosion of Trust:** Unequal partnerships undermine trust and mutual respect.

- **Stifled Growth:** The relationship may not grow or thrive due to the imbalance.

Addressing Unequal Partnership

If you notice an unequal partnership in your relationship, consider these steps:

- **Communicate Openly:** Discuss the imbalance and its impact on your relationship. Proverbs 15:22 says, "Plans fail for lack of counsel, but with many advisers they succeed."

- **Share Responsibilities:** Work towards a fair distribution of responsibilities and decision-making.

- **Value Contributions:** Acknowledge and value each other's contributions and efforts.

- **Seek Counseling:** Consider professional counseling to address underlying issues and improve partnership dynamics.

- **Pray for Balance:** Pray together for balance, mutual respect, and shared responsibilities. Philippians 2:3-4 advises, "Do nothing out of selfish ambition or vain conceit. Rather, in humility value others above yourselves, not looking to your own interests but each of you to the interests of the others."

Reflection Questions
1. How does an unequal partnership affect your emotional well-being and relationship?
2. Have you discussed the impact of this behavior on your mutual respect and trust?
3. What steps can you take together to promote equality and shared responsibilities?
4. How can you support each other in maintaining a balanced and healthy partnership?

Conclusion
An unequal partnership is a significant relationship red flag that can undermine the health and balance of a relationship. Addressing this issue is crucial for fostering a loving and respectful marriage. As Christians, we are called to mutual submission and partnership. Ecclesiastes 4:9-10 reminds us, "Two are better than one, because they have a good return for their labor: If either of them falls down, one can help the other up. But pity anyone who falls and has no one to help them up." Strive to cultivate a relationship based on mutual respect and shared responsibilities, seeking God's guidance and wisdom.

39. Overly Dependent

Understanding Overly Dependent Behavior
Overly dependent behavior involves relying excessively on a partner for emotional, financial, or physical support to the point where it hinders personal growth and creates an unhealthy dynamic. While support in a relationship is essential, excessive dependence can lead to imbalance and strain. The Bible encourages self-reliance and diligence. Proverbs 6:6-8 says, "Go to the ant, you sluggard; consider its ways and be wise! It has no commander, no overseer or ruler, yet it stores its provisions in summer and gathers its food at harvest."

Biblical Perspective on Self-Reliance
The Bible emphasizes the importance of individual responsibility and diligence. Galatians 6:5 states, "For each one should carry their own load." A healthy relationship involves both partners contributing and supporting each other without creating dependency.

Identifying Overly Dependent Behavior
Signs of overly dependent behavior in a partner include:
- **Constant Need for Reassurance:** Regularly seeking affirmation and reassurance.

- **Inability to Make Decisions:** Reluctance or inability to make decisions independently.

- **Avoiding Responsibilities:** Relying on the partner to handle all responsibilities.

- **Lack of Initiative:** Showing little initiative in personal or professional life.

- **Emotional Clinginess:** Displaying excessive emotional reliance on the partner.

Consequences of Overly Dependent Behavior

Overly dependent behavior can have several negative impacts on a relationship:

- **Imbalance:** Creates an imbalance where one partner feels overwhelmed.

- **Stunted Growth:** Hinders personal growth and development.

- **Resentment:** Can lead to feelings of resentment and frustration.

- **Emotional Strain:** Places emotional strain on the supporting partner.

- **Decreased Intimacy:** Can reduce intimacy and mutual respect.

Addressing Overly Dependent Behavior

If you notice overly dependent behavior in your partner, consider these steps:

- **Encourage Independence:** Promote activities and decisions that foster independence. Philippians 4:13 reminds us, "I can do all this through him who gives me strength."

- **Set Boundaries:** Establish clear boundaries to ensure a healthy balance of support.

- **Support Growth:** Encourage your partner to pursue personal growth and development.

- **Seek Counseling:** Consider professional counseling to address dependency issues.

- **Pray for Strength:** Pray together for strength and self-reliance. Isaiah 40:31 encourages, "But those who hope in the Lord will renew their strength. They will soar on wings like eagles; they will run and not grow weary, they will walk and not be faint."

Reflection Questions

1. How does overly dependent behavior affect your emotional well-being and relationship?
2. Have you discussed the impact of this behavior on your mutual growth and development?
3. What steps can you take together to promote independence and balance?
4. How can you support each other in maintaining a healthy dynamic?

Conclusion

Overly dependent behavior is a significant relationship red flag that can undermine the health and balance of a relationship. Addressing this issue is crucial for fostering a loving and respectful partnership. As Christians, we are called to be diligent and self-reliant. Proverbs 31:17 says, "She sets about her work vigorously; her arms are strong for her tasks." Strive to cultivate a relationship where both partners are empowered and supportive, seeking God's guidance and wisdom.

40. Disrespect for Boundaries

Understanding Disrespect for Boundaries
Disrespect for boundaries involves ignoring or violating a partner's personal, emotional, or physical limits. This behavior can lead to feelings of discomfort, resentment, and a lack of trust. The Bible teaches us to respect others' boundaries and to treat them with love and consideration. Matthew 7:12 says, "So in everything, do to others what you would have them do to you, for this sums up the Law and the Prophets."

Biblical Perspective on Respecting Boundaries
The Bible emphasizes the importance of respecting others and their boundaries. Philippians 2:4 states, "Not looking to your own interests but each of you to the interests of the others." Healthy relationships involve understanding and honoring each other's limits.

Identifying Disrespect for Boundaries
Signs of disrespect for boundaries in a partner include:

- **Ignoring Limits:** Disregarding your expressed limits and wishes.

- **Overstepping:** Consistently invading your personal space or privacy.

- **Pressuring:** Pressuring you to do things you are uncomfortable with.

- **Invalidating Feelings:** Dismissing or invalidating your feelings and preferences.

- **Control:** Attempting to control your actions, decisions, or relationships.

Consequences of Disrespect for Boundaries

Disrespect for boundaries can have several negative impacts on a relationship:

- **Erosion of Trust:** Undermines trust and mutual respect.

- **Emotional Distress:** Causes significant emotional pain and discomfort.

- **Conflict:** Leads to frequent arguments and tension.

- **Resentment:** Can result in feelings of resentment and anger.

- **Loss of Autonomy:** Reduces a sense of independence and self-worth.

Addressing Disrespect for Boundaries

If you notice disrespect for boundaries in your partner, consider these steps:

- **Communicate Clearly:** Discuss your boundaries and how their behavior affects you. Ephesians 4:15 advises, "Instead, speaking the truth in love, we will grow to become in every respect the mature body of him who is the head, that is, Christ."

- **Set Firm Boundaries:** Establish and maintain clear boundaries to protect your well-being.

- **Seek Mutual Respect:** Promote a culture of mutual respect and understanding in your relationship.

- **Seek Counseling:** Consider professional counseling to address underlying issues.

- **Pray for Understanding:** Pray together for understanding and respect in your relationship. Proverbs 3:5-6 encourages, "Trust in the Lord with all your heart and lean not on your own understanding; in all your ways submit to him, and he will make your paths straight."

Reflection Questions

1. How does disrespect for boundaries affect your emotional well-being and relationship?
2. Have you discussed the impact of this behavior on your trust and mutual respect?
3. What steps can you take together to promote respect for boundaries?
4. How can you support each other in maintaining healthy boundaries?

Conclusion

Disrespect for boundaries is a significant relationship red flag that can undermine the health and trust of a partnership. Addressing this issue is crucial for fostering a loving and respectful marriage. As Christians, we are called to respect and honor each other. Romans 12:10 reminds us, "Be devoted to one another in love. Honor one another above yourselves." Strive to cultivate a relationship where boundaries are respected, seeking God's guidance and wisdom as you grow together.

Chapter 5: Lifestyle and Habits

41. Substance Abuse
Understanding Substance Abuse

Substance abuse involves the excessive use of alcohol, drugs, or other substances that impair judgment and behavior. This can lead to health problems, relationship issues, and financial difficulties. The Bible warns against overindulgence and losing self-control. Proverbs 20:1 says, "Wine is a mocker and beer a brawler; whoever is led astray by them is not wise."

Biblical Perspective on Sobriety

The Bible encourages sobriety and self-control. Ephesians 5:18 states, "Do not get drunk on wine, which leads to debauchery. Instead, be filled with the Spirit." Maintaining control over one's actions and avoiding substance abuse is crucial for a healthy and stable life.

Identifying Substance Abuse

Signs of substance abuse in a partner include:

- **Frequent Intoxication:** Regularly getting drunk or high.

- **Neglecting Responsibilities:** Failing to meet work, family, or social obligations due to substance use.

- **Health Problems:** Experiencing health issues related to substance use.

- **Financial Issues:** Spending excessive amounts of money on substances.

- **Denial:** Refusing to acknowledge the problem or its impact on their life and relationships.

Consequences of Substance Abuse

Substance abuse can have several severe impacts on a relationship:

- **Health Risks:** Increased risk of physical and mental health problems.

- **Trust Issues:** Erosion of trust due to unpredictable behavior.
- **Financial Strain:** Financial instability caused by spending on substances.

- **Emotional Pain:** Emotional distress and fear for the partner's well-being.

- **Conflict:** Frequent arguments and tension related to substance use.

Addressing Substance Abuse

If you notice substance abuse in your partner, consider these steps:

- **Communicate Concern:** Express your concerns about their substance use and its impact. Galatians 6:1 advises, "Brothers and sisters, if someone is caught in a sin, you who live by the Spirit should restore that person gently."

- **Encourage Treatment:** Encourage your partner to seek professional help or join a support group.

- **Set Boundaries:** Establish clear boundaries to protect yourself and your relationship.

- **Seek Support:** Engage with support groups or counselors for guidance and assistance.

- **Pray for Healing:** Pray together for healing and strength to overcome substance abuse. Psalm 147:3 says, "He heals the brokenhearted and binds up their wounds."

Reflection Questions

1. How does substance abuse affect your relationship and emotional well-being?
2. Have you discussed the impact of this behavior on your future together?
3. What steps can you take to encourage treatment and recovery?
4. How can you support each other in maintaining a substance-free lifestyle?

Conclusion

Substance abuse is a significant lifestyle red flag that can severely impact a relationship. Addressing this issue is crucial for fostering a healthy and stable partnership. As Christians, we are called to live sober and self-controlled lives. 1 Peter 5:8 reminds us, "Be alert and of sober mind. Your enemy the devil prowls around like a roaring lion looking for someone to devour." Strive to support each other in maintaining sobriety and seeking God's guidance and strength.

42. Addictive Behaviors
Understanding Addictive Behaviors

Addictive behaviors involve compulsive engagement in activities such as gambling, gaming, shopping, or internet use that interfere with daily life and responsibilities. These behaviors can become destructive and lead to significant personal and relational issues. The Bible cautions against being enslaved by anything other than God. 1 Corinthians 6:12 says, "I have the right to do anything," you say—but not everything is beneficial. "I have the right to do anything"—but I will not be mastered by anything."

Biblical Perspective on Self-Control

The Bible emphasizes the importance of self-control and avoiding behaviors that can lead to addiction. Galatians 5:22-23 highlights self-control as a fruit of the Spirit: "But the fruit of the Spirit is love, joy, peace, forbearance, kindness, goodness, faithfulness, gentleness and self-control. Against such things there is no law."

Identifying Addictive Behaviors

Signs of addictive behaviors in a partner include:

- **Neglecting Responsibilities:** Failing to meet obligations due to the addictive behavior.

- **Preoccupation:** Constantly thinking about or engaging in the addictive activity.

- **Loss of Interest:** Losing interest in activities once enjoyed.

- **Secrecy:** Hiding the extent of the behavior from others.

- **Negative Consequences:** Continuing the behavior despite negative consequences.

Consequences of Addictive Behaviors

Addictive behaviors can have several negative impacts on a relationship:

- **Emotional Distance:** Creating emotional distance and reducing intimacy.

- **Financial Strain:** Leading to financial problems due to excessive spending.

- **Health Issues:** Causing physical and mental health problems.

- **Trust Issues:** Eroding trust due to secrecy and dishonesty.

- **Increased Conflict:** Leading to frequent arguments and tension.

Addressing Addictive Behaviors

If you notice addictive behaviors in your partner, consider these steps:

- **Express Concern:** Share your concerns about their behavior and its impact. Proverbs 27:5 says, "Better is open rebuke than hidden love."

- **Encourage Professional Help:** Suggest seeking help from a counselor or support group.

- **Set Boundaries:** Establish boundaries to protect yourself and encourage change.

- **Seek Support:** Engage with support groups or counselors for guidance and assistance.

- **Pray for Deliverance:** Pray together for deliverance and self-control. Philippians 4:13 reminds us, "I can do all this through him who gives me strength."

Reflection Questions

1. How do addictive behaviors affect your relationship and daily life?
2. Have you discussed the impact of this behavior on your future together?
3. What steps can you take to encourage seeking help and recovery?
4. How can you support each other in overcoming addictive behaviors?

Conclusion

Addictive behaviors are significant lifestyle red flags that can severely impact a relationship. Addressing this issue is crucial for fostering a healthy and balanced partnership. As Christians, we are called to exercise self-control and avoid being mastered by anything other than God. 2 Timothy 1:7 encourages, "For the Spirit God gave us does not make us timid, but gives us power, love and self-discipline." Strive to support each other in overcoming addictive behaviors, seeking God's guidance and strength as you pursue a healthy lifestyle.

43. Unhealthy Lifestyle Choices

Understanding Unhealthy Lifestyle Choices
Unhealthy lifestyle choices involve behaviors that negatively impact physical and mental health, such as poor diet, lack of exercise, smoking, excessive drinking, and inadequate sleep. These choices can lead to chronic health issues and affect overall well-being. The Bible encourages us to take care of our bodies as temples of the Holy Spirit. 1 Corinthians 6:19-20 says, "Do you not know that your bodies are temples of the Holy Spirit, who is in you, whom you have received from God? You are not your own; you were bought at a price. Therefore honor God with your bodies."

Biblical Perspective on Healthy Living
The Bible emphasizes the importance of maintaining good health and treating our bodies with respect. Proverbs 3:7-8 advises, "Do not be wise in your own eyes; fear the Lord and shun evil. This will bring health to your body and nourishment to your bones." Embracing healthy habits is part of honoring God with our bodies.

Identifying Unhealthy Lifestyle Choices
Signs of unhealthy lifestyle choices in a partner include:
- **Poor Diet:** Consistently consuming unhealthy foods and neglecting nutritional needs.

- **Lack of Exercise:** Avoiding physical activity and leading a sedentary lifestyle.

- **Substance Use:** Smoking, excessive drinking, or using drugs.

- **Inadequate Sleep:** Not getting enough rest or maintaining irregular sleep patterns.

- **Neglecting Health:** Ignoring health problems or avoiding medical check-ups.

Consequences of Unhealthy Lifestyle Choices

Unhealthy lifestyle choices can have several negative impacts on a relationship:

- **Health Problems:** Increased risk of chronic diseases and health complications.

- **Emotional Strain:** Stress and worry about a partner's health can cause emotional strain.

- **Decreased Quality of Life:** Reduced energy, mood swings, and overall well-being.

- **Financial Strain:** Increased medical expenses and potential loss of income due to illness.

- **Relationship Tension:** Conflicts arising from differing lifestyle habits and priorities.

Addressing Unhealthy Lifestyle Choices

If you notice unhealthy lifestyle choices in your partner, consider these steps:

- **Communicate Concerns:** Share your concerns about their health and the impact on your relationship. Ephesians 4:15 encourages, "Instead, speaking the truth in love, we will grow to become in every respect the mature body of him who is the head, that is, Christ."

- **Promote Healthy Habits:** Encourage adopting healthier habits together, such as cooking nutritious meals or exercising.

- **Support and Encourage:** Offer support and encouragement for making positive changes.

- **Lead by Example:** Model healthy lifestyle choices in your own behavior.

- **Pray for Health:** Pray together for strength and motivation to make healthier choices. 3 John 1:2 says, "Dear friend, I pray that you may enjoy good health and that all may go well with you, even as your soul is getting along well."

Reflection Questions
1. How do unhealthy lifestyle choices affect your partner's well-being and your relationship?
2. Have you discussed the impact of these behaviors on your future together?
3. What steps can you take to promote healthier habits in your relationship?
4. How can you support each other in maintaining a healthy lifestyle?

Conclusion
Unhealthy lifestyle choices are significant red flags that can affect both individual well-being and relationship health. Addressing this issue is crucial for fostering a loving and supportive partnership. As Christians, we are called to honor God with our bodies and embrace healthy living. Proverbs 4:20-22 reminds us, "My son, pay attention to what I say; turn your ear to my words. Do not let them out of your sight, keep them within your heart; for they are life to those who find them and health to one's whole body." Strive to support each other in making healthy choices, seeking God's guidance and strength.

44. Lack of Ambition
Understanding Lack of Ambition

Lack of ambition involves a disinterest or unwillingness to set and pursue personal or professional goals. This behavior can lead to stagnation and dissatisfaction in life. The Bible encourages diligence and striving towards goals. Proverbs 13:4 says, "A sluggard's appetite is never filled, but the desires of the diligent are fully satisfied."

Biblical Perspective on Diligence and Purpose

The Bible emphasizes the importance of working diligently and fulfilling our God-given purposes. Colossians 3:23-24 instructs, "Whatever you do, work at it with all your heart, as working for the Lord, not for human masters, since you know that you will receive an inheritance from the Lord as a reward. It is the Lord Christ you are serving."

Identifying Lack of Ambition

Signs of lack of ambition in a partner include:

- **No Goals:** Having no personal or professional goals or plans for the future.

- **Procrastination:** Consistently putting off tasks and responsibilities.

- **Contentment with Stagnation:** Showing no interest in growth or improvement.

- **Dependence:** Relying on others for motivation and direction.

- **Avoidance of Challenges:** Avoiding opportunities that require effort or commitment.

Consequences of Lack of Ambition

Lack of ambition can have several negative impacts on a relationship:

- **Stagnation:** Both personal and relational growth can become stagnant.

- **Frustration:** One partner may feel frustrated or burdened by the imbalance.

- **Financial Strain:** Lack of ambition can lead to financial instability and dependency.

- **Conflict:** Differing levels of ambition can lead to disagreements and tension.

- **Unfulfilled Potential:** The partner may not reach their full potential, leading to dissatisfaction.

Addressing Lack of Ambition

If you notice a lack of ambition in your partner, consider these steps:

- **Discuss Aspirations:** Have an open conversation about dreams, goals, and aspirations. Proverbs 20:5 says, "The purposes of a person's heart are deep waters, but one who has insight draws them out."

- **Encourage Goal Setting:** Help your partner set realistic and achievable goals.

- **Provide Support:** Offer support and encouragement to pursue these goals.

- **Celebrate Progress:** Acknowledge and celebrate achievements, no matter how small.

- **Pray for Motivation:** Pray together for inspiration and motivation to pursue meaningful goals. Philippians 4:13 reminds us, "I can do all this through him who gives me strength."

Reflection Questions

1. How does a lack of ambition affect your partner's personal growth and your relationship?
2. Have you discussed the impact of this behavior on your mutual goals and future?
3. What steps can you take to encourage ambition and goal setting in your relationship?
4. How can you support each other in pursuing personal and professional growth?

Conclusion

Lack of ambition is a significant red flag that can affect both personal fulfillment and relationship dynamics. Addressing this issue is crucial for fostering a motivated and supportive partnership. As Christians, we are called to work diligently and pursue our God-given purposes. Ecclesiastes 9:10 encourages, "Whatever your hand finds to do, do it with all your might." Strive to support each other in setting and achieving meaningful goals, seeking God's guidance and strength as you grow together.

45. Poor Hygiene

Understanding Poor Hygiene
Poor hygiene involves neglecting personal cleanliness and grooming, which can lead to health issues and affect social interactions. This behavior can be problematic in a relationship, as it may cause discomfort and concern. The Bible highlights the importance of cleanliness and taking care of oneself. Leviticus 11:44 says, "I am the Lord your God; consecrate yourselves and be holy, because I am holy."

Biblical Perspective on Cleanliness
The Bible encourages us to maintain cleanliness and present ourselves well. 1 Corinthians 6:19-20 reminds us, "Do you not know that your bodies are temples of the Holy Spirit, who is in you, whom you have received from God? You are not your own; you were bought at a price. Therefore honor God with your bodies." Taking care of our bodies through proper hygiene is a way of honoring God.

Identifying Poor Hygiene
Signs of poor hygiene in a partner include:
- **Neglecting Daily Hygiene:** Not bathing regularly or neglecting oral hygiene.

- **Untidy Appearance:** Consistently wearing dirty or unkempt clothes.

- **Bad Breath or Body Odor:** Persistent bad breath or body odor due to lack of hygiene.

- **Neglecting Grooming:** Ignoring basic grooming practices like haircuts, nail trimming, etc.

- **Avoiding Cleanliness Routines:** Skipping regular hygiene routines such as handwashing.

Consequences of Poor Hygiene

Poor hygiene can have several negative impacts on a relationship:

- **Health Issues:** Increased risk of infections and illnesses.

- **Social Discomfort:** Causing discomfort in social interactions and intimacy.

- **Reduced Attraction:** Affecting physical attraction between partners.

- **Embarrassment:** Leading to embarrassment in social settings.

- **Conflict:** Creating tension and conflict due to differing standards of cleanliness.

Addressing Poor Hygiene

If you notice poor hygiene in your partner, consider these steps:

- **Communicate Clearly:** Discuss your concerns about their hygiene in a loving and respectful manner. Ephesians 4:15 advises, "Instead, speaking the truth in love, we will grow to become in every respect the mature body of him who is the head, that is, Christ."

- **Encourage Good Habits:** Encourage and support your partner in establishing good hygiene practices.

- **Offer Solutions:** Suggest practical solutions, such as setting reminders or creating a hygiene routine together.

- **Lead by Example:** Model good hygiene practices in your own behavior.

- **Pray for Improvement:** Pray together for the motivation and commitment to maintain good hygiene. Philippians 4:13 reminds us, "I can do all this through him who gives me strength."

Reflection Questions
1. How does poor hygiene affect your relationship and daily interactions?
2. Have you discussed the impact of this behavior on your comfort and health?
3. What steps can you take together to promote better hygiene practices?
4. How can you support each other in maintaining personal cleanliness?

Conclusion
Poor hygiene is a significant lifestyle red flag that can impact both personal well-being and relationship dynamics. Addressing this issue is crucial for fostering a healthy and comfortable partnership. As Christians, we are called to honor God with our bodies and maintain cleanliness. Proverbs 31:17 says, "She sets about her work vigorously; her arms are strong for her tasks." Strive to support each other in maintaining good hygiene practices, seeking God's guidance and strength.

46. Disregard for Health
Understanding Disregard for Health

Disregard for health involves neglecting physical and mental well-being through unhealthy behaviors such as poor diet, lack of exercise, neglecting medical care, and ignoring mental health needs. This behavior can lead to serious health issues and affect the quality of life. The Bible emphasizes the importance of taking care of our bodies. 3 John 1:2 says, "Dear friend, I pray that you may enjoy good health and that all may go well with you, even as your soul is getting along well."

Biblical Perspective on Health

The Bible encourages us to maintain our health and well-being as a way of honoring God. Proverbs 4:20-22 advises, "My son, pay attention to what I say; turn your ear to my words. Do not let them out of your sight, keep them within your heart; for they are life to those who find them and health to one's whole body." Embracing healthy habits is part of our stewardship of the bodies God has given us.

Identifying Disregard for Health

Signs of disregard for health in a partner include:

- **Unhealthy Eating:** Consistently consuming a poor diet and neglecting nutritional needs.

- **Sedentary Lifestyle:** Avoiding physical activity and exercise.

- **Ignoring Medical Care:** Neglecting regular medical check-ups and ignoring health problems.

- **Mental Health Neglect:** Ignoring mental health needs and refusing to seek help when needed.

- **Risky Behaviors:** Engaging in behaviors that put their health at risk.

Consequences of Disregard for Health

Disregard for health can have several negative impacts on a relationship:

- **Health Problems:** Increased risk of chronic diseases and health complications.

- **Emotional Strain:** Worry and stress about a partner's health can cause emotional strain.

- **Financial Strain:** Increased medical expenses and potential loss of income due to illness.

- **Reduced Quality of Life:** Decreased energy, mood swings, and overall well-being.

- **Relationship Tension:** Conflicts arising from differing health habits and priorities.

Addressing Disregard for Health

If you notice a disregard for health in your partner, consider these steps:

- **Communicate Concerns:** Share your concerns about their health and the impact on your relationship. Proverbs 27:17 says, "As iron sharpens iron, so one person sharpens another."

- **Promote Healthy Habits:** Encourage adopting healthier habits together, such as cooking nutritious meals or exercising.

- **Support and Encourage:** Offer support and encouragement for making positive changes.

- **Lead by Example:** Model healthy lifestyle choices in your own behavior.

- **Pray for Health:** Pray together for strength and motivation to maintain good health. Isaiah 40:31 says, "But those who hope in the Lord will renew their strength. They will soar on wings like eagles; they will run and not grow weary, they will walk and not be faint."

Reflection Questions
1. How does disregard for health affect your partner's well-being and your relationship?
2. Have you discussed the impact of these behaviors on your future together?
3. What steps can you take to promote healthier habits in your relationship?
4. How can you support each other in maintaining physical and mental health?

Conclusion
Disregard for health is a significant lifestyle red flag that can affect both individual well-being and relationship health. Addressing this issue is crucial for fostering a loving and supportive partnership. As Christians, we are called to honor God with our bodies and embrace healthy living. 1 Corinthians 10:31 reminds us, "So whether you eat or drink or whatever you do, do it all for the glory of God." Strive to support each other in making healthy choices, seeking God's guidance and strength.

47. Excessive Gaming or TV Watching

Understanding Excessive Gaming or TV Watching

Excessive gaming or TV watching involves spending an inordinate amount of time engaged in these activities to the detriment of other important aspects of life, such as relationships, responsibilities, and personal growth. This behavior can lead to neglect of duties and strained relationships. The Bible encourages us to use our time wisely. Ephesians 5:15-16 says, "Be very careful, then, how you live — not as unwise but as wise, making the most of every opportunity, because the days are evil."

Biblical Perspective on Time Management

The Bible emphasizes the importance of managing our time well and engaging in activities that are edifying and productive. Colossians 3:17 advises, "And whatever you do, whether in word or deed, do it all in the name of the Lord Jesus, giving thanks to God the Father through him." Balancing leisure activities with responsibilities is crucial for a healthy life.

Identifying Excessive Gaming or TV Watching

Signs of excessive gaming or TV watching in a partner include:

- **Neglecting Responsibilities:** Ignoring household chores, work, or other obligations.

- **Social Withdrawal:** Avoiding social interactions and activities in favor of gaming or TV.

- **Increased Screen Time:** Spending many hours daily on gaming or watching TV.

- **Irritability:** Becoming irritable or defensive when asked to reduce screen time.

- **Health Issues:** Developing health problems such as eye strain, poor posture, or sleep deprivation.

Consequences of Excessive Gaming or TV Watching

Excessive gaming or TV watching can have several negative impacts on a relationship:

- **Neglect of Relationship:** Reduced quality time and interaction with a partner.

- **Decreased Productivity:** Lower productivity at work or home.

- **Health Problems:** Physical health issues due to prolonged inactivity.

- **Financial Strain:** Potential financial strain from spending on gaming or streaming services.

- **Conflict:** Frequent arguments over screen time and neglected responsibilities.

Addressing Excessive Gaming or TV Watching

If you notice excessive gaming or TV watching in your partner, consider these steps:

- **Communicate Concerns:** Share your concerns about the impact of their behavior on your relationship. Proverbs 27:5 says, "Better is open rebuke than hidden love."

- **Set Limits:** Agree on reasonable limits for screen time to ensure a healthy balance.

- **Encourage Other Activities:** Promote engagement in other activities such as hobbies, exercise, or socializing.

- **Plan Quality Time:** Schedule regular quality time together without screens.

- **Pray for Balance:** Pray together for wisdom to balance leisure activities with responsibilities. Psalm 90:12 says, "Teach us to number our days, that we may gain a heart of wisdom."

Reflection Questions

1. How does excessive gaming or TV watching affect your relationship and daily life?
2. Have you discussed the impact of this behavior on your mutual goals and responsibilities?
3. What steps can you take together to promote a healthier balance of activities?
4. How can you support each other in managing screen time effectively?

Conclusion

Excessive gaming or TV watching is a significant lifestyle red flag that can impact personal well-being and relationship health. Addressing this issue is crucial for fostering a balanced and fulfilling partnership. As Christians, we are called to manage our time wisely and engage in edifying activities. 1 Corinthians 6:12 reminds us, "I have the right to do anything," you say—but not everything is beneficial. "I have the right to do anything"—but I will not be mastered by anything." Strive to support each other in maintaining a healthy balance of activities, seeking God's guidance and strength.

48. Irresponsible Hobbies

Understanding Irresponsible Hobbies

Irresponsible hobbies involve engaging in activities that are excessively costly, time-consuming, or dangerous, often to the detriment of personal responsibilities and relationships. While hobbies can be a healthy outlet, they should not overshadow other important aspects of life. The Bible calls for moderation and wisdom in all things. Proverbs 25:28 says, "Like a city whose walls are broken through is a person who lacks self-control."

Biblical Perspective on Moderation

The Bible encourages moderation and balance in our pursuits. Philippians 4:5 advises, "Let your gentleness be evident to all. The Lord is near." Engaging in hobbies responsibly ensures they remain a source of joy and not a source of conflict or neglect.

Identifying Irresponsible Hobbies

Signs of irresponsible hobbies in a partner include:

- **Excessive Spending:** Spending large sums of money on hobbies, leading to financial strain.

- **Neglecting Responsibilities:** Ignoring work, family, or other duties to engage in hobbies.

- **Risky Behavior:** Participating in activities that are dangerous or harmful.

- **Isolation:** Preferring hobbies over spending time with family or friends.

- **Addictive Patterns:** Showing signs of addiction to the hobby, such as withdrawal symptoms when unable to participate.

Consequences of Irresponsible Hobbies

Irresponsible hobbies can have several negative impacts on a relationship:

- **Financial Strain:** Increased debt and financial instability due to excessive spending.

- **Neglect of Relationship:** Reduced quality time and interaction with a partner.

- **Health Risks:** Potential physical harm from dangerous activities.

- **Conflict:** Frequent arguments over time and money spent on hobbies.

- **Emotional Distance:** Growing emotional distance due to lack of shared activities and interests.

Addressing Irresponsible Hobbies

If you notice irresponsible hobbies in your partner, consider these steps:

- **Communicate Concerns:** Share your concerns about their hobbies and the impact on your relationship. Ephesians 4:29 encourages, "Do not let any unwholesome talk come out of your mouths, but only what is helpful for building others up according to their needs, that it may benefit those who listen."

- **Set Boundaries:** Establish boundaries to ensure hobbies do not interfere with responsibilities and relationship quality.

- **Encourage Balance:** Promote a healthy balance between hobbies and other aspects of life.

- **Find Shared Interests:** Discover activities you can enjoy together to strengthen your bond.

- **Pray for Wisdom:** Pray together for wisdom and moderation in pursuing hobbies. James 1:5 says, "If any of you lacks wisdom, you should ask God, who gives generously to all without finding fault, and it will be given to you."

Reflection Questions
1. How do irresponsible hobbies affect your relationship and financial stability?
2. Have you discussed the impact of these behaviors on your mutual goals and responsibilities?
3. What steps can you take together to promote responsible engagement in hobbies?
4. How can you support each other in finding a healthy balance between hobbies and other aspects of life?

Conclusion
Irresponsible hobbies are significant lifestyle red flags that can impact both personal well-being and relationship health. Addressing this issue is crucial for fostering a balanced and fulfilling partnership. As Christians, we are called to exercise self-control and seek moderation. 1 Corinthians 10:31 reminds us, "So whether you eat or drink or whatever you do, do it all for the glory of God." Strive to support each other in maintaining a healthy balance of activities, seeking God's guidance and wisdom.

49. Workaholism

Understanding Workaholism
Workaholism involves an unhealthy obsession with work, where a person spends an excessive amount of time and energy on their job at the expense of personal relationships and well-being. This behavior can lead to burnout and strain relationships. The Bible calls for a balanced approach to work and rest. Ecclesiastes 4:6 says, "Better one handful with tranquility than two handfuls with toil and chasing after the wind."

Biblical Perspective on Work-Life Balance
The Bible encourages us to work diligently but also to rest and enjoy the fruits of our labor. Exodus 20:9-10 instructs, "Six days you shall labor and do all your work, but the seventh day is a sabbath to the Lord your God. On it you shall not do any work." Maintaining a healthy work-life balance is crucial for overall well-being and relationships.

Identifying Workaholism
Signs of workaholism in a partner include:
- **Long Hours:** Consistently working long hours and bringing work home.

- **Neglecting Relationships:** Prioritizing work over spending time with family and friends.

- **Health Issues:** Experiencing stress-related health problems due to overwork.

- **Avoiding Rest:** Feeling guilty or anxious when not working.

- **Reduced Leisure Activities:** Neglecting hobbies and leisure activities.

Consequences of Workaholism

Workaholism can have several negative impacts on a relationship:

- **Emotional Distance:** Reduced quality time and emotional connection with a partner.

- **Health Problems:** Increased risk of physical and mental health issues.

- **Burnout:** Higher likelihood of burnout and exhaustion.
- **Conflict:** Frequent arguments over time spent on work.

- **Decreased Satisfaction:** Overall decrease in life satisfaction and happiness.

Addressing Workaholism

If you notice workaholism in your partner, consider these steps:

- **Communicate Concerns:** Share your concerns about their work habits and the impact on your relationship. Proverbs 27:5 says, "Better is open rebuke than hidden love."

- **Encourage Boundaries:** Encourage setting clear boundaries between work and personal time.

- **Promote Rest:** Emphasize the importance of rest and leisure activities for well-being.

- **Support Balance:** Help your partner find a healthy balance between work and personal life.

- **Pray for Guidance:** Pray together for wisdom to manage work responsibilities and maintain a balanced life. Matthew 11:28-30 encourages, "Come to me, all you who are weary and burdened, and I will give you rest. Take my yoke upon you and learn from me, for I am gentle and humble in heart, and you will find rest for your souls. For my yoke is easy and my burden is light."

Reflection Questions
1. How does workaholism affect your relationship and emotional connection?
2. Have you discussed the impact of this behavior on your mutual goals and well-being?
3. What steps can you take together to promote a healthier work-life balance?
4. How can you support each other in maintaining rest and leisure activities?

Conclusion
Workaholism is a significant lifestyle red flag that can impact personal well-being and relationship health. Addressing this issue is crucial for fostering a balanced and fulfilling partnership. As Christians, we are called to work diligently but also to rest and enjoy life. Psalm 127:2 reminds us, "In vain you rise early and stay up late, toiling for food to eat—for he grants sleep to those he loves." Strive to support each other in maintaining a healthy work-life balance, seeking God's guidance and strength.

50. Unstable Living Situation
Understanding Unstable Living Situation

An unstable living situation involves frequent moves, lack of a permanent residence, or living in conditions that are unsafe or unsuitable. This instability can cause significant stress and affect the overall quality of life. The Bible values stability and security in our living conditions. Proverbs 24:3-4 says, "By wisdom a house is built, and through understanding it is established; through knowledge its rooms are filled with rare and beautiful treasures."

Biblical Perspective on Stability

The Bible emphasizes the importance of having a stable and secure home. Psalm 91:1 states, "Whoever dwells in the shelter of the Most High will rest in the shadow of the Almighty." A stable home environment is essential for peace and well-being.

Identifying Unstable Living Situation

Signs of an unstable living situation include:
- **Frequent Moves:** Regularly moving from place to place without stability.

- **Unsuitable Conditions:** Living in unsafe, overcrowded, or unhealthy conditions.

- **Financial Instability:** Struggling to afford rent or mortgage payments.

- **Lack of Permanent Residence:** Living with friends, family, or in temporary housing.

- **Stress and Anxiety:** Experiencing stress and anxiety due to housing instability.

Consequences of Unstable Living Situation

An unstable living situation can have several negative impacts on a relationship:

- **Emotional Stress:** Increased stress and anxiety due to lack of stability.

- **Health Problems:** Potential health issues from living in unsuitable conditions.

- **Financial Strain:** Ongoing financial strain from frequent moves or high housing costs.

- **Relationship Tension:** Conflicts arising from the stress of instability.

- **Lack of Security:** Feeling insecure and unsettled without a stable home.

Addressing Unstable Living Situation

If you notice an unstable living situation in your relationship, consider these steps:

- **Communicate Concerns:** Discuss the impact of housing instability on your well-being and relationship. Proverbs 16:3 says, "Commit to the Lord whatever you do, and he will establish your plans."

- **Plan for Stability:** Work together to create a plan for achieving a stable living situation.

- **Seek Financial Advice:** Consider seeking financial advice to manage housing costs and budgeting.

- **Prioritize Safety:** Ensure that your living conditions are safe and suitable.

- **Pray for Provision:** Pray together for God's provision and guidance in finding a stable home. Philippians 4:19 says, "And my God will meet all your needs according to the riches of his glory in Christ Jesus."

Reflection Questions

1. How does an unstable living situation affect your relationship and overall well-being?
2. Have you discussed the impact of this situation on your future plans?
3. What steps can you take together to achieve a stable and secure living environment?
4. How can you support each other in finding and maintaining suitable housing?

Conclusion

An unstable living situation is a significant lifestyle red flag that can impact personal well-being and relationship health. Addressing this issue is crucial for fostering a stable and fulfilling partnership. As Christians, we are called to seek stability and security in our lives. Proverbs 3:5-6 encourages, "Trust in the Lord with all your heart and lean not on your own understanding; in all your ways submit to him, and he will make your paths straight." Strive to support each other in finding a stable and secure living environment, seeking God's guidance and provision.

Chapter 6: Family and Background

51. Dysfunctional Family Dynamics

Understanding Dysfunctional Family Dynamics
Dysfunctional family dynamics involve patterns of behavior within a family that are unhealthy, disruptive, or abusive. These patterns can include constant conflict, lack of communication, neglect, or abusive behavior. Such dynamics can significantly affect an individual's emotional well-being and relationships. The Bible encourages healthy and loving family relationships. Colossians 3:21 says, "Fathers, do not embitter your children, or they will become discouraged."

Biblical Perspective on Family Relationships
The Bible teaches us to nurture loving and respectful family relationships. Ephesians 6:1-4 advises, "Children, obey your parents in the Lord, for this is right. 'Honor your father and mother' — which is the first commandment with a promise — 'so that it may go well with you and that you may enjoy long life on the earth.' Fathers, do not exasperate your children; instead, bring them up in the training and instruction of the Lord."

Identifying Dysfunctional Family Dynamics
Signs of dysfunctional family dynamics include:
- **Constant Conflict:** Frequent arguments and unresolved conflicts.

- **Lack of Communication:** Poor communication or complete breakdown of communication.

- **Neglect or Abuse:** Emotional, physical, or psychological neglect or abuse.

- **Manipulation:** Manipulative behaviors to control or influence family members.

- **Enmeshment:** Lack of healthy boundaries and excessive involvement in each other's lives.

Consequences of Dysfunctional Family Dynamics

Dysfunctional family dynamics can have several negative impacts on a relationship:

- **Emotional Trauma:** Carrying emotional scars from past family experiences.

- **Trust Issues:** Difficulty trusting others due to past betrayals or conflicts.

- **Conflict Resolution Issues:** Struggling with healthy conflict resolution in relationships.

- **Emotional Distance:** Difficulty forming close and intimate relationships.

- **Stress and Anxiety:** Increased stress and anxiety from unresolved family issues.

Addressing Dysfunctional Family Dynamics

If your partner comes from a background of dysfunctional family dynamics, consider these steps:

- **Communicate Openly:** Encourage open and honest communication about family experiences and their impact. Proverbs 16:24 says, "Gracious words are a honeycomb, sweet to the soul and healing to the bones."

- **Seek Counseling:** Suggest seeking professional counseling to address past traumas and develop healthy relationship patterns.

- **Establish Boundaries:** Work together to establish healthy boundaries with family members.

- **Provide Support:** Offer support and understanding as your partner navigates their family dynamics.

- **Pray for Healing:** Pray together for healing and restoration. Psalm 147:3 says, "He heals the brokenhearted and binds up their wounds."

Reflection Questions
1. How do dysfunctional family dynamics affect your partner's emotional well-being and your relationship?

2. Have you discussed the impact of these dynamics on your future together?

3. What steps can you take to promote healing and healthy relationship patterns?

4. How can you support each other in establishing healthy boundaries with family members?

Conclusion
Dysfunctional family dynamics are significant red flags that can impact personal well-being and relationship health. Addressing these issues is crucial for fostering a loving and supportive partnership. As Christians, we are called to nurture healthy and respectful family relationships. Ephesians 4:32 reminds us, "Be kind and compassionate to one another, forgiving each other, just as in Christ God forgave you." Strive to support each other in healing from past family traumas and establishing healthy relationship patterns, seeking God's guidance and strength.

52. Negative Influence from Family

Understanding Negative Influence from Family
Negative influence from family involves family members who consistently exert a harmful or disruptive impact on an individual's life and relationships. This can include pressure, manipulation, criticism, or discouragement. The Bible encourages us to seek wise counsel and avoid negative influences. Proverbs 13:20 says, "Walk with the wise and become wise, for a companion of fools suffers harm."

Biblical Perspective on Influence
The Bible emphasizes the importance of surrounding ourselves with positive influences and avoiding those that lead us astray. 1 Corinthians 15:33 states, "Do not be misled: 'Bad company corrupts good character.'" It is essential to discern and limit negative influences to protect our well-being and relationships.

Identifying Negative Influence from Family
Signs of negative influence from family include:
- **Criticism and Discouragement:** Consistently criticizing or discouraging your goals and decisions.

- **Manipulation:** Using guilt, pressure, or manipulation to control your actions.

- **Interference:** Excessive involvement in your personal life and decisions.

- **Undermining Relationships:** Attempting to create conflict or division in your relationships.

- **Negative Behaviors:** Encouraging or modeling negative behaviors such as dishonesty, addiction, or disrespect.

Consequences of Negative Influence from Family

Negative influence from family can have several detrimental impacts on a relationship:

- **Conflict:** Increased conflicts and tension within the relationship.

- **Stress and Anxiety:** Heightened stress and anxiety due to family interference.

- **Erosion of Trust:** Trust issues arising from external manipulation and pressure.

- **Emotional Distress:** Emotional turmoil caused by family criticism and negativity.

- **Relationship Strain:** Strain on the relationship due to differing loyalties and influences.

Addressing Negative Influence from Family

If you notice negative influence from family affecting your relationship, consider these steps:

- **Communicate Boundaries:** Discuss and establish clear boundaries with family members. Matthew 18:15 advises, "If your brother or sister sins, go and point out their fault, just between the two of you. If they listen to you, you have won them over."

- **Limit Exposure:** Limit exposure to negative family influences and seek support from positive role models.

- **Strengthen Unity:** Work together to strengthen your relationship and present a united front.

- **Seek Counsel:** Consider seeking guidance from a counselor or trusted advisor.

- **Pray for Wisdom:** Pray together for wisdom and discernment in handling negative influences. James 1:5 says, "If any of you lacks wisdom, you should ask God, who gives generously to all without finding fault, and it will be given to you."

Reflection Questions

1. How does negative influence from family affect your relationship and well-being?
2. Have you discussed the impact of these influences on your future together?
3. What steps can you take to protect your relationship from negative family influences?
4. How can you support each other in establishing healthy boundaries with family members?

Conclusion

Negative influence from family is a significant red flag that can impact personal well-being and relationship health. Addressing this issue is crucial for fostering a loving and supportive partnership. As Christians, we are called to seek wise counsel and avoid negative influences. Proverbs 27:17 reminds us, "As iron sharpens iron, so one person sharpens another." Strive to support each other in managing family influences and protecting your relationship, seeking God's guidance and strength.

53. Unresolved Family Issues

Understanding Unresolved Family Issues

Unresolved family issues involve lingering conflicts, traumas, or misunderstandings within a family that have not been addressed or healed. These issues can cause ongoing stress and affect an individual's emotional health and relationships. The Bible encourages reconciliation and healing in relationships. Matthew 5:23-24 says, "Therefore, if you are offering your gift at the altar and there remember that your brother or sister has something against you, leave your gift there in front of the altar. First go and be reconciled to them; then come and offer your gift."

Biblical Perspective on Reconciliation

The Bible emphasizes the importance of resolving conflicts and seeking reconciliation. Colossians 3:13 advises, "Bear with each other and forgive one another if any of you has a grievance against someone. Forgive as the Lord forgave you." Addressing unresolved family issues is crucial for emotional healing and healthy relationships.

Identifying Unresolved Family Issues

Signs of unresolved family issues in a partner include:

- **Lingering Resentment:** Holding onto past hurts and resentments.

- **Avoidance:** Avoiding family members or topics related to past conflicts.

- **Emotional Triggers:** Becoming easily triggered by certain family-related topics or behaviors.

- **Conflict Repetition:** Repeating similar conflicts and patterns in current relationships.

- **Inability to Forgive:** Struggling to forgive past wrongs and move forward.

Consequences of Unresolved Family Issues

Unresolved family issues can have several negative impacts on a relationship:

- **Emotional Baggage:** Carrying emotional baggage from past conflicts into the relationship.

- **Trust Issues:** Difficulty trusting others due to past betrayals or conflicts.

- **Conflict Resolution Issues:** Struggling with healthy conflict resolution in relationships.

- **Emotional Distance:** Difficulty forming close and intimate relationships.

- **Stress and Anxiety:** Increased stress and anxiety from unresolved issues.

Addressing Unresolved Family Issues

If your partner has unresolved family issues, consider these steps:

- **Communicate Openly:** Encourage open and honest communication about past family experiences and their impact. Proverbs 15:22 says, "Plans fail for lack of counsel, but with many advisers they succeed."

- **Seek Counseling:** Suggest seeking professional counseling to address past traumas and develop healthy relationship patterns.

- **Promote Forgiveness:** Encourage forgiveness and reconciliation, where possible, to promote healing.

- **Provide Support:** Offer support and understanding as your partner navigates their family dynamics.

- **Pray for Healing:** Pray together for healing and restoration. 2 Corinthians 5:18 reminds us, "All this is from God, who reconciled us to himself through Christ and gave us the ministry of reconciliation."

Reflection Questions

1. How do unresolved family issues affect your partner's emotional well-being and your relationship?
2. Have you discussed the impact of these issues on your future together?
3. What steps can you take to promote healing and reconciliation?
4. How can you support each other in addressing and resolving family issues?

Conclusion

Unresolved family issues are significant red flags that can impact personal well-being and relationship health. Addressing these issues is crucial for fostering a loving and supportive partnership. As Christians, we are called to seek reconciliation and healing in our relationships. Ephesians 4:31-32 encourages, "Get rid of all bitterness, rage and anger, brawling and slander, along with every form of malice. Be kind and compassionate to one another, forgiving each other, just as in Christ God forgave you." Strive to support each other in healing from past family traumas and establishing healthy relationship patterns, seeking God's guidance and strength.

54. Cultural or Religious Conflicts

Understanding Cultural or Religious Conflicts
Cultural or religious conflicts arise when partners have differing cultural backgrounds or religious beliefs, leading to misunderstandings and disagreements. These conflicts can create significant challenges in a relationship, affecting mutual respect and unity. The Bible encourages harmony and understanding. Romans 14:19 says, "Let us therefore make every effort to do what leads to peace and to mutual edification."

Biblical Perspective on Unity
The Bible emphasizes the importance of unity and peace, even amidst differences. Ephesians 4:3 advises, "Make every effort to keep the unity of the Spirit through the bond of peace." Embracing each other's backgrounds with respect and understanding is essential for a harmonious relationship.

Identifying Cultural or Religious Conflicts
Signs of cultural or religious conflicts in a relationship include:
- **Frequent Disagreements:** Regular arguments over cultural or religious practices.

- **Lack of Understanding:** Difficulty understanding or respecting each other's beliefs.

- **Pressure to Conform:** Pressuring one partner to adopt the other's cultural or religious practices.

- **Isolation:** Feeling isolated or unsupported due to differing backgrounds.

- **Conflict Over Traditions:** Disagreements about family traditions, holidays, and celebrations.

Consequences of Cultural or Religious Conflicts

Cultural or religious conflicts can have several negative impacts on a relationship:

- **Emotional Distance:** Growing emotional distance due to lack of understanding and respect.

- **Stress and Anxiety:** Increased stress and anxiety from ongoing conflicts.

- **Reduced Unity:** Difficulty achieving unity and mutual support.

- **Negative Impact on Family:** Strain on family relationships and dynamics.

- **Decreased Relationship Satisfaction:** Overall decrease in relationship satisfaction and happiness.

Addressing Cultural or Religious Conflicts

If cultural or religious conflicts are affecting your relationship, consider these steps:

- **Communicate Openly:** Discuss your beliefs and practices openly and respectfully. Proverbs 15:1 says, "A gentle answer turns away wrath, but a harsh word stirs up anger."

- **Seek Understanding:** Make an effort to understand and respect each other's backgrounds.

- **Find Common Ground:** Identify shared values and practices that can strengthen your bond.

- **Celebrate Diversity:** Embrace and celebrate the diversity in your relationship.

- **Pray for Unity:** Pray together for unity and mutual respect. Colossians 3:14 says, "And over all these virtues put on love, which binds them all together in perfect unity."

Reflection Questions
1. How do cultural or religious conflicts affect your relationship and mutual respect?
2. Have you discussed the impact of these differences on your future together?
3. What steps can you take to promote understanding and unity in your relationship?
4. How can you support each other in embracing and celebrating your diverse backgrounds?

Conclusion
Cultural or religious conflicts are significant red flags that can impact relationship health and harmony. Addressing these issues is crucial for fostering a loving and respectful partnership. As Christians, we are called to seek peace and unity. Romans 12:18 reminds us, "If it is possible, as far as it depends on you, live at peace with everyone." Strive to support each other in understanding and respecting your diverse backgrounds, seeking God's guidance and strength.

55. Unwillingness to Integrate Families

Understanding Unwillingness to Integrate Families
Unwillingness to integrate families involves a lack of effort to blend and unite both partners' families. This can lead to tension, isolation, and conflict, making it difficult to create a cohesive family unit. The Bible encourages unity and love within families. Psalm 133:1 says, "How good and pleasant it is when God's people live together in unity!"

Biblical Perspective on Family Unity
The Bible emphasizes the importance of unity and harmony within families. Ephesians 4:2-3 advises, "Be completely humble and gentle; be patient, bearing with one another in love. Make every effort to keep the unity of the Spirit through the bond of peace." Integrating families with love and patience is essential for a harmonious relationship.

Identifying Unwillingness to Integrate Families
Signs of unwillingness to integrate families include:
- **Avoidance:** Avoiding interactions and events involving the other partner's family.

- **Exclusion:** Excluding the partner's family from important events and celebrations.

- **Negative Attitude:** Displaying a negative attitude towards the other partner's family.

- **Lack of Effort:** Making little or no effort to build relationships with the partner's family.

- **Conflict:** Frequent conflicts arising from family interactions.

Consequences of Unwillingness to Integrate Families

Unwillingness to integrate families can have several negative impacts on a relationship:

- **Isolation:** Feeling isolated and unsupported by family members.

- **Increased Conflict:** Frequent arguments and tension related to family interactions.

- **Emotional Strain:** Emotional strain from navigating family dynamics alone.

- **Reduced Family Support:** Lack of family support and unity.
- **Decreased Relationship Satisfaction:** Overall decrease in relationship satisfaction and harmony.

Addressing Unwillingness to Integrate Families

If you notice an unwillingness to integrate families in your relationship, consider these steps:

- **Communicate Openly:** Discuss the importance of integrating families and the impact on your relationship. Proverbs 18:15 says, "The heart of the discerning acquires knowledge, for the ears of the wise seek it out."

- **Encourage Participation:** Encourage your partner to participate in family events and interactions.

- **Build Relationships:** Make an effort to build positive relationships with each other's families.

- **Seek Common Ground:** Find common interests and activities that can help bring families together.

- **Pray for Unity:** Pray together for unity and harmony within your families. Romans 15:5-6 says, "May the God who gives endurance and encouragement give you the same attitude of mind toward each other that Christ Jesus had, so that with one mind and one voice you may glorify the God and Father of our Lord Jesus Christ."

Reflection Questions
1. How does unwillingness to integrate families affect your relationship and family dynamics?
2. Have you discussed the impact of this behavior on your mutual goals and future together?
3. What steps can you take to promote family unity and integration?
4. How can you support each other in building positive relationships with your families?

Conclusion
Unwillingness to integrate families is a significant red flag that can impact relationship health and family harmony. Addressing this issue is crucial for fostering a loving and supportive partnership. As Christians, we are called to seek unity and harmony within our families. 1 Peter 3:8 reminds us, "Finally, all of you, be like-minded, be sympathetic, love one another, be compassionate and humble." Strive to support each other in integrating your families, seeking God's guidance and strength.

56. Disrespect for Your Family

Understanding Disrespect for Your Family
Disrespect for your family involves negative attitudes, behaviors, or comments towards your family members. This can lead to tension, conflict, and hurt feelings, affecting the overall harmony of the relationship. The Bible calls us to honor and respect our families. Exodus 20:12 says, "Honor your father and your mother, so that you may live long in the land the Lord your God is giving you."

Biblical Perspective on Family Respect
The Bible emphasizes the importance of respecting and honoring family members. Ephesians 6:2-3 advises, "Honor your father and mother"—which is the first commandment with a promise—"so that it may go well with you and that you may enjoy long life on the earth." Respecting each other's families is essential for a healthy relationship.

Identifying Disrespect for Your Family
Signs of disrespect for your family in a partner include:
- **Negative Comments:** Making negative or derogatory comments about your family members.

- **Avoidance:** Avoiding interactions with your family.

- **Undermining Relationships:** Attempting to create conflict or division within your family.

- **Disregard:** Disregarding your family's opinions, traditions, or values.

- **Rudeness:** Displaying rude or disrespectful behavior towards your family members.

Consequences of Disrespect for Your Family

Disrespect for your family can have several negative impacts on a relationship:

- **Emotional Hurt:** Causing emotional pain and resentment.

- **Family Conflict:** Creating tension and conflict within your family.

- **Relationship Strain:** Straining your relationship due to differing loyalties.

- **Isolation:** Leading to feelings of isolation and lack of support.

- **Decreased Relationship Satisfaction:** Overall decrease in relationship satisfaction and harmony.

Addressing Disrespect for Your Family

If you notice disrespect for your family in your partner, consider these steps:

- **Communicate Clearly:** Discuss your concerns and the importance of respecting your family. Proverbs 12:18 says, "The words of the reckless pierce like swords, but the tongue of the wise brings healing."

- **Set Boundaries:** Establish clear boundaries to ensure respectful interactions.

- **Encourage Positive Behavior:** Encourage positive and respectful behavior towards your family.

- **Lead by Example:** Model respect and honor in your interactions with your partner's family.

- **Pray for Respect:** Pray together for mutual respect and understanding. Romans 12:10 says, "Be devoted to one another in love. Honor one another above yourselves."

Reflection Questions

1. How does disrespect for your family affect your relationship and emotional well-being?
2. Have you discussed the impact of this behavior on your family dynamics?
3. What steps can you take together to promote respect and harmony within your families?
4. How can you support each other in honoring and respecting your families?

Conclusion

Disrespect for your family is a significant red flag that can impact relationship health and family harmony. Addressing this issue is crucial for fostering a loving and respectful partnership. As Christians, we are called to honor and respect our families. Colossians 3:21 advises, "Fathers, do not embitter your children, or they will become discouraged." Strive to support each other in respecting and honoring your families, seeking God's guidance and strength.

57. Overdependence on Family

Understanding Overdependence on Family

Overdependence on family involves relying excessively on family members for emotional, financial, or decision-making support. This can hinder personal growth and create an imbalance in the relationship. The Bible encourages leaving and cleaving to one's spouse. Genesis 2:24 says, "That is why a man leaves his father and mother and is united to his wife, and they become one flesh."

Biblical Perspective on Independence

The Bible emphasizes the importance of establishing independence and unity in marriage. Ephesians 5:31 reiterates, "For this reason a man will leave his father and mother and be united to his wife, and the two will become one flesh." Building a strong, independent partnership is essential for a healthy marriage.

Identifying Overdependence on Family

Signs of overdependence on family in a partner include:

- **Frequent Consultation:** Consulting family members for every decision, big or small.

- **Financial Dependence:** Relying on family for financial support.

- **Emotional Reliance:** Seeking emotional support primarily from family rather than the partner.

- **Involvement in Conflicts:** Involving family members in personal or relationship conflicts.

- **Lack of Boundaries:** Difficulty establishing boundaries with family members.

Consequences of Overdependence on Family

Overdependence on family can have several negative impacts on a relationship:

- **Lack of Independence:** Hindering personal growth and independence.

- **Relationship Imbalance:** Creating an imbalance in the relationship dynamics.

- **Conflict:** Frequent conflicts over family involvement and boundaries.

- **Emotional Strain:** Emotional strain from navigating multiple relationships.

- **Decreased Intimacy:** Reduced intimacy and connection with the partner.

Addressing Overdependence on Family

If you notice overdependence on family in your partner, consider these steps:

- **Communicate Clearly:** Discuss the importance of establishing independence and unity in your relationship. Proverbs 18:1 says, "An unfriendly person pursues selfish ends and against all sound judgment starts quarrels."

- **Set Boundaries:** Establish clear boundaries with family members to protect your relationship.

- **Encourage Independence:** Encourage your partner to make decisions independently and seek support from you.

- **Strengthen Your Bond:** Focus on building a strong and intimate relationship with your partner.

- **Pray for Guidance:** Pray together for wisdom and strength to establish a healthy balance. Proverbs 3:5-6 advises, "Trust in the Lord with all your heart and lean not on your own understanding; in all your ways submit to him, and he will make your paths straight."

Reflection Questions

1. How does overdependence on family affect your relationship and personal growth?
2. Have you discussed the impact of this behavior on your mutual goals and future together?
3. What steps can you take together to promote independence and unity in your relationship?
4. How can you support each other in establishing healthy boundaries with family members?

Conclusion

Overdependence on family is a significant red flag that can impact relationship health and personal growth. Addressing this issue is crucial for fostering a strong and independent partnership. As Christians, we are called to establish independence and unity in our marriages. Matthew 19:5 reminds us, "For this reason a man will leave his father and mother and be united to his wife, and the two will become one flesh." Strive to support each other in building a strong, independent relationship, seeking God's guidance and strength.

58. History of Abuse

Understanding a History of Abuse
A history of abuse involves experiences of physical, emotional, or sexual abuse in one's past. This can deeply affect an individual's mental health and relationship dynamics. The Bible emphasizes the need for healing and restoration. Psalm 34:18 says, "The Lord is close to the brokenhearted and saves those who are crushed in spirit."

Biblical Perspective on Healing and Restoration
The Bible encourages us to seek healing and restoration from past hurts. Isaiah 61:1 says, "The Spirit of the Sovereign Lord is on me, because the Lord has anointed me to proclaim good news to the poor. He has sent me to bind up the brokenhearted, to proclaim freedom for the captives and release from darkness for the prisoners." Seeking God's help and professional support is essential for healing from past abuse.

Identifying a History of Abuse
Signs that a partner may have a history of abuse include:
- **Emotional Triggers:** Intense emotional reactions to certain situations or topics.

- **Trust Issues:** Difficulty trusting others or forming close relationships.

- **Hypervigilance:** Constantly being on guard or easily startled.

- **Low Self-Esteem:** Struggling with feelings of worthlessness or inadequacy.

- **Flashbacks:** Experiencing flashbacks or intrusive memories of the abuse.

Consequences of a History of Abuse

A history of abuse can have several negative impacts on a relationship:

- **Emotional Trauma:** Ongoing emotional pain and trauma affecting daily life and relationships.

- **Trust Issues:** Difficulty building trust and intimacy with a partner.

- **Conflict:** Increased potential for misunderstandings and conflicts.

- **Mental Health Struggles:** Higher risk of anxiety, depression, and other mental health issues.

- **Impact on Communication:** Challenges in open and honest communication due to past experiences.

Addressing a History of Abuse

If your partner has a history of abuse, consider these steps:

- **Communicate Sensitively:** Approach discussions with sensitivity and compassion. Proverbs 15:1 says, "A gentle answer turns away wrath, but a harsh word stirs up anger."

- **Encourage Professional Help:** Encourage seeking therapy or counseling for healing and support.

- **Build Trust:** Foster a safe and trusting environment in your relationship.

- **Be Patient:** Understand that healing takes time and be patient with your partner's process.

- **Pray for Healing:** Pray together for God's healing and strength. Psalm 147:3 says, "He heals the brokenhearted and binds up their wounds."

Reflection Questions
1. How does a history of abuse affect your partner's emotional well-being and your relationship?
2. Have you discussed the impact of past abuse on your future together?
3. What steps can you take to support your partner's healing process?
4. How can you create a safe and trusting environment in your relationship?

Conclusion
A history of abuse is a significant red flag that can deeply impact personal well-being and relationship health. Addressing this issue is crucial for fostering a loving and supportive partnership. As Christians, we are called to seek healing and restoration. Jeremiah 30:17 says, "But I will restore you to health and heal your wounds," declares the Lord. Strive to support each other in the healing process, seeking God's guidance and strength.

59. Secretive About Past

Understanding Being Secretive About the Past

Being secretive about the past involves withholding significant information about previous experiences, relationships, or events. This lack of transparency can create trust issues and hinder intimacy. The Bible encourages honesty and transparency. Proverbs 12:22 says, "The Lord detests lying lips, but he delights in people who are trustworthy."

Biblical Perspective on Honesty

The Bible emphasizes the importance of honesty and integrity in relationships. Ephesians 4:25 advises, "Therefore each of you must put off falsehood and speak truthfully to your neighbor, for we are all members of one body." Open and honest communication is essential for building trust and closeness.

Identifying Secretive Behavior

Signs that a partner may be secretive about their past include:

- **Avoidance:** Avoiding discussions about their past or providing vague answers.

- **Inconsistencies:** Providing inconsistent or contradictory information about past events.

- **Defensiveness:** Becoming defensive or angry when asked about their past.

- **Lack of Disclosure:** Failing to share significant past experiences or relationships.

- **Privacy:** Keeping personal documents or items hidden.

Consequences of Being Secretive About the Past

Being secretive about the past can have several negative impacts on a relationship:

- **Trust Issues:** Erosion of trust due to lack of transparency.

- **Emotional Distance:** Difficulty building emotional intimacy and connection.

- **Conflict:** Increased potential for misunderstandings and conflicts.

- **Insecurity:** Creating feelings of insecurity and suspicion in the relationship.

- **Communication Barriers:** Hindering open and honest communication.

Addressing Secretive Behavior

If you notice secretive behavior in your partner, consider these steps:

- **Communicate Clearly:** Discuss the importance of transparency and its impact on your relationship. Proverbs 16:13 says, "Kings take pleasure in honest lips; they value the one who speaks what is right."

- **Build Trust:** Foster a safe and trusting environment where your partner feels comfortable sharing.

- **Be Patient:** Understand that sharing personal information can be difficult and be patient with your partner.

- **Encourage Openness:** Encourage open and honest communication about past experiences.

- **Pray for Openness:** Pray together for honesty and transparency in your relationship. John 8:32 says, "Then you will know the truth, and the truth will set you free."

Reflection Questions

1. How does secretive behavior affect your trust and emotional connection in the relationship?
2. Have you discussed the impact of this behavior on your mutual goals and future together?
3. What steps can you take to promote transparency and trust in your relationship?
4. How can you support each other in being open and honest about your pasts?

Conclusion

Being secretive about the past is a significant red flag that can impact relationship health and trust. Addressing this issue is crucial for fostering a loving and transparent partnership. As Christians, we are called to live in truth and honesty. Proverbs 28:13 reminds us, "Whoever conceals their sins does not prosper, but the one who confesses and renounces them finds mercy." Strive to support each other in being open and honest, seeking God's guidance and strength.

60. Conflict with Family Members

Understanding Conflict with Family Members
Conflict with family members involves ongoing disputes, misunderstandings, or strained relationships with one's own family or the partner's family. These conflicts can create stress and tension, affecting the overall harmony of the relationship. The Bible encourages reconciliation and peace. Matthew 5:9 says, "Blessed are the peacemakers, for they will be called children of God."

Biblical Perspective on Reconciliation
The Bible emphasizes the importance of seeking peace and resolving conflicts. Romans 12:18 advises, "If it is possible, as far as it depends on you, live at peace with everyone." Working towards reconciliation and harmony is essential for a healthy relationship.

Identifying Conflict with Family Members
Signs of conflict with family members include:
- **Frequent Arguments:** Regular disputes and disagreements with family members.

- **Avoidance:** Avoiding family gatherings or interactions to prevent conflict.

- **Resentment:** Holding onto feelings of anger or resentment towards family members.

- **Lack of Communication:** Poor or no communication with certain family members.

- **Emotional Distress:** Feeling stressed or anxious about family interactions.

Consequences of Conflict with Family Members

Conflict with family members can have several negative impacts on a relationship:

- **Emotional Strain:** Increased emotional stress and anxiety.

- **Relationship Tension:** Tension and conflict within the relationship due to family issues.

- **Isolation:** Feeling isolated from family support and connections.

- **Negative Impact on Partner:** Strain on the partner due to divided loyalties.

- **Decreased Relationship Satisfaction:** Overall decrease in relationship satisfaction and harmony.

Addressing Conflict with Family Members

If you notice ongoing conflict with family members, consider these steps:

- **Communicate Openly:** Discuss the impact of family conflicts on your relationship. Proverbs 15:22 says, "Plans fail for lack of counsel, but with many advisers they succeed."

- **Seek Reconciliation:** Encourage efforts towards reconciliation and resolving misunderstandings.

- **Set Boundaries:** Establish healthy boundaries to protect your relationship from ongoing conflicts.

- **Provide Support:** Offer support and understanding as your partner navigates family conflicts.

- **Pray for Peace:** Pray together for peace and reconciliation within your families. Colossians 3:15 says, "Let the peace of Christ rule in your hearts, since as members of one body you were called to peace. And be thankful."

Reflection Questions
1. How does conflict with family members affect your emotional well-being and relationship?
2. Have you discussed the impact of these conflicts on your future together?
3. What steps can you take to promote peace and reconciliation within your families?
4. How can you support each other in navigating and resolving family conflicts?

Conclusion
Conflict with family members is a significant red flag that can impact relationship health and harmony. Addressing this issue is crucial for fostering a loving and peaceful partnership. As Christians, we are called to seek reconciliation and peace. Hebrews 12:14 reminds us, "Make every effort to live in peace with everyone and to be holy; without holiness no one will see the Lord." Strive to support each other in resolving family conflicts, seeking God's guidance and strength.

Chapter 7: Emotional and Mental Health

61. Unaddressed Mental Health Issues

Understanding Unaddressed Mental Health Issues

Unaddressed mental health issues involve ignoring or failing to seek treatment for conditions such as depression, anxiety, bipolar disorder, PTSD, and others. This neglect can have serious implications for an individual's well-being and relationship dynamics. The Bible encourages seeking healing and restoration. Psalm 34:17-18 says, "The righteous cry out, and the Lord hears them; he delivers them from all their troubles. The Lord is close to the brokenhearted and saves those who are crushed in spirit."

Biblical Perspective on Seeking Help

The Bible emphasizes the importance of seeking help and healing for our afflictions. James 5:14-15 advises, "Is anyone among you sick? Let them call the elders of the church to pray over them and anoint them with oil in the name of the Lord. And the prayer offered in faith will make the sick person well; the Lord will raise them up. If they have sinned, they will be forgiven."

Identifying Unaddressed Mental Health Issues

Signs of unaddressed mental health issues in a partner include:

- **Persistent Sadness:** Ongoing feelings of sadness or hopelessness.

- **Anxiety:** Constant worry, fear, or panic attacks.

- **Withdrawal:** Avoiding social interactions and activities once enjoyed.

- **Mood Changes:** Noticeable shifts in mood, energy, or behavior.

- **Lack of Self-Care:** Neglecting personal hygiene, health, and responsibilities.

Consequences of Unaddressed Mental Health Issues

Unaddressed mental health issues can have several negative impacts on a relationship:

- **Emotional Strain:** Increased emotional stress and anxiety for both partners.

- **Communication Problems:** Difficulty communicating and understanding each other's needs.

- **Decreased Intimacy:** Reduced emotional and physical intimacy.

- **Conflict:** Frequent misunderstandings and conflicts.

- **Impact on Daily Life:** Challenges in managing daily responsibilities and maintaining stability.

Addressing Unaddressed Mental Health Issues

If you notice unaddressed mental health issues in your partner, consider these steps:

- **Communicate with Compassion:** Discuss your concerns with empathy and understanding. Proverbs 16:24 says, "Gracious words are a honeycomb, sweet to the soul and healing to the bones."

- **Encourage Professional Help:** Encourage seeking therapy or counseling for proper diagnosis and treatment.

- **Offer Support:** Provide emotional support and patience as your partner seeks help.

- **Create a Supportive Environment:** Foster a safe and supportive environment to promote healing.

- **Pray for Healing:** Pray together for God's healing and strength. Psalm 147:3 says, "He heals the brokenhearted and binds up their wounds."

Reflection Questions

1. How do unaddressed mental health issues affect your partner's well-being and your relationship?
2. Have you discussed the impact of these issues on your mutual goals and future together?
3. What steps can you take to support your partner in seeking help and healing?
4. How can you create a supportive environment for addressing mental health issues?

Conclusion

Unaddressed mental health issues are a significant red flag that can impact personal well-being and relationship health. Addressing this issue is crucial for fostering a loving and supportive partnership. As Christians, we are called to seek healing and support. Galatians 6:2 reminds us, "Carry each other's burdens, and in this way you will fulfill the law of Christ." Strive to support each other in seeking help and healing, seeking God's guidance and strength.

62. Emotional Unavailability
Understanding Emotional Unavailability

Emotional unavailability involves difficulty in expressing feelings, forming emotional connections, and being present in a relationship. This can create barriers to intimacy and understanding. The Bible encourages us to love and connect deeply with others. 1 Peter 4:8 says, "Above all, love each other deeply, because love covers over a multitude of sins."

Biblical Perspective on Emotional Availability

The Bible emphasizes the importance of being emotionally available and connected in relationships. Romans 12:15 advises, "Rejoice with those who rejoice; mourn with those who mourn." Being present emotionally is essential for a healthy and supportive relationship.

Identifying Emotional Unavailability

Signs of emotional unavailability in a partner include:

- **Avoiding Intimacy:** Shying away from emotional or physical intimacy.

- **Withholding Feelings:** Difficulty expressing emotions or discussing feelings.

- **Disengagement:** Being distant or disengaged in conversations and activities.

- **Inconsistent Communication:** Inconsistent or minimal communication about personal matters.

- **Reluctance to Commit:** Hesitation or reluctance to commit to the relationship fully.

Consequences of Emotional Unavailability

Emotional unavailability can have several negative impacts on a relationship:

- **Lack of Intimacy:** Difficulty building emotional and physical intimacy.

- **Misunderstandings:** Increased potential for misunderstandings and conflicts.

- **Emotional Distance:** Growing emotional distance and disconnection.

- **Insecurity:** Creating feelings of insecurity and doubt in the relationship.

- **Decreased Satisfaction:** Overall decrease in relationship satisfaction and happiness.

Addressing Emotional Unavailability

If you notice emotional unavailability in your partner, consider these steps:

- **Communicate Needs:** Discuss your emotional needs and the impact on your relationship. Ephesians 4:15 says, "Instead, speaking the truth in love, we will grow to become in every respect the mature body of him who is the head, that is, Christ."

- **Encourage Vulnerability:** Encourage your partner to open up and share their feelings.

- **Be Patient:** Understand that becoming emotionally available takes time and patience.

- **Create a Safe Space:** Foster a safe and supportive environment for sharing emotions.

- **Pray for Connection:** Pray together for emotional connection and understanding. Colossians 3:14 says, "And over all these virtues put on love, which binds them all together in perfect unity."

Reflection Questions

1. How does emotional unavailability affect your relationship and intimacy?
2. Have you discussed the impact of this behavior on your mutual goals and future together?
3. What steps can you take to promote emotional availability and connection?
4. How can you support each other in becoming more emotionally available?

Conclusion

Emotional unavailability is a significant red flag that can impact relationship health and intimacy. Addressing this issue is crucial for fostering a loving and connected partnership. As Christians, we are called to love deeply and connect with others. 1 Thessalonians 5:11 reminds us, "Therefore encourage one another and build each other up, just as in fact you are doing." Strive to support each other in becoming emotionally available, seeking God's guidance and strength.

63. Mood Swings

Understanding Mood Swings

Mood swings involve rapid and intense changes in mood, which can be challenging for both the individual experiencing them and their partner. These fluctuations can create instability and unpredictability in the relationship. The Bible encourages us to seek stability and self-control. Proverbs 25:28 says, "Like a city whose walls are broken through is a person who lacks self-control."

Biblical Perspective on Stability and Self-Control

The Bible emphasizes the importance of stability and self-control in our lives. Galatians 5:22-23 highlights self-control as a fruit of the Spirit: "But the fruit of the Spirit is love, joy, peace, forbearance, kindness, goodness, faithfulness, gentleness and self-control. Against such things there is no law."

Identifying Mood Swings

Signs of mood swings in a partner include:

- **Rapid Mood Changes:** Frequent and sudden changes in mood, from happiness to anger or sadness.

- **Emotional Intensity:** Intense emotional reactions that seem disproportionate to the situation.

- **Unpredictability:** Unpredictable behavior and reactions.

- **Impact on Daily Life:** Difficulty managing daily responsibilities due to mood fluctuations.

- **Strained Relationships:** Struggles in maintaining stable relationships due to mood changes.

Consequences of Mood Swings

Mood swings can have several negative impacts on a relationship:

- **Emotional Strain:** Increased emotional stress and anxiety for both partners.

- **Communication Challenges:** Difficulty communicating effectively due to unpredictable moods.

- **Conflict:** Frequent misunderstandings and conflicts arising from mood changes.

- **Instability:** Creating an unstable and unpredictable relationship environment.

- **Decreased Relationship Satisfaction:** Overall decrease in relationship satisfaction and harmony.

Addressing Mood Swings

If you notice mood swings in your partner, consider these steps:

- **Communicate with Empathy:** Discuss your concerns with empathy and understanding. Proverbs 17:17 says, "A friend loves at all times, and a brother is born for a time of adversity."

- **Encourage Professional Help:** Encourage seeking therapy or counseling for managing mood swings.

- **Provide Support:** Offer emotional support and patience as your partner seeks help.

- **Create a Stable Environment:** Foster a stable and supportive environment to promote emotional balance.

- **Pray for Stability:** Pray together for emotional stability and self-control. 2 Timothy 1:7 says, "For the Spirit God gave us does not make us timid, but gives us power, love and self-discipline."

Reflection Questions

1. How do mood swings affect your relationship and daily interactions?
2. Have you discussed the impact of these mood changes on your mutual goals and future together?
3. What steps can you take to support your partner in managing mood swings?
4. How can you create a stable and supportive environment in your relationship?

Conclusion

Mood swings are a significant red flag that can impact relationship health and stability. Addressing this issue is crucial for fostering a loving and stable partnership. As Christians, we are called to seek stability and self-control. Proverbs 16:32 reminds us, "Better a patient person than a warrior, one with self-control than one who takes a city." Strive to support each other in managing mood swings, seeking God's guidance and strength.

64. Unresolved Trauma

Understanding Unresolved Trauma
Unresolved trauma refers to the lingering emotional and psychological effects of a past traumatic experience that has not been adequately addressed or healed. This can significantly impact an individual's mental health and relationships. The Bible encourages seeking healing and restoration. Psalm 147:3 says, "He heals the brokenhearted and binds up their wounds."

Biblical Perspective on Healing
The Bible emphasizes the importance of seeking healing and wholeness. Isaiah 61:1 says, "The Spirit of the Sovereign Lord is on me, because the Lord has anointed me to proclaim good news to the poor. He has sent me to bind up the brokenhearted, to proclaim freedom for the captives and release from darkness for the prisoners." God's desire is for us to be healed and restored.

Identifying Unresolved Trauma
Signs of unresolved trauma in a partner include:
- **Flashbacks:** Experiencing flashbacks or intrusive memories of the trauma.

- **Avoidance:** Avoiding places, people, or activities that remind them of the trauma.

- **Emotional Numbness:** Feeling detached or emotionally numb.

- **Hypervigilance:** Being easily startled or constantly on edge.

- **Mood Swings:** Intense and unpredictable mood changes.

Consequences of Unresolved Trauma

Unresolved trauma can have several negative impacts on a relationship:

- **Emotional Distance:** Difficulty forming close emotional connections.

- **Communication Barriers:** Challenges in open and honest communication.

- **Trust Issues:** Difficulty trusting others due to past experiences.

- **Conflict:** Increased potential for misunderstandings and conflicts.

- **Mental Health Struggles:** Higher risk of anxiety, depression, and other mental health issues.

Addressing Unresolved Trauma

If your partner has unresolved trauma, consider these steps:

- **Communicate with Compassion:** Approach discussions with empathy and understanding. Proverbs 12:25 says, "Anxiety weighs down the heart, but a kind word cheers it up."

- **Encourage Professional Help:** Encourage seeking therapy or counseling for trauma.

- **Offer Support:** Provide emotional support and patience as your partner works through their trauma.

- **Create a Safe Environment:** Foster a safe and supportive environment for healing.

- **Pray for Healing:** Pray together for God's healing and strength. Psalm 34:18 says, "The Lord is close to the brokenhearted and saves those who are crushed in spirit."

Reflection Questions
1. How does unresolved trauma affect your partner's emotional well-being and your relationship?
2. Have you discussed the impact of these issues on your mutual goals and future together?
3. What steps can you take to support your partner in seeking help and healing?
4. How can you create a safe and supportive environment for addressing trauma?

Conclusion
Unresolved trauma is a significant red flag that can impact personal well-being and relationship health. Addressing this issue is crucial for fostering a loving and supportive partnership. As Christians, we are called to seek healing and restoration. Jeremiah 30:17 says, "But I will restore you to health and heal your wounds," declares the Lord. Strive to support each other in the healing process, seeking God's guidance and strength.

65. Lack of Emotional Regulation

Understanding Lack of Emotional Regulation
Lack of emotional regulation involves difficulty in managing and responding to emotions in a healthy and balanced way. This can lead to intense emotional reactions and instability in relationships. The Bible encourages self-control and emotional maturity. Proverbs 25:28 says, "Like a city whose walls are broken through is a person who lacks self-control."

Biblical Perspective on Self-Control
The Bible emphasizes the importance of self-control and emotional maturity. Galatians 5:22-23 highlights self-control as a fruit of the Spirit: "But the fruit of the Spirit is love, joy, peace, forbearance, kindness, goodness, faithfulness, gentleness and self-control. Against such things there is no law."

Identifying Lack of Emotional Regulation
Signs of lack of emotional regulation in a partner include:
- **Intense Reactions:** Having extreme emotional reactions to minor incidents.

- **Impulsivity:** Acting impulsively without considering the consequences.

- **Frequent Mood Swings:** Experiencing frequent and intense mood swings.

- **Difficulty Calming Down:** Struggling to calm down after being upset.

- **Emotional Outbursts:** Having frequent emotional outbursts, such as yelling or crying.

Consequences of Lack of Emotional Regulation

Lack of emotional regulation can have several negative impacts on a relationship:

- **Emotional Strain:** Increased emotional stress and anxiety for both partners.

- **Communication Problems:** Difficulty communicating effectively due to unpredictable emotions.

- **Conflict:** Frequent misunderstandings and conflicts arising from emotional reactions.

- **Instability:** Creating an unstable and unpredictable relationship environment.

- **Decreased Relationship Satisfaction:** Overall decrease in relationship satisfaction and harmony.

Addressing Lack of Emotional Regulation

If you notice a lack of emotional regulation in your partner, consider these steps:

- **Communicate with Empathy:** Discuss your concerns with empathy and understanding. Proverbs 15:1 says, "A gentle answer turns away wrath, but a harsh word stirs up anger."

- **Encourage Professional Help:** Encourage seeking therapy or counseling for emotional regulation skills.

- **Provide Support:** Offer emotional support and patience as your partner works on improving emotional regulation.

- **Create a Stable Environment:** Foster a stable and supportive environment to promote emotional balance.

- **Pray for Self-Control:** Pray together for emotional stability and self-control. 2 Timothy 1:7 says, "For the Spirit God gave us does not make us timid, but gives us power, love and self-discipline."

Reflection Questions
1. How does lack of emotional regulation affect your relationship and daily interactions?
2. Have you discussed the impact of these emotional challenges on your mutual goals and future together?
3. What steps can you take to support your partner in improving emotional regulation?
4. How can you create a stable and supportive environment for emotional growth?

Conclusion
Lack of emotional regulation is a significant red flag that can impact relationship health and stability. Addressing this issue is crucial for fostering a loving and stable partnership. As Christians, we are called to seek self-control and emotional maturity. Proverbs 16:32 reminds us, "Better a patient person than a warrior, one with self-control than one who takes a city." Strive to support each other in improving emotional regulation, seeking God's guidance and strength.

66. Dependency on You for Emotional Stability
Understanding Dependency on You for Emotional Stability

Dependency on a partner for emotional stability involves relying excessively on them for emotional support and regulation, often leading to an imbalance in the relationship. This can place significant pressure on the partner and hinder personal growth. The Bible encourages us to find our primary strength and stability in God. Psalm 62:5-6 says, "Yes, my soul, find rest in God; my hope comes from him. Truly he is my rock and my salvation; he is my fortress, I will not be shaken."

Biblical Perspective on Emotional Dependence

The Bible emphasizes the importance of finding our primary emotional support and stability in God. Philippians 4:6-7 advises, "Do not be anxious about anything, but in every situation, by prayer and petition, with thanksgiving, present your requests to God. And the peace of God, which transcends all understanding, will guard your hearts and your minds in Christ Jesus."

Identifying Emotional Dependency

Signs of emotional dependency in a partner include:

- **Constant Reassurance:** Frequently seeking reassurance and validation from you.

- **Inability to Self-Soothe:** Struggling to manage emotions without your support.

- **Clinginess:** Being overly clingy or dependent on your presence.

- **Avoidance of Independence:** Avoiding activities or decisions that require independence.

- **Emotional Instability:** Experiencing significant emotional distress when you are not available.

Consequences of Emotional Dependency

Emotional dependency can have several negative impacts on a relationship:

- **Imbalance:** Creating an imbalance where one partner feels overwhelmed by the other's emotional needs.

- **Stifled Growth:** Hindering personal growth and self-reliance.

- **Emotional Strain:** Increased emotional strain and pressure on the supportive partner.

- **Conflict:** Frequent conflicts arising from unmet emotional needs and expectations.

- **Decreased Intimacy:** Reduced intimacy and connection due to emotional imbalance.

Addressing Emotional Dependency

If you notice emotional dependency in your partner, consider these steps:

- **Communicate Clearly:** Discuss the importance of emotional independence and its impact on your relationship. Galatians 6:5 says, "For each one should carry their own load."

- **Encourage Self-Reliance:** Encourage your partner to develop emotional self-reliance and coping skills.

- **Provide Support:** Offer support and understanding while promoting independence.

- **Seek Professional Help:** Consider seeking counseling to address emotional dependency issues.

- **Pray for Balance:** Pray together for emotional balance and stability. Psalm 55:22 says, "Cast your cares on the Lord and he will sustain you; he will never let the righteous be shaken."

Reflection Questions

1. How does emotional dependency affect your relationship and personal well-being?
2. Have you discussed the impact of this dependency on your mutual goals and future together?
3. What steps can you take to support your partner in developing emotional self-reliance?
4. How can you create a balanced and supportive environment for emotional growth?

Conclusion

Dependency on you for emotional stability is a significant red flag that can impact relationship health and personal growth. Addressing this issue is crucial for fostering a balanced and fulfilling partnership. As Christians, we are called to find our primary emotional support in God. Isaiah 26:3 reminds us, "You will keep in perfect peace those whose minds are steadfast, because they trust in you." Strive to support each other in developing emotional self-reliance, seeking God's guidance and strength.

67. Inability to Handle Stress

Understanding Inability to Handle Stress
Inability to handle stress involves struggling to manage and cope with stress in a healthy and effective manner. This can lead to heightened anxiety, emotional outbursts, and difficulty managing daily responsibilities. The Bible encourages us to cast our burdens on God and seek His peace. Matthew 11:28 says, "Come to me, all you who are weary and burdened, and I will give you rest."

Biblical Perspective on Stress Management
The Bible emphasizes the importance of seeking God's help in managing stress and finding peace. Philippians 4:6-7 advises, "Do not be anxious about anything, but in every situation, by prayer and petition, with thanksgiving, present your requests to God. And the peace of God, which transcends all understanding, will guard your hearts and your minds in Christ Jesus."

Identifying Inability to Handle Stress
Signs of inability to handle stress in a partner include:
- **Overwhelmed:** Feeling overwhelmed by daily responsibilities and challenges.

- **Emotional Outbursts:** Having frequent emotional outbursts, such as anger or tears.

- **Avoidance:** Avoiding stressful situations or tasks.

- **Physical Symptoms:** Experiencing physical symptoms of stress, such as headaches or fatigue.

- **Ineffective Coping:** Using unhealthy coping mechanisms, such as substance use or withdrawal.

Consequences of Inability to Handle Stress

Inability to handle stress can have several negative impacts on a relationship:

- **Emotional Strain:** Increased emotional stress and anxiety for both partners.

- **Conflict:** Frequent conflicts arising from stress-related issues.

- **Instability:** Creating an unstable and unpredictable relationship environment.

- **Health Problems:** Potential physical and mental health problems due to unmanaged stress.

- **Decreased Relationship Satisfaction:** Overall decrease in relationship satisfaction and harmony.

Addressing Inability to Handle Stress

If you notice an inability to handle stress in your partner, consider these steps:

- **Communicate with Empathy:** Discuss your concerns with empathy and understanding. Proverbs 12:25 says, "Anxiety weighs down the heart, but a kind word cheers it up."

- **Encourage Stress Management Techniques:** Encourage your partner to practice healthy stress management techniques, such as exercise, meditation, or journaling.

- **Provide Support:** Offer emotional support and patience as your partner learns to manage stress.

- **Create a Calm Environment:** Foster a calm and supportive environment to reduce stress.

- **Pray for Peace:** Pray together for God's peace and guidance in managing stress. John 14:27 says, "Peace I leave with you; my peace I give you. I do not give to you as the world gives. Do not let your hearts be troubled and do not be afraid."

Reflection Questions
1. How does inability to handle stress affect your relationship and daily interactions?
2. Have you discussed the impact of stress management issues on your mutual goals and future together?
3. What steps can you take to support your partner in managing stress effectively?
4. How can you create a calm and supportive environment for stress management?

Conclusion
Inability to handle stress is a significant red flag that can impact relationship health and stability. Addressing this issue is crucial for fostering a loving and supportive partnership. As Christians, we are called to seek God's peace and guidance in managing stress. Psalm 55:22 reminds us, "Cast your cares on the Lord and he will sustain you; he will never let the righteous be shaken." Strive to support each other in developing effective stress management techniques, seeking God's guidance and strength.

68. Frequent Feelings of Hopelessness

Understanding Frequent Feelings of Hopelessness
Frequent feelings of hopelessness involve persistent thoughts and emotions of despair, believing that things will never improve. This can be a sign of underlying mental health issues such as depression. The Bible encourages us to find hope and strength in God. Romans 15:13 says, "May the God of hope fill you with all joy and peace as you trust in him, so that you may overflow with hope by the power of the Holy Spirit."

Biblical Perspective on Hope
The Bible emphasizes the importance of hope and trusting in God's promises. Jeremiah 29:11 says, "For I know the plans I have for you," declares the Lord, "plans to prosper you and not to harm you, plans to give you hope and a future." Trusting in God's plans can help restore hope and purpose.

Identifying Frequent Feelings of Hopelessness
Signs of frequent feelings of hopelessness in a partner include:
- **Persistent Sadness:** Constantly feeling sad or down without relief.

- **Lack of Motivation:** Finding it difficult to get motivated or take interest in activities.

- **Negative Self-Talk:** Regularly engaging in negative self-talk and self-criticism.

- **Isolation:** Withdrawing from social interactions and activities.

- **Talk of Worthlessness:** Expressing feelings of worthlessness or thoughts of giving up.

Consequences of Frequent Feelings of Hopelessness

Frequent feelings of hopelessness can have several negative impacts on a relationship:

- **Emotional Strain:** Increased emotional stress and anxiety for both partners.

- **Communication Barriers:** Difficulty communicating effectively due to persistent sadness.

- **Reduced Intimacy:** Decreased emotional and physical intimacy.

- **Conflict:** Frequent misunderstandings and conflicts arising from emotional distress.

- **Impact on Daily Life:** Challenges in managing daily responsibilities and maintaining stability.

Addressing Frequent Feelings of Hopelessness

If you notice frequent feelings of hopelessness in your partner, consider these steps:

- **Communicate with Compassion:** Discuss your concerns with empathy and understanding. Proverbs 16:24 says, "Gracious words are a honeycomb, sweet to the soul and healing to the bones."

- **Encourage Professional Help:** Encourage seeking therapy or counseling for proper diagnosis and treatment.

- **Offer Support:** Provide emotional support and patience as your partner seeks help.

- **Create a Supportive Environment:** Foster a safe and supportive environment to promote healing.

- **Pray for Hope:** Pray together for God's hope and strength. Psalm 42:11 says, "Why, my soul, are you downcast? Why so disturbed within me? Put your hope in God, for I will yet praise him, my Savior and my God."

Reflection Questions
1. How do frequent feelings of hopelessness affect your partner's well-being and your relationship?
2. Have you discussed the impact of these feelings on your mutual goals and future together?
3. What steps can you take to support your partner in seeking help and finding hope?
4. How can you create a supportive environment for addressing feelings of hopelessness?

Conclusion
Frequent feelings of hopelessness are a significant red flag that can impact personal well-being and relationship health. Addressing this issue is crucial for fostering a loving and supportive partnership. As Christians, we are called to find hope in God's promises. Romans 12:12 reminds us, "Be joyful in hope, patient in affliction, faithful in prayer." Strive to support each other in seeking hope and healing, seeking God's guidance and strength.

69. Negative Outlook on Life

Understanding Negative Outlook on Life

A negative outlook on life involves consistently viewing situations, the future, and oneself in a pessimistic and hopeless manner. This mindset can affect motivation, relationships, and overall well-being. The Bible encourages a positive and hopeful perspective. Philippians 4:8 says, "Finally, brothers and sisters, whatever is true, whatever is noble, whatever is right, whatever is pure, whatever is lovely, whatever is admirable — if anything is excellent or praiseworthy — think about such things."

Biblical Perspective on Positivity

The Bible emphasizes the importance of maintaining a positive and hopeful mindset. Romans 15:13 says, "May the God of hope fill you with all joy and peace as you trust in him, so that you may overflow with hope by the power of the Holy Spirit." Focusing on God's promises can help foster a positive outlook.

Identifying a Negative Outlook on Life

Signs of a negative outlook on life in a partner include:

- **Pessimism:** Consistently expecting the worst in situations.

- **Negative Self-Talk:** Regularly engaging in self-critical and negative thoughts.

- **Hopelessness:** Expressing a lack of hope for the future.

- **Criticism:** Frequently criticizing oneself and others.

- **Lack of Gratitude:** Difficulty recognizing and appreciating positive aspects of life.

Consequences of a Negative Outlook on Life

A negative outlook on life can have several negative impacts on a relationship:

- **Emotional Strain:** Increased emotional stress and tension for both partners.

- **Communication Challenges:** Difficulty maintaining positive and constructive communication.

- **Reduced Intimacy:** Decreased emotional and physical intimacy due to negativity.

- **Conflict:** Frequent misunderstandings and conflicts arising from a pessimistic perspective.

- **Impact on Well-Being:** Challenges in maintaining mental and emotional well-being.

Addressing a Negative Outlook on Life

If you notice a negative outlook on life in your partner, consider these steps:

- **Communicate Positively:** Encourage positive and hopeful communication. Proverbs 17:22 says, "A cheerful heart is good medicine, but a crushed spirit dries up the bones."

- **Encourage Professional Help:** Encourage seeking therapy or counseling for support in developing a positive mindset.

- **Practice Gratitude:** Encourage practicing gratitude and focusing on positive aspects of life.

- **Offer Support:** Provide emotional support and understanding as your partner works on changing their outlook.

- **Pray for Positivity:** Pray together for a positive and hopeful perspective. Romans 12:2 says, "Do not conform to the pattern of this world, but be transformed by the renewing of your mind. Then you will be able to test and approve what God's will is—his good, pleasing and perfect will."

Reflection Questions

1. How does a negative outlook on life affect your relationship and mutual goals?
2. Have you discussed the impact of this mindset on your future together?
3. What steps can you take to support your partner in developing a positive outlook?
4. How can you create a supportive environment for fostering positivity and hope?

Conclusion

A negative outlook on life is a significant red flag that can impact personal well-being and relationship health. Addressing this issue is crucial for fostering a loving and hopeful partnership. As Christians, we are called to maintain a positive and hopeful mindset. Proverbs 4:23 reminds us, "Above all else, guard your heart, for everything you do flows from it." Strive to support each other in developing a positive outlook, seeking God's guidance and strength.

70. Avoidance of Professional Help

Understanding Avoidance of Professional Help
Avoidance of professional help involves refusing to seek or accept assistance from mental health professionals, counselors, or therapists despite needing support. This can prevent individuals from addressing and overcoming their issues. The Bible encourages seeking wisdom and counsel. Proverbs 11:14 says, "For lack of guidance a nation falls, but victory is won through many advisers."

Biblical Perspective on Seeking Help
The Bible emphasizes the importance of seeking wise counsel and guidance. Proverbs 19:20 says, "Listen to advice and accept discipline, and at the end you will be counted among the wise." Seeking professional help is a valuable step towards healing and growth.

Identifying Avoidance of Professional Help
Signs of avoidance of professional help in a partner include:
- **Denial:** Denying the existence or severity of issues.

- **Stigma:** Fearing the stigma associated with seeking mental health support.

- **Fear:** Feeling afraid of confronting personal issues or change.

- **Minimization:** Minimizing the impact of issues on well-being and relationships.

- **Reluctance:** Showing reluctance or refusal to consider therapy or counseling.

Consequences of Avoidance of Professional Help

Avoidance of professional help can have several negative impacts on a relationship:

- **Emotional Strain:** Increased emotional stress and tension due to unresolved issues.

- **Communication Barriers:** Difficulty communicating effectively about problems.

- **Stagnation:** Lack of progress in personal growth and relationship dynamics.

- **Conflict:** Frequent conflicts arising from unaddressed issues.
- **Impact on Well-Being:** Challenges in maintaining mental and emotional well-being.

Addressing Avoidance of Professional Help

If you notice avoidance of professional help in your partner, consider these steps:

- **Communicate with Understanding:** Discuss the importance of seeking help with empathy and understanding. Proverbs 12:15 says, "The way of fools seems right to them, but the wise listen to advice."

- **Reduce Stigma:** Work to reduce the stigma associated with seeking mental health support.

- **Encourage Small Steps:** Encourage taking small steps towards seeking help, such as researching therapists or attending a support group.

- **Offer Support:** Provide emotional support and understanding as your partner considers professional help.

- **Pray for Openness:** Pray together for openness to seeking and accepting help. James 1:5 says, "If any of you lacks wisdom, you should ask God, who gives generously to all without finding fault, and it will be given to you."

Reflection Questions

1. How does avoidance of professional help affect your relationship and personal growth?
2. Have you discussed the impact of this avoidance on your mutual goals and future together?
3. What steps can you take to support your partner in seeking professional help?
4. How can you create a supportive environment for encouraging openness to help?

Conclusion

Avoidance of professional help is a significant red flag that can impact personal well-being and relationship health. Addressing this issue is crucial for fostering a supportive and growth-oriented partnership. As Christians, we are called to seek wise counsel and guidance. Proverbs 15:22 reminds us, "Plans fail for lack of counsel, but with many advisers they succeed." Strive to support each other in seeking and accepting help, seeking God's guidance and strength.

Chapter 8: Compatibility and Values

71. Different Life Goals

Understanding Different Life Goals
Different life goals refer to significant disparities in what partners want to achieve in their personal and professional lives. These differences can create tension and conflict, making it difficult to build a harmonious future together. The Bible emphasizes the importance of shared vision and unity in relationships. Amos 3:3 says, "Do two walk together unless they have agreed to do so?"

Biblical Perspective on Shared Vision
The Bible encourages unity and shared purpose in relationships. Philippians 2:2 advises, "Then make my joy complete by being like-minded, having the same love, being one in spirit and of one mind." Aligning life goals is essential for a harmonious and fulfilling relationship.

Identifying Different Life Goals
Signs of different life goals in a relationship include:

- **Career Aspirations:** Differing aspirations regarding career paths and professional achievements.

- **Family Plans:** Conflicting desires about having children or the timing of starting a family.

- **Lifestyle Choices:** Varied preferences for lifestyle choices, such as where to live or how to spend leisure time.

- **Financial Goals:** Discrepancies in financial goals and priorities.

- **Personal Development:** Differing views on personal growth and education.

Consequences of Different Life Goals

Different life goals can have several negative impacts on a relationship:

- **Tension:** Increased tension and conflict over future plans.

- **Emotional Distance:** Growing emotional distance due to lack of alignment.

- **Unfulfilled Dreams:** Risk of unfulfilled dreams and dissatisfaction.

- **Compromised Stability:** Difficulty achieving stability and security together.

- **Decreased Relationship Satisfaction:** Overall decrease in relationship satisfaction and harmony.

Addressing Different Life Goals

If you notice different life goals in your relationship, consider these steps:

- **Communicate Openly:** Discuss your life goals and how they align or conflict. Proverbs 15:22 says, "Plans fail for lack of counsel, but with many advisers they succeed."

- **Seek Common Ground:** Identify areas where your goals align and work towards compromise in areas of conflict.

- **Set Joint Goals:** Establish joint goals that reflect both partners' aspirations and desires.

- **Pray for Guidance:** Pray together for God's guidance in aligning your life goals. Psalm 37:4 says, "Take delight in the Lord, and he will give you the desires of your heart."

Reflection Questions

1. How do different life goals affect your relationship and future plans?
2. Have you discussed the impact of these differences on your mutual goals and future together?
3. What steps can you take to align your life goals and work towards a shared vision?
4. How can you support each other in achieving your individual and joint goals?

Conclusion

Different life goals are a significant red flag that can impact relationship health and harmony. Addressing this issue is crucial for fostering a unified and fulfilling partnership. As Christians, we are called to seek unity and shared purpose. Proverbs 16:3 reminds us, "Commit to the Lord whatever you do, and he will establish your plans." Strive to support each other in aligning your life goals, seeking God's guidance and strength.

72. Conflicting Values

Understanding Conflicting Values
Conflicting values involve fundamental differences in beliefs and principles that guide behavior and decision-making. These differences can create tension and discord in a relationship. The Bible emphasizes the importance of shared values and harmony in relationships. 2 Corinthians 6:14 says, "Do not be yoked together with unbelievers. For what do righteousness and wickedness have in common? Or what fellowship can light have with darkness?"

Biblical Perspective on Shared Values
The Bible encourages us to build relationships based on shared values and principles. Amos 3:3 states, "Do two walk together unless they have agreed to do so?" Shared values are essential for a strong and cohesive partnership.

Identifying Conflicting Values
Signs of conflicting values in a relationship include:
- **Moral Beliefs:** Differing beliefs about what is right and wrong.

- **Ethical Standards:** Varied standards of ethics and integrity.

- **Lifestyle Choices:** Different preferences for lifestyle and daily habits.

- **Political Views:** Conflicting political beliefs and priorities.

- **Social Issues:** Differing views on social and cultural issues.

Consequences of Conflicting Values

Conflicting values can have several negative impacts on a relationship:

- **Tension:** Increased tension and conflict over fundamental beliefs.

- **Emotional Distance:** Growing emotional distance due to lack of alignment.

- **Decision-Making Challenges:** Difficulty making joint decisions.

- **Erosion of Trust:** Potential erosion of trust and respect.

- **Decreased Relationship Satisfaction:** Overall decrease in relationship satisfaction and harmony.

Addressing Conflicting Values

If you notice conflicting values in your relationship, consider these steps:

- **Communicate Openly:** Discuss your values and how they align or conflict. Proverbs 27:17 says, "As iron sharpens iron, so one person sharpens another."

- **Seek Understanding:** Make an effort to understand each other's values and beliefs.

- **Find Common Ground:** Identify shared values and work towards compromise in areas of conflict.

- **Pray for Unity:** Pray together for God's guidance in aligning your values. Romans 15:5-6 says, "May the God who gives endurance and encouragement give you the same attitude of mind toward each other that Christ Jesus had, so that with one mind and one voice you may glorify the God and Father of our Lord Jesus Christ."

Reflection Questions
1. How do conflicting values affect your relationship and mutual goals?
2. Have you discussed the impact of these differences on your future together?
3. What steps can you take to align your values and work towards a shared understanding?
4. How can you support each other in respecting and understanding each other's values?

Conclusion
Conflicting values are a significant red flag that can impact relationship health and harmony. Addressing this issue is crucial for fostering a unified and respectful partnership. As Christians, we are called to build relationships based on shared values and principles. Ephesians 4:2-3 reminds us, "Be completely humble and gentle; be patient, bearing with one another in love. Make every effort to keep the unity of the Spirit through the bond of peace." Strive to support each other in aligning your values, seeking God's guidance and strength.

73. Religious Incompatibility

Understanding Religious Incompatibility
Religious incompatibility involves significant differences in religious beliefs and practices that can create tension and conflict in a relationship. These differences can affect various aspects of life, including values, traditions, and raising children. The Bible emphasizes the importance of spiritual unity in relationships. 2 Corinthians 6:14 says, "Do not be yoked together with unbelievers. For what do righteousness and wickedness have in common? Or what fellowship can light have with darkness?"

Biblical Perspective on Spiritual Unity
The Bible encourages spiritual unity and shared faith in relationships. Ephesians 4:3-6 advises, "Make every effort to keep the unity of the Spirit through the bond of peace. There is one body and one Spirit, just as you were called to one hope when you were called; one Lord, one faith, one baptism; one God and Father of all, who is over all and through all and in all."

Identifying Religious Incompatibility
Signs of religious incompatibility in a relationship include:
- **Differing Beliefs:** Holding different core beliefs and doctrines.

- **Varied Practices:** Practicing different religious rituals and traditions.

- **Conflicting Values:** Having conflicting values and moral standards based on religious beliefs.

- **Disagreements on Worship:** Disagreeing on places of worship or spiritual practices.

- **Challenges in Raising Children:** Differing views on religious upbringing for children.

Consequences of Religious Incompatibility

Religious incompatibility can have several negative impacts on a relationship:

- **Tension:** Increased tension and conflict over religious beliefs and practices.

- **Emotional Distance:** Growing emotional distance due to lack of spiritual alignment.

- **Decision-Making Challenges:** Difficulty making joint decisions on religious matters.

- **Impact on Family Dynamics:** Potential strain on family relationships and raising children.

- **Decreased Relationship Satisfaction:** Overall decrease in relationship satisfaction and harmony.

Addressing Religious Incompatibility

If you notice religious incompatibility in your relationship, consider these steps:

- **Communicate Respectfully:** Discuss your religious beliefs and practices with respect and understanding. Proverbs 18:15 says, "The heart of the discerning acquires knowledge, for the ears of the wise seek it out."

- **Seek Common Ground:** Identify shared values and beliefs that can strengthen your relationship.

- **Respect Differences:** Respect each other's religious beliefs and practices.

- **Find Compromise:** Work towards compromise in areas of conflict, especially regarding family and children.

- **Pray for Unity:** Pray together for God's guidance in finding spiritual unity. Colossians 3:14 says, "And over all these virtues put on love, which binds them all together in perfect unity."

Reflection Questions
1. How does religious incompatibility affect your relationship and mutual goals?
2. Have you discussed the impact of these differences on your future together?
3. What steps can you take to respect each other's religious beliefs and practices?
4. How can you support each other in finding spiritual unity and common ground?

Conclusion
Religious incompatibility is a significant red flag that can impact relationship health and harmony. Addressing this issue is crucial for fostering a unified and respectful partnership. As Christians, we are called to seek spiritual unity and shared faith. Philippians 2:2 reminds us, "Then make my joy complete by being like-minded, having the same love, being one in spirit and of one mind." Strive to support each other in finding common ground and spiritual unity, seeking God's guidance and strength.

74. Different Parenting Views

Understanding Different Parenting Views
Different parenting views involve varying beliefs and practices regarding raising children, including discipline, education, and values. These differences can lead to conflicts and tension in a relationship, especially when deciding on parenting strategies. The Bible emphasizes the importance of raising children with wisdom and guidance. Proverbs 22:6 says, "Start children off on the way they should go, and even when they are old they will not turn from it."

Biblical Perspective on Parenting
The Bible encourages parents to raise their children in a nurturing and godly environment. Ephesians 6:4 advises, "Fathers, do not exasperate your children; instead, bring them up in the training and instruction of the Lord." Aligning parenting views is essential for creating a harmonious family life.

Identifying Different Parenting Views
Signs of different parenting views in a relationship include:

- **Discipline:** Differing opinions on methods of discipline and correction.

- **Education:** Conflicting views on educational choices and priorities.

- **Values and Morals:** Varying beliefs about instilling values and morals in children.

- **Health and Nutrition:** Differing approaches to health, nutrition, and wellness.

- **Family Roles:** Different expectations of parental roles and responsibilities.

Consequences of Different Parenting Views

Different parenting views can have several negative impacts on a relationship:

- **Conflict:** Frequent arguments and disagreements over parenting decisions.

- **Inconsistency:** Inconsistent parenting approaches leading to confusion for children.

- **Emotional Strain:** Increased emotional stress and tension for both partners.

- **Undermining:** Potential undermining of each other's authority and decisions.

- **Decreased Relationship Satisfaction:** Overall decrease in relationship satisfaction and family harmony.

Addressing Different Parenting Views

If you notice different parenting views in your relationship, consider these steps:

- **Communicate Openly:** Discuss your parenting views and the importance of aligning your approaches. Proverbs 15:22 says, "Plans fail for lack of counsel, but with many advisers they succeed."

- **Seek Common Ground:** Identify areas where your views align and work towards compromise in areas of conflict.

- **Establish Joint Guidelines:** Create joint parenting guidelines that reflect both partners' values and beliefs.

- **Pray for Guidance:** Pray together for God's wisdom in parenting. James 1:5 says, "If any of you lacks wisdom, you should ask God, who gives generously to all without finding fault, and it will be given to you."

Reflection Questions

1. How do different parenting views affect your relationship and family dynamics?
2. Have you discussed the impact of these differences on your children and family harmony?
3. What steps can you take to align your parenting views and establish joint guidelines?
4. How can you support each other in implementing consistent and godly parenting practices?

Conclusion

Different parenting views are a significant red flag that can impact relationship health and family harmony. Addressing this issue is crucial for fostering a unified and supportive partnership. As Christians, we are called to raise our children in a nurturing and godly environment. Proverbs 29:17 reminds us, "Discipline your children, and they will give you peace; they will bring you the delights you desire." Strive to support each other in aligning your parenting views, seeking God's guidance and strength.

75. Political Differences

Understanding Political Differences
Political differences involve varying beliefs and opinions regarding political issues, policies, and leadership. These differences can create tension and conflict, particularly in today's polarized political climate. The Bible encourages us to live in harmony and peace with one another. Romans 12:18 says, "If it is possible, as far as it depends on you, live at peace with everyone."

Biblical Perspective on Harmony
The Bible emphasizes the importance of living in harmony and respecting differing opinions. Philippians 2:3-4 advises, "Do nothing out of selfish ambition or vain conceit. Rather, in humility value others above yourselves, not looking to your own interests but each of you to the interests of the others." Finding common ground and respecting each other's views is essential for maintaining harmony in a relationship.

Identifying Political Differences
Signs of political differences in a relationship include:
- **Differing Beliefs:** Holding different core beliefs about political issues and policies.

- **Conflicting Values:** Having conflicting values and priorities based on political views.

- **Disagreements:** Frequently disagreeing on political topics and current events.

- **Debates:** Engaging in heated debates or arguments about politics.

- **Social Circle:** Differing preferences for social circles and political affiliations.

Consequences of Political Differences

Political differences can have several negative impacts on a relationship:

- **Tension:** Increased tension and conflict over political beliefs and discussions.

- **Emotional Strain:** Emotional stress and anxiety due to disagreements.

- **Communication Barriers:** Difficulty maintaining positive and constructive communication.

- **Impact on Family Dynamics:** Potential strain on family relationships and interactions.

- **Decreased Relationship Satisfaction:** Overall decrease in relationship satisfaction and harmony.

Addressing Political Differences

If you notice political differences in your relationship, consider these steps:

- **Communicate Respectfully:** Discuss your political views with respect and understanding. Proverbs 18:15 says, "The heart of the discerning acquires knowledge, for the ears of the wise seek it out."

- **Seek Understanding:** Make an effort to understand each other's perspectives and beliefs.

- **Find Common Ground:** Identify shared values and priorities that can strengthen your relationship.

- **Respect Differences:** Respect each other's political views and avoid contentious debates.

- **Pray for Unity:** Pray together for God's guidance in finding harmony and peace. Colossians 3:14 says, "And over all these virtues put on love, which binds them all together in perfect unity."

Reflection Questions

1. How do political differences affect your relationship and mutual goals?
2. Have you discussed the impact of these differences on your future together?
3. What steps can you take to respect each other's political views and find common ground?
4. How can you support each other in maintaining harmony and respect despite political differences?

Conclusion

Political differences are a significant red flag that can impact relationship health and harmony. Addressing this issue is crucial for fostering a respectful and supportive partnership. As Christians, we are called to live in harmony and respect differing opinions. Ephesians 4:2-3 reminds us, "Be completely humble and gentle; be patient, bearing with one another in love. Make every effort to keep the unity of the Spirit through the bond of peace." Strive to support each other in finding common ground and respecting political differences, seeking God's guidance and strength.

76. Different Views on Marriage Roles

Understanding Different Views on Marriage Roles
Different views on marriage roles involve varying beliefs and expectations regarding the roles and responsibilities of each partner within the marriage. These differences can lead to misunderstandings and conflicts, especially when expectations are not aligned. The Bible provides guidance on marriage roles, emphasizing mutual love and respect. Ephesians 5:21 says, "Submit to one another out of reverence for Christ."

Biblical Perspective on Marriage Roles
The Bible emphasizes mutual love, respect, and submission in marriage. Ephesians 5:22-25 advises, "Wives, submit yourselves to your own husbands as you do to the Lord. For the husband is the head of the wife as Christ is the head of the church, his body, of which he is the Savior. Now as the church submits to Christ, so also wives should submit to their husbands in everything. Husbands, love your wives, just as Christ loved the church and gave himself up for her."

Identifying Different Views on Marriage Roles
Signs of different views on marriage roles in a relationship include:
- **Role Expectations:** Differing expectations regarding the roles and responsibilities of each partner.

- **Decision-Making:** Conflicting beliefs about who should make major decisions.

- **Work and Home Balance:** Varying views on balancing work and home responsibilities.

- **Leadership and Submission:** Differing beliefs about leadership and submission within the marriage.

- **Conflict Resolution:** Conflicting approaches to resolving conflicts and making compromises.

Consequences of Different Views on Marriage Roles

Different views on marriage roles can have several negative impacts on a relationship:

- **Tension:** Increased tension and conflict over roles and responsibilities.

- **Emotional Strain:** Emotional stress and frustration due to unmet expectations.

- **Communication Barriers:** Difficulty maintaining positive and constructive communication.

- **Imbalance:** Creating an imbalance in the relationship dynamics.

- **Decreased Relationship Satisfaction:** Overall decrease in relationship satisfaction and harmony.

Addressing Different Views on Marriage Roles

If you notice different views on marriage roles in your relationship, consider these steps:

- **Communicate Openly:** Discuss your views on marriage roles and how they align or conflict. Proverbs 15:22 says, "Plans fail for lack of counsel, but with many advisers they succeed."

- **Seek Understanding:** Make an effort to understand each other's perspectives and beliefs.

- **Find Common Ground:** Identify shared values and work towards compromise in areas of conflict.

- **Establish Joint Roles:** Create joint guidelines for roles and responsibilities that reflect both partners' values and beliefs.

- **Pray for Unity:** Pray together for God's guidance in aligning your views on marriage roles. Colossians 3:14 says, "And over all these virtues put on love, which binds them all together in perfect unity."

Reflection Questions

1. How do different views on marriage roles affect your relationship and mutual goals?
2. Have you discussed the impact of these differences on your future together?
3. What steps can you take to align your views on marriage roles and establish joint guidelines?
4. How can you support each other in implementing godly and respectful marriage roles?

Conclusion

Different views on marriage roles are a significant red flag that can impact relationship health and harmony. Addressing this issue is crucial for fostering a unified and supportive partnership. As Christians, we are called to embrace mutual love, respect, and submission in marriage. Ephesians 5:33 reminds us, "However, each one of you also must love his wife as he loves himself, and the wife must respect her husband." Strive to support each other in aligning your views on marriage roles, seeking God's guidance and strength.

77. Incompatible Lifestyles

Understanding Incompatible Lifestyles

Incompatible lifestyles refer to significant differences in daily habits, routines, and preferences that can create tension and conflict in a relationship. These differences can range from work-life balance to leisure activities and overall lifestyle choices. The Bible encourages us to live in harmony and be considerate of one another. Romans 12:16 says, "Live in harmony with one another. Do not be proud, but be willing to associate with people of low position. Do not be conceited."

Biblical Perspective on Harmony

The Bible emphasizes the importance of living in harmony and being considerate of each other's needs and preferences. Philippians 2:4 advises, "Not looking to your own interests but each of you to the interests of the others." Aligning lifestyles requires mutual respect and consideration.

Identifying Incompatible Lifestyles

Signs of incompatible lifestyles in a relationship include:

- **Different Routines:** Conflicting daily schedules and routines.

- **Leisure Activities:** Differing preferences for leisure activities and hobbies.

- **Work-Life Balance:** Varied approaches to balancing work and personal life.

- **Health and Fitness:** Differing priorities regarding health, fitness, and wellness.

- **Social Preferences:** Varied preferences for socializing and spending time with others.

Consequences of Incompatible Lifestyles

Incompatible lifestyles can have several negative impacts on a relationship:

- **Tension:** Increased tension and conflict over daily habits and routines.

- **Emotional Distance:** Growing emotional distance due to lack of alignment.

- **Resentment:** Potential resentment arising from unmet expectations and compromises.

- **Communication Barriers:** Difficulty maintaining positive and constructive communication.

- **Decreased Relationship Satisfaction:** Overall decrease in relationship satisfaction and harmony.

Addressing Incompatible Lifestyles

If you notice incompatible lifestyles in your relationship, consider these steps:

- **Communicate Openly:** Discuss your lifestyles and how they align or conflict. Proverbs 15:22 says, "Plans fail for lack of counsel, but with many advisers they succeed."

- **Seek Compromise:** Identify areas where compromise is possible and work towards finding a balance.

- **Respect Differences:** Respect each other's lifestyle choices and preferences.

- **Create Joint Routines:** Establish joint routines and activities that reflect both partners' lifestyles.

- **Pray for Harmony:** Pray together for God's guidance in aligning your lifestyles. Romans 15:5-6 says, "May the God who gives endurance and encouragement give you the same attitude of mind toward each other that Christ Jesus had, so that with one mind and one voice you may glorify the God and Father of our Lord Jesus Christ."

Reflection Questions

1. How do incompatible lifestyles affect your relationship and daily interactions?
2. Have you discussed the impact of these differences on your mutual goals and future together?
3. What steps can you take to align your lifestyles and find a balance?
4. How can you support each other in respecting and accommodating each other's lifestyle choices?

Conclusion

Incompatible lifestyles are a significant red flag that can impact relationship health and harmony. Addressing this issue is crucial for fostering a balanced and respectful partnership. As Christians, we are called to live in harmony and be considerate of each other's needs. Ephesians 4:2-3 reminds us, "Be completely humble and gentle; be patient, bearing with one another in love. Make every effort to keep the unity of the Spirit through the bond of peace." Strive to support each other in aligning your lifestyles, seeking God's guidance and strength.

78. Lack of Shared Interests

Understanding Lack of Shared Interests
Lack of shared interests refers to having few or no common hobbies, activities, or interests that you both enjoy together. This can lead to a lack of connection and bonding opportunities, impacting the overall quality of the relationship. The Bible encourages shared joy and unity. Philippians 2:2 says, "Then make my joy complete by being like-minded, having the same love, being one in spirit and of one mind."

Biblical Perspective on Shared Interests
The Bible emphasizes the importance of unity and shared joy in relationships. Amos 3:3 states, "Do two walk together unless they have agreed to do so?" Having shared interests can strengthen the bond and create meaningful connections.

Identifying Lack of Shared Interests
Signs of lack of shared interests in a relationship include:
- **Separate Activities:** Frequently engaging in activities separately rather than together.

- **Different Hobbies:** Having different hobbies and interests with little overlap.

- **Limited Bonding Time:** Spending limited quality time together due to differing interests.

- **Lack of Enthusiasm:** Showing little enthusiasm for each other's interests.

- **Struggles in Planning:** Difficulty planning activities or outings that both enjoy.

Consequences of Lack of Shared Interests

Lack of shared interests can have several negative impacts on a relationship:

- **Emotional Distance:** Growing emotional distance due to lack of bonding activities.

- **Boredom:** Potential boredom and dissatisfaction in the relationship.

- **Limited Quality Time:** Reduced quality time spent together.

- **Communication Barriers:** Difficulty maintaining positive and engaging communication.

- **Decreased Relationship Satisfaction:** Overall decrease in relationship satisfaction and harmony.

Addressing Lack of Shared Interests

If you notice a lack of shared interests in your relationship, consider these steps:

- **Communicate Openly:** Discuss your interests and explore potential shared activities. Proverbs 27:9 says, "Perfume and incense bring joy to the heart, and the pleasantness of a friend springs from their heartfelt advice."

- **Try New Activities:** Be open to trying new activities together to discover common interests.

- **Show Support:** Support and encourage each other's hobbies and interests.

- **Plan Joint Activities:** Schedule regular activities and outings that you both enjoy.

- **Pray for Unity:** Pray together for God's guidance in finding and nurturing shared interests. Colossians 3:14 says, "And over all these virtues put on love, which binds them all together in perfect unity."

Reflection Questions
1. How does the lack of shared interests affect your relationship and bonding opportunities?
2. Have you discussed the impact of these differences on your mutual goals and future together?
3. What steps can you take to discover and nurture shared interests?
4. How can you support each other in exploring and enjoying each other's hobbies?

Conclusion
Lack of shared interests is a significant red flag that can impact relationship health and bonding. Addressing this issue is crucial for fostering a unified and engaging partnership. As Christians, we are called to seek unity and shared joy. Romans 15:5-6 reminds us, "May the God who gives endurance and encouragement give you the same attitude of mind toward each other that Christ Jesus had, so that with one mind and one voice you may glorify the God and Father of our Lord Jesus Christ." Strive to support each other in finding and nurturing shared interests, seeking God's guidance and strength.

79. Differing Social Lives

Understanding Differing Social Lives

Differing social lives refer to having distinct social circles, preferences, and activities that can create challenges in spending quality time together and maintaining a unified relationship. The Bible encourages fellowship and unity. Hebrews 10:24-25 says, "And let us consider how we may spur one another on toward love and good deeds, not giving up meeting together, as some are in the habit of doing, but encouraging one another — and all the more as you see the Day approaching."

Biblical Perspective on Fellowship

The Bible emphasizes the importance of fellowship and unity in relationships. 1 Thessalonians 5:11 advises, "Therefore encourage one another and build each other up, just as in fact you are doing." Finding a balance in social lives is essential for maintaining a strong connection.

Identifying Differing Social Lives

Signs of differing social lives in a relationship include:

- **Separate Social Circles:** Maintaining distinct and separate social circles with little overlap.

- **Different Social Preferences:** Having different preferences for social activities and events.

- **Limited Shared Social Time:** Spending limited social time together due to differing interests.

- **Conflict Over Plans:** Frequent conflicts over social plans and activities.

- **Isolation:** Feeling isolated or left out of each other's social lives.

Consequences of Differing Social Lives

Differing social lives can have several negative impacts on a relationship:

- **Emotional Distance:** Growing emotional distance due to lack of shared social experiences.

- **Conflict:** Increased conflict over social plans and priorities.

- **Isolation:** Potential feelings of isolation and exclusion.

- **Communication Barriers:** Difficulty maintaining positive and engaging communication.

- **Decreased Relationship Satisfaction:** Overall decrease in relationship satisfaction and harmony.

Addressing Differing Social Lives

If you notice differing social lives in your relationship, consider these steps:

- **Communicate Openly:** Discuss your social preferences and how they align or conflict. Proverbs 27:17 says, "As iron sharpens iron, so one person sharpens another."

- **Find Balance:** Seek a balance between individual social activities and shared social time.

- **Integrate Social Circles:** Make an effort to integrate your social circles and activities.

- **Respect Differences:** Respect each other's social preferences and friends.

- **Pray for Unity:** Pray together for God's guidance in balancing and integrating your social lives. Romans 12:10 says, "Be devoted to one another in love. Honor one another above yourselves."

Reflection Questions

1. How do differing social lives affect your relationship and quality time together?
2. Have you discussed the impact of these differences on your mutual goals and future together?
3. What steps can you take to integrate and balance your social lives?
4. How can you support each other in respecting and enjoying each other's social preferences?

Conclusion

Differing social lives are a significant red flag that can impact relationship health and unity. Addressing this issue is crucial for fostering a balanced and engaging partnership. As Christians, we are called to seek fellowship and unity. Hebrews 10:24-25 reminds us, "And let us consider how we may spur one another on toward love and good deeds, not giving up meeting together, as some are in the habit of doing, but encouraging one another—and all the more as you see the Day approaching." Strive to support each other in balancing and integrating your social lives, seeking God's guidance and strength.

80. Unresolved Deal-Breakers
Understanding Unresolved Deal-Breakers

Unresolved deal-breakers refer to significant issues or differences that are critical to one or both partners but have not been addressed or resolved. These can include fundamental values, behaviors, or expectations that are non-negotiable. The Bible emphasizes the importance of addressing and resolving conflicts. Matthew 18:15 says, "If your brother or sister sins, go and point out their fault, just between the two of you. If they listen to you, you have won them over."

Biblical Perspective on Resolution

The Bible encourages resolving conflicts and addressing important issues in relationships. Ephesians 4:2-3 advises, "Be completely humble and gentle; be patient, bearing with one another in love. Make every effort to keep the unity of the Spirit through the bond of peace." Addressing deal-breakers is essential for a healthy and harmonious relationship.

Identifying Unresolved Deal-Breakers

Signs of unresolved deal-breakers in a relationship include:

- **Significant Issues:** Presence of major issues or differences that have not been addressed.

- **Avoidance:** Avoiding discussions about critical and non-negotiable topics.

- **Conflict:** Frequent conflicts arising from unresolved issues.

- **Emotional Strain:** Increased emotional stress and tension due to unresolved differences.

- **Decision-Making Challenges:** Difficulty making joint decisions due to fundamental disagreements.

Consequences of Unresolved Deal-Breakers

Unresolved deal-breakers can have several negative impacts on a relationship:

- **Tension:** Increased tension and conflict over unresolved issues.

- **Emotional Distance:** Growing emotional distance due to lack of resolution.

- **Resentment:** Potential resentment arising from unmet expectations and unresolved conflicts.

- **Communication Barriers:** Difficulty maintaining positive and constructive communication.

- **Decreased Relationship Satisfaction:** Overall decrease in relationship satisfaction and harmony.

Addressing Unresolved Deal-Breakers

If you notice unresolved deal-breakers in your relationship, consider these steps:

- **Communicate Openly:** Discuss the deal-breakers and their impact on your relationship. Proverbs 27:5 says, "Better is open rebuke than hidden love."

- **Seek Resolution:** Make a concerted effort to address and resolve these critical issues.

- **Consider Counseling:** Seek professional counseling to facilitate resolution and understanding.

- **Establish Boundaries:** Set clear boundaries and guidelines to prevent future conflicts.

- **Pray for Wisdom:** Pray together for God's wisdom and guidance in resolving deal-breakers. James 1:5 says, "If any of you lacks wisdom, you should ask God, who gives generously to all without finding fault, and it will be given to you."

Reflection Questions
1. How do unresolved deal-breakers affect your relationship and mutual goals?
2. Have you discussed the impact of these issues on your future together?
3. What steps can you take to address and resolve these deal-breakers?
4. How can you support each other in maintaining a healthy and respectful relationship?

Conclusion
Unresolved deal-breakers are a significant red flag that can impact relationship health and harmony. Addressing this issue is crucial for fostering a unified and supportive partnership. As Christians, we are called to resolve conflicts and seek peace. Colossians 3:13 reminds us, "Bear with each other and forgive one another if any of you has a grievance against someone. Forgive as the Lord forgave you." Strive to support each other in addressing and resolving deal-breakers, seeking God's guidance and strength.

Chapter 9: Future Plans and Expectations

81. Unclear Future Plans

Understanding Unclear Future Plans
Unclear future plans refer to a lack of concrete goals and direction regarding the future of the relationship. This uncertainty can create confusion and insecurity, making it difficult to build a stable and committed partnership. The Bible encourages us to plan wisely and seek God's guidance for the future. Proverbs 16:9 says, "In their hearts humans plan their course, but the Lord establishes their steps."

Biblical Perspective on Planning
The Bible emphasizes the importance of planning and seeking God's wisdom in our decisions. Proverbs 19:21 advises, "Many are the plans in a person's heart, but it is the Lord's purpose that prevails." Having clear and aligned future plans is essential for a strong relationship.

Identifying Unclear Future Plans
Signs of unclear future plans in a relationship include:
- **Vague Goals:** Lack of specific and concrete goals for the future.

- **Avoidance:** Avoiding discussions about long-term plans and commitments.

- **Inconsistency:** Frequently changing or inconsistent plans and goals.

- **Indecision:** Difficulty making decisions about significant life events.

- **Uncertainty:** Feeling uncertain or insecure about the direction of the relationship.

Consequences of Unclear Future Plans

Unclear future plans can have several negative impacts on a relationship:

- **Insecurity:** Increased insecurity and anxiety about the future.

- **Emotional Strain:** Emotional stress and tension due to lack of direction.

- **Conflict:** Frequent conflicts arising from differing expectations and uncertainty.

- **Lack of Progress:** Difficulty making progress towards shared goals.

- **Decreased Relationship Satisfaction:** Overall decrease in relationship satisfaction and stability.

Addressing Unclear Future Plans

If you notice unclear future plans in your relationship, consider these steps:

- **Communicate Openly:** Discuss your future goals and expectations with clarity and honesty. Proverbs 15:22 says, "Plans fail for lack of counsel, but with many advisers they succeed."

- **Set Concrete Goals:** Establish specific and realistic goals for your future together.

- **Create a Plan:** Develop a clear and actionable plan to achieve your shared goals.

- **Seek God's Guidance:** Pray together for God's wisdom and guidance in planning your future. Jeremiah 29:11 says, "For I know the plans I have for you," declares the Lord, "plans to prosper you and not to harm you, plans to give you hope and a future."

Reflection Questions

1. How do unclear future plans affect your relationship and mutual goals?
2. Have you discussed the impact of this uncertainty on your future together?
3. What steps can you take to establish clear and concrete future plans?
4. How can you support each other in achieving your shared goals and seeking God's guidance?

Conclusion

Unclear future plans are a significant red flag that can impact relationship health and stability. Addressing this issue is crucial for fostering a unified and committed partnership. As Christians, we are called to plan wisely and seek God's guidance for our future. Proverbs 3:5-6 reminds us, "Trust in the Lord with all your heart and lean not on your own understanding; in all your ways submit to him, and he will make your paths straight." Strive to support each other in establishing clear future plans, seeking God's wisdom and strength.

82. Unrealistic Expectations

Understanding Unrealistic Expectations

Unrealistic expectations involve having impractical or idealistic beliefs about what the relationship or partner should be like. These expectations can create disappointment and frustration when reality does not align with them. The Bible encourages realistic and humble expectations. Romans 12:3 says, "For by the grace given me I say to every one of you: Do not think of yourself more highly than you ought, but rather think of yourself with sober judgment, in accordance with the faith God has distributed to each of you."

Biblical Perspective on Expectations

The Bible emphasizes the importance of humility and realistic expectations in relationships. Philippians 2:3-4 advises, "Do nothing out of selfish ambition or vain conceit. Rather, in humility value others above yourselves, not looking to your own interests but each of you to the interests of the others." Having realistic and humble expectations fosters a healthy relationship.

Identifying Unrealistic Expectations

Signs of unrealistic expectations in a relationship include:

- **Perfectionism:** Expecting perfection from your partner or the relationship.

- **Idealization:** Holding idealistic beliefs about how your partner should behave or what the relationship should be like.

- **Disappointment:** Frequently feeling disappointed when expectations are not met.

- **Criticism:** Regularly criticizing your partner for not meeting unrealistic standards.

- **Pressure:** Placing undue pressure on your partner to fulfill impractical expectations.

Consequences of Unrealistic Expectations

Unrealistic expectations can have several negative impacts on a relationship:

- **Disappointment:** Increased disappointment and frustration when expectations are not met.

- **Conflict:** Frequent conflicts arising from unmet expectations and criticism.

- **Emotional Strain:** Emotional stress and tension due to unrealistic standards.

- **Erosion of Trust:** Potential erosion of trust and respect.

- **Decreased Relationship Satisfaction:** Overall decrease in relationship satisfaction and harmony.

Addressing Unrealistic Expectations

If you notice unrealistic expectations in your relationship, consider these steps:

- **Communicate Honestly:** Discuss your expectations and assess their realism. Proverbs 27:17 says, "As iron sharpens iron, so one person sharpens another."

- **Adjust Expectations:** Work together to adjust your expectations to be more realistic and achievable.

- **Practice Humility:** Embrace humility and appreciate your partner's strengths and weaknesses.

- **Seek Growth:** Focus on personal and mutual growth rather than perfection.

- **Pray for Wisdom:** Pray together for God's wisdom and guidance in managing expectations. James 1:5 says, "If any of you lacks wisdom, you should ask God, who gives generously to all without finding fault, and it will be given to you."

Reflection Questions

1. How do unrealistic expectations affect your relationship and mutual goals?
2. Have you discussed the impact of these expectations on your future together?
3. What steps can you take to adjust your expectations and foster a healthy relationship?
4. How can you support each other in practicing humility and seeking mutual growth?

Conclusion

Unrealistic expectations are a significant red flag that can impact relationship health and harmony. Addressing this issue is crucial for fostering a humble and supportive partnership. As Christians, we are called to have realistic and humble expectations. Philippians 4:8 reminds us, "Finally, brothers and sisters, whatever is true, whatever is noble, whatever is right, whatever is pure, whatever is lovely, whatever is admirable — if anything is excellent or praiseworthy — think about such things." Strive to support each other in adjusting expectations and fostering mutual growth, seeking God's wisdom and strength.

83. Lack of Long-Term Commitment

Understanding Lack of Long-Term Commitment
Lack of long-term commitment involves uncertainty or unwillingness to commit to a future together. This can create insecurity and instability in the relationship, making it difficult to build a lasting partnership. The Bible emphasizes the importance of commitment and faithfulness in relationships. Ruth 1:16-17 says, "But Ruth replied, 'Don't urge me to leave you or to turn back from you. Where you go I will go, and where you stay I will stay. Your people will be my people and your God my God. Where you die I will die, and there I will be buried. May the Lord deal with me, be it ever so severely, if even death separates you and me.'"

Biblical Perspective on Commitment
The Bible encourages commitment and faithfulness in relationships. Ecclesiastes 4:9-10 advises, "Two are better than one, because they have a good return for their labor: If either of them falls down, one can help the other up. But pity anyone who falls and has no one to help them up." Long-term commitment is essential for building a strong and lasting relationship.

Identifying Lack of Long-Term Commitment
Signs of lack of long-term commitment in a relationship include:
- **Indecision:** Indecisiveness about the future of the relationship.

- **Avoidance:** Avoiding discussions about long-term plans and commitments.

- **Inconsistency:** Inconsistent actions and statements regarding commitment.

- **Reluctance:** Reluctance to make long-term plans or take significant steps in the relationship.

- **Insecurity:** Feeling insecure or uncertain about the partner's commitment.

Consequences of Lack of Long-Term Commitment

Lack of long-term commitment can have several negative impacts on a relationship:

- **Insecurity:** Increased insecurity and anxiety about the future.

- **Emotional Strain:** Emotional stress and tension due to lack of commitment.

- **Conflict:** Frequent conflicts arising from uncertainty and insecurity.

- **Lack of Progress:** Difficulty making progress towards shared goals.

- **Decreased Relationship Satisfaction:** Overall decrease in relationship satisfaction and stability.

Addressing Lack of Long-Term Commitment

If you notice lack of long-term commitment in your relationship, consider these steps:

- **Communicate Clearly:** Discuss your expectations and desires for long-term commitment. Proverbs 16:3 says, "Commit to the Lord whatever you do, and he will establish your plans."

- **Set Goals:** Establish clear and mutual goals for the future of your relationship.

- **Build Trust:** Focus on building trust and demonstrating commitment through actions.

- **Seek Counsel:** Consider seeking counsel or guidance to address commitment issues.

- **Pray for Guidance:** Pray together for God's wisdom and guidance in fostering long-term commitment. Proverbs 3:5-6 says, "Trust in the Lord with all your heart and lean not on your own understanding; in all your ways submit to him, and he will make your paths straight."

Reflection Questions
1. How does lack of long-term commitment affect your relationship and mutual goals?
2. Have you discussed the impact of this issue on your future together?
3. What steps can you take to build trust and demonstrate commitment?
4. How can you support each other in fostering long-term commitment and stability?

Conclusion
Lack of long-term commitment is a significant red flag that can impact relationship health and stability. Addressing this issue is crucial for fostering a committed and secure partnership. As Christians, we are called to embrace commitment and faithfulness. Proverbs 18:22 reminds us, "He who finds a wife finds what is good and receives favor from the Lord." Strive to support each other in fostering long-term commitment, seeking God's wisdom and strength.

84. Indecisiveness About Marriage

Understanding Indecisiveness About Marriage
Indecisiveness about marriage refers to uncertainty or hesitation in making a firm decision about getting married. This can create anxiety and insecurity in the relationship, making it difficult to build a future together. The Bible emphasizes the importance of commitment and decisiveness in relationships. James 1:8 says, "Such a person is double-minded and unstable in all they do."

Biblical Perspective on Commitment
The Bible encourages decisiveness and commitment in relationships. Proverbs 16:3 advises, "Commit to the Lord whatever you do, and he will establish your plans." Making a clear decision about marriage is essential for a stable and secure relationship.

Identifying Indecisiveness About Marriage
Signs of indecisiveness about marriage in a relationship include:

- **Avoidance:** Avoiding discussions about marriage and long-term commitment.

- **Hesitation:** Showing hesitation or reluctance to make a decision about getting married.

- **Inconsistent Statements:** Making inconsistent statements about marriage plans.

- **Delay:** Frequently delaying or postponing discussions or decisions about marriage.

- **Uncertainty:** Expressing uncertainty or confusion about the future of the relationship.

Consequences of Indecisiveness About Marriage

Indecisiveness about marriage can have several negative impacts on a relationship:

- **Insecurity:** Increased insecurity and anxiety about the future.

- **Emotional Strain:** Emotional stress and tension due to lack of commitment.

- **Conflict:** Frequent conflicts arising from uncertainty and hesitation.

- **Lack of Progress:** Difficulty making progress towards shared goals.

- **Decreased Relationship Satisfaction:** Overall decrease in relationship satisfaction and stability.

Addressing Indecisiveness About Marriage

If you notice indecisiveness about marriage in your relationship, consider these steps:

- **Communicate Clearly:** Discuss your expectations and desires for marriage. Proverbs 3:5-6 says, "Trust in the Lord with all your heart and lean not on your own understanding; in all your ways submit to him, and he will make your paths straight."

- **Seek Understanding:** Try to understand the reasons behind the indecisiveness and address any underlying concerns.

- **Set a Timeline:** Agree on a reasonable timeline for making a decision about marriage.

- **Seek Counsel:** Consider seeking guidance from a trusted mentor or counselor.

- **Pray for Clarity:** Pray together for God's wisdom and clarity in making a decision. James 1:5 says, "If any of you lacks wisdom, you should ask God, who gives generously to all without finding fault, and it will be given to you."

Reflection Questions

1. How does indecisiveness about marriage affect your relationship and mutual goals?
2. Have you discussed the impact of this indecisiveness on your future together?
3. What steps can you take to gain clarity and make a firm decision about marriage?
4. How can you support each other in addressing concerns and seeking God's guidance?

Conclusion

Indecisiveness about marriage is a significant red flag that can impact relationship health and stability. Addressing this issue is crucial for fostering a committed and secure partnership. As Christians, we are called to embrace decisiveness and commitment. Proverbs 16:9 reminds us, "In their hearts humans plan their course, but the Lord establishes their steps." Strive to support each other in making a clear decision about marriage, seeking God's wisdom and strength.

85. Unwillingness to Plan Together

Understanding Unwillingness to Plan Together
Unwillingness to plan together refers to a lack of interest or effort in making joint plans for the future. This can create a sense of disconnection and uncertainty in the relationship, making it difficult to achieve shared goals. The Bible encourages unity and cooperation in relationships. Ecclesiastes 4:9 says, "Two are better than one, because they have a good return for their labor."

Biblical Perspective on Cooperation
The Bible emphasizes the importance of working together and making joint plans. Amos 3:3 states, "Do two walk together unless they have agreed to do so?" Planning together is essential for a unified and harmonious relationship.

Identifying Unwillingness to Plan Together
Signs of unwillingness to plan together in a relationship include:
- **Avoidance:** Avoiding discussions about future plans and goals.

- **Indifference:** Showing indifference or lack of interest in making joint plans.

- **Solo Planning:** Preferring to make plans independently rather than as a couple.

- **Resistance:** Resisting efforts to create shared goals and strategies.

- **Lack of Initiative:** Failing to take the initiative in planning for the future together.

Consequences of Unwillingness to Plan Together

Unwillingness to plan together can have several negative impacts on a relationship:

- **Disconnection:** Increased emotional disconnection and lack of unity.

- **Uncertainty:** Growing uncertainty and insecurity about the future.

- **Conflict:** Frequent conflicts arising from differing expectations and plans.

- **Stagnation:** Difficulty making progress towards shared goals and aspirations.

- **Decreased Relationship Satisfaction:** Overall decrease in relationship satisfaction and harmony.

Addressing Unwillingness to Plan Together

If you notice unwillingness to plan together in your relationship, consider these steps:

- **Communicate Clearly:** Discuss the importance of making joint plans and working towards shared goals. Proverbs 15:22 says, "Plans fail for lack of counsel, but with many advisers they succeed."

- **Identify Common Goals:** Identify common goals and aspirations that you can work towards together.

- **Create a Plan:** Develop a clear and actionable plan to achieve your shared goals.

- **Encourage Participation:** Encourage your partner to take an active role in planning for the future.

- **Pray for Unity:** Pray together for God's guidance in fostering unity and cooperation. Colossians 3:14 says, "And over all these virtues put on love, which binds them all together in perfect unity."

Reflection Questions

1. How does unwillingness to plan together affect your relationship and mutual goals?
2. Have you discussed the impact of this issue on your future together?
3. What steps can you take to encourage joint planning and cooperation?
4. How can you support each other in working towards shared goals and aspirations?

Conclusion

Unwillingness to plan together is a significant red flag that can impact relationship health and unity. Addressing this issue is crucial for fostering a cooperative and harmonious partnership. As Christians, we are called to work together and make joint plans. Proverbs 16:3 reminds us, "Commit to the Lord whatever you do, and he will establish your plans." Strive to support each other in planning for the future together, seeking God's guidance and strength.

86. Inconsistent Life Goals
Understanding Inconsistent Life Goals

Inconsistent life goals refer to significant differences or frequent changes in what partners want to achieve in their personal and professional lives. These inconsistencies can create confusion and conflict, making it difficult to build a stable and unified future together. The Bible encourages us to seek God's guidance and wisdom in our plans. Proverbs 16:9 says, "In their hearts humans plan their course, but the Lord establishes their steps."

Biblical Perspective on Alignment

The Bible emphasizes the importance of aligning our goals with God's will and seeking unity in our relationships. Philippians 2:2 advises, "Then make my joy complete by being like-minded, having the same love, being one in spirit and of one mind." Having consistent and aligned life goals is essential for a strong and harmonious relationship.

Identifying Inconsistent Life Goals

Signs of inconsistent life goals in a relationship include:

- **Frequent Changes:** Regularly changing or conflicting goals and aspirations.

- **Differing Priorities:** Having different priorities and values that influence life goals.

- **Lack of Agreement:** Difficulty agreeing on significant life decisions and plans.

- **Confusion:** Feeling confused or uncertain about the direction of the relationship.

- **Conflict:** Frequent conflicts arising from differing goals and expectations.

Consequences of Inconsistent Life Goals

Inconsistent life goals can have several negative impacts on a relationship:

- **Confusion:** Increased confusion and uncertainty about the future.

- **Conflict:** Frequent conflicts arising from differing expectations and plans.

- **Emotional Strain:** Emotional stress and tension due to lack of alignment.

- **Lack of Progress:** Difficulty making progress towards shared goals and aspirations.

- **Decreased Relationship Satisfaction:** Overall decrease in relationship satisfaction and stability.

Addressing Inconsistent Life Goals

If you notice inconsistent life goals in your relationship, consider these steps:

- **Communicate Clearly:** Discuss your life goals and how they align or conflict. Proverbs 15:22 says, "Plans fail for lack of counsel, but with many advisers they succeed."

- **Seek Alignment:** Identify areas where your goals align and work towards finding common ground.

- **Set Joint Goals:** Establish joint goals that reflect both partners' aspirations and desires.

- **Create a Plan:** Develop a clear and actionable plan to achieve your shared goals.

- **Pray for Unity:** Pray together for God's guidance in aligning your life goals. Jeremiah 29:11 says, "For I know the plans I have for you," declares the Lord, "plans to prosper you and not to harm you, plans to give you hope and a future."

Reflection Questions

1. How do inconsistent life goals affect your relationship and mutual goals?
2. Have you discussed the impact of these differences on your future together?
3. What steps can you take to align your life goals and find common ground?
4. How can you support each other in achieving your individual and joint aspirations?

Conclusion

Inconsistent life goals are a significant red flag that can impact relationship health and stability. Addressing this issue is crucial for fostering a unified and purposeful partnership. As Christians, we are called to seek alignment and unity in our relationships. Proverbs 16:3 reminds us, "Commit to the Lord whatever you do, and he will establish your plans." Strive to support each other in aligning your life goals, seeking God's guidance and strength.

87. Disinterest in Marriage Counseling

Understanding Disinterest in Marriage Counseling
Disinterest in marriage counseling involves a reluctance or refusal to seek professional help to address relationship issues. This can prevent the couple from resolving conflicts and improving their relationship. The Bible emphasizes the importance of seeking wisdom and counsel. Proverbs 11:14 says, "For lack of guidance a nation falls, but victory is won through many advisers."

Biblical Perspective on Seeking Help
The Bible encourages us to seek wise counsel and guidance in all aspects of life, including relationships. Proverbs 19:20 advises, "Listen to advice and accept discipline, and at the end you will be counted among the wise." Seeking marriage counseling can provide valuable insights and strategies for improving the relationship.

Identifying Disinterest in Marriage Counseling
Signs of disinterest in marriage counseling in a relationship include:

- **Refusal:** Refusing to consider marriage counseling as an option.

- **Minimization:** Minimizing the importance or effectiveness of counseling.

- **Avoidance:** Avoiding discussions about seeking professional help.

- **Excuses:** Making excuses to avoid attending counseling sessions.

- **Lack of Initiative:** Failing to take the initiative to find a counselor or schedule sessions.

Consequences of Disinterest in Marriage Counseling

Disinterest in marriage counseling can have several negative impacts on a relationship:

- **Unresolved Issues:** Increased likelihood of unresolved conflicts and issues.

- **Emotional Strain:** Emotional stress and tension due to lack of resolution.

- **Communication Barriers:** Difficulty improving communication and understanding.

- **Stagnation:** Lack of progress in relationship growth and improvement.

- **Decreased Relationship Satisfaction:** Overall decrease in relationship satisfaction and stability.

Addressing Disinterest in Marriage Counseling

If you notice disinterest in marriage counseling in your relationship, consider these steps:

- **Communicate Openly:** Discuss the importance of marriage counseling and its potential benefits. Proverbs 15:22 says, "Plans fail for lack of counsel, but with many advisers they succeed."

- **Share Concerns:** Express your concerns about unresolved issues and the need for professional help.

- **Provide Information:** Provide information about the benefits and effectiveness of marriage counseling.

- **Encourage Participation:** Encourage your partner to give counseling a try, even if they are initially reluctant.

- **Pray for Openness:** Pray together for openness to seeking and accepting help. James 1:5 says, "If any of you lacks wisdom, you should ask God, who gives generously to all without finding fault, and it will be given to you."

Reflection Questions

1. How does disinterest in marriage counseling affect your relationship and mutual goals?
2. Have you discussed the impact of unresolved issues on your future together?
3. What steps can you take to encourage participation in marriage counseling?
4. How can you support each other in seeking and benefiting from professional help?

Conclusion

Disinterest in marriage counseling is a significant red flag that can impact relationship health and stability. Addressing this issue is crucial for fostering a supportive and growth-oriented partnership. As Christians, we are called to seek wise counsel and guidance. Proverbs 12:15 reminds us, "The way of fools seems right to them, but the wise listen to advice." Strive to support each other in seeking and accepting help, seeking God's guidance and strength.

88. Avoidance of Future Discussions
Understanding Avoidance of Future Discussions

Avoidance of future discussions involves reluctance or refusal to talk about plans, goals, and expectations for the future. This can create uncertainty and insecurity in the relationship, making it difficult to build a stable and committed partnership. The Bible encourages us to plan wisely and seek God's guidance. Proverbs 16:3 says, "Commit to the Lord whatever you do, and he will establish your plans."

Biblical Perspective on Planning

The Bible emphasizes the importance of planning and seeking God's wisdom for the future. Proverbs 21:5 advises, "The plans of the diligent lead to profit as surely as haste leads to poverty." Having open discussions about the future is essential for a strong and stable relationship.

Identifying Avoidance of Future Discussions

Signs of avoidance of future discussions in a relationship include:

- **Reluctance:** Reluctance to engage in conversations about future plans and goals.

- **Deflection:** Deflecting or changing the subject when future discussions arise.

- **Inconsistency:** Providing inconsistent or vague responses about future plans.

- **Indecision:** Showing indecision or lack of interest in planning for the future.

- **Anxiety:** Expressing anxiety or discomfort about discussing long-term commitments.

Consequences of Avoidance of Future Discussions
Avoidance of future discussions can have several negative impacts on a relationship:

- **Uncertainty:** Increased uncertainty and insecurity about the future.

- **Emotional Strain:** Emotional stress and tension due to lack of clarity and direction.

- **Conflict:** Frequent conflicts arising from differing expectations and plans.

- **Lack of Progress:** Difficulty making progress towards shared goals and aspirations.

- **Decreased Relationship Satisfaction:** Overall decrease in relationship satisfaction and stability.

Addressing Avoidance of Future Discussions
If you notice avoidance of future discussions in your relationship, consider these steps:

- **Communicate Clearly:** Discuss the importance of future planning and its impact on your relationship. Proverbs 15:22 says, "Plans fail for lack of counsel, but with many advisers they succeed."

- **Express Concerns:** Share your concerns about the lack of future discussions and its effects.

- **Set a Time:** Agree on a specific time to have an open and honest conversation about future plans.

- **Encourage Openness:** Encourage your partner to express their thoughts, fears, and expectations.

- **Pray for Clarity:** Pray together for God's wisdom and clarity in planning your future. Jeremiah 29:11 says, "For I know the plans I have for you," declares the Lord, "plans to prosper you and not to harm you, plans to give you hope and a future."

Reflection Questions

1. How does avoidance of future discussions affect your relationship and mutual goals?
2. Have you discussed the impact of this avoidance on your future together?
3. What steps can you take to encourage open and honest discussions about the future?
4. How can you support each other in planning and achieving your shared goals and aspirations?

Conclusion

Avoidance of future discussions is a significant red flag that can impact relationship health and stability. Addressing this issue is crucial for fostering a committed and secure partnership. As Christians, we are called to plan wisely and seek God's guidance for our future. Proverbs 3:5-6 reminds us, "Trust in the Lord with all your heart and lean not on your own understanding; in all your ways submit to him, and he will make your paths straight." Strive to support each other in having open discussions about the future, seeking God's wisdom and strength.

89. Different Views on Children

Understanding Different Views on Children
Different views on children involve varying beliefs and expectations about having and raising children. These differences can create significant tension and conflict in a relationship, particularly when making decisions about starting a family. The Bible emphasizes the blessing of children and the importance of unity in family decisions. Psalm 127:3 says, "Children are a heritage from the Lord, offspring a reward from him."

Biblical Perspective on Children
The Bible encourages viewing children as a blessing and making unified decisions about family matters. Ephesians 6:4 advises, "Fathers, do not exasperate your children; instead, bring them up in the training and instruction of the Lord." Aligning views on children is essential for a harmonious family life.

Identifying Different Views on Children
Signs of different views on children in a relationship include:
- **Differing Desires:** Conflicting desires about whether to have children or not.

- **Timing Disagreements:** Disagreements about the timing of starting a family.

- **Parenting Styles:** Differing beliefs about parenting styles and discipline.

- **Family Size:** Varied expectations about the number of children to have.

- **Child-Rearing Values:** Conflicting values and priorities regarding raising children.

Consequences of Different Views on Children

Different views on children can have several negative impacts on a relationship:

- **Conflict:** Frequent conflicts arising from differing expectations and desires.

- **Emotional Strain:** Emotional stress and tension due to unresolved differences.

- **Insecurity:** Increased insecurity and anxiety about the future of the relationship.

- **Decision-Making Challenges:** Difficulty making unified decisions about family planning.

- **Decreased Relationship Satisfaction:** Overall decrease in relationship satisfaction and harmony.

Addressing Different Views on Children

If you notice different views on children in your relationship, consider these steps:

- **Communicate Openly:** Discuss your views on children and how they align or conflict. Proverbs 18:15 says, "The heart of the discerning acquires knowledge, for the ears of the wise seek it out."

- **Seek Understanding:** Make an effort to understand each other's perspectives and desires.

- **Find Common Ground:** Identify shared values and work towards compromise in areas of conflict.

- **Set Joint Goals:** Establish joint goals and plans for your family's future.

- **Pray for Unity:** Pray together for God's guidance in aligning your views on children. Psalm 37:4 says, "Take delight in the Lord, and he will give you the desires of your heart."

Reflection Questions

1. How do different views on children affect your relationship and mutual goals?
2. Have you discussed the impact of these differences on your future together?
3. What steps can you take to align your views on children and find common ground?
4. How can you support each other in making unified decisions about family planning?

Conclusion

Different views on children are a significant red flag that can impact relationship health and harmony. Addressing this issue is crucial for fostering a unified and supportive partnership. As Christians, we are called to view children as a blessing and make unified family decisions. Proverbs 22:6 reminds us, "Start children off on the way they should go, and even when they are old they will not turn from it." Strive to support each other in aligning your views on children, seeking God's guidance and strength.

90. Unwillingness to Grow Together

Understanding Unwillingness to Grow Together
Unwillingness to grow together involves a lack of interest or effort in personal and mutual growth within the relationship. This can hinder the development of a strong and lasting partnership. The Bible emphasizes the importance of growth and unity in relationships. Ephesians 4:15-16 says, "Instead, speaking the truth in love, we will grow to become in every respect the mature body of him who is the head, that is, Christ. From him the whole body, joined and held together by every supporting ligament, grows and builds itself up in love, as each part does its work."

Biblical Perspective on Growth
The Bible encourages continuous growth and unity in relationships. Colossians 2:6-7 advises, "So then, just as you received Christ Jesus as Lord, continue to live your lives in him, rooted and built up in him, strengthened in the faith as you were taught, and overflowing with thankfulness." Growing together is essential for a strong and fulfilling partnership.

Identifying Unwillingness to Grow Together
Signs of unwillingness to grow together in a relationship include:

- **Lack of Effort:** Showing little or no effort in working on personal and mutual growth.

- **Resistance to Change:** Resisting changes that promote growth and improvement.

- **Indifference:** Indifference towards opportunities for growth and development.

- **Stagnation:** Experiencing stagnation in the relationship without progress.

- **Avoidance:** Avoiding discussions or activities that promote growth and unity.

Consequences of Unwillingness to Grow Together
Unwillingness to grow together can have several negative impacts on a relationship:

- **Stagnation:** Increased stagnation and lack of progress in the relationship.

- **Emotional Distance:** Growing emotional distance due to lack of shared growth experiences.

- **Conflict:** Frequent conflicts arising from differing attitudes towards growth.

- **Resentment:** Potential resentment due to unmet expectations and lack of improvement.

- **Decreased Relationship Satisfaction:** Overall decrease in relationship satisfaction and harmony.

Addressing Unwillingness to Grow Together
If you notice unwillingness to grow together in your relationship, consider these steps:

- **Communicate Openly:** Discuss the importance of growth and its impact on your relationship. Proverbs 27:17 says, "As iron sharpens iron, so one person sharpens another."

- **Set Goals:** Establish personal and mutual growth goals that reflect your aspirations.

- **Encourage Participation:** Encourage each other to participate in activities that promote growth.

- **Seek Opportunities:** Look for opportunities for growth, such as workshops, counseling, or spiritual activities.

- **Pray for Growth:** Pray together for God's guidance and strength in fostering growth and unity. Colossians 1:10 says, "So that you may live a life worthy of the Lord and please him in every way: bearing fruit in every good work, growing in the knowledge of God."

Reflection Questions
1. How does unwillingness to grow together affect your relationship and mutual goals?
2. Have you discussed the impact of this issue on your future together?
3. What steps can you take to encourage personal and mutual growth?
4. How can you support each other in seeking opportunities for growth and improvement?

Conclusion
Unwillingness to grow together is a significant red flag that can impact relationship health and fulfillment. Addressing this issue is crucial for fostering a growth-oriented and supportive partnership. As Christians, we are called to seek continuous growth and unity. Ephesians 4:15-16 reminds us, "Instead, speaking the truth in love, we will grow to become in every respect the mature body of him who is the head, that is, Christ. From him the whole body, joined and held together by every supporting ligament, grows and builds itself up in love, as each part does its work." Strive to support each other in fostering growth and unity, seeking God's guidance and strength.

Chapter 10: Behavior in Conflict

91. Frequent Arguments

Understanding Frequent Arguments
Frequent arguments refer to regular and intense conflicts that arise in a relationship. These conflicts can create a hostile environment, affecting the emotional well-being of both partners and the overall health of the relationship. The Bible encourages us to pursue peace and harmony in our relationships. Proverbs 15:1 says, "A gentle answer turns away wrath, but a harsh word stirs up anger."

Biblical Perspective on Peace
The Bible emphasizes the importance of maintaining peace and resolving conflicts in a gentle manner. Romans 12:18 advises, "If it is possible, as far as it depends on you, live at peace with everyone." Striving for peace and understanding is essential for a healthy relationship.

Identifying Frequent Arguments
Signs of frequent arguments in a relationship include:
- **Constant Disputes:** Regularly engaging in disputes and disagreements.

- **High Intensity:** Conflicts that escalate quickly and become intense.

- **Repetition:** Arguing about the same issues repeatedly without resolution.

- **Emotional Strain:** Feeling emotionally drained and stressed due to frequent conflicts.

- **Communication Breakdown:** Difficulty maintaining positive and constructive communication.

Consequences of Frequent Arguments

Frequent arguments can have several negative impacts on a relationship:

- **Emotional Stress:** Increased emotional stress and anxiety for both partners.

- **Trust Issues:** Erosion of trust and respect due to ongoing conflicts.

- **Communication Barriers:** Difficulty communicating effectively and openly.

- **Instability:** Creating an unstable and hostile relationship environment.

- **Decreased Relationship Satisfaction:** Overall decrease in relationship satisfaction and harmony.

Addressing Frequent Arguments

If you notice frequent arguments in your relationship, consider these steps:

- **Communicate Calmly:** Approach discussions with calmness and respect. Proverbs 15:18 says, "A hot-tempered person stirs up conflict, but the one who is patient calms a quarrel."

- **Identify Triggers:** Identify the triggers and underlying issues that lead to arguments.

- **Seek Resolution:** Focus on resolving conflicts rather than winning arguments.

- **Practice Active Listening:** Listen actively to each other's perspectives and feelings.

- **Pray for Peace:** Pray together for God's guidance in fostering peace and understanding. Philippians 4:6-7 says, "Do not be anxious about anything, but in every situation, by prayer and petition, with thanksgiving, present your requests to God. And the peace of God, which transcends all understanding, will guard your hearts and your minds in Christ Jesus."

Reflection Questions

1. How do frequent arguments affect your relationship and emotional well-being?
2. Have you discussed the impact of these conflicts on your future together?
3. What steps can you take to reduce the frequency and intensity of arguments?
4. How can you support each other in fostering a peaceful and understanding relationship?

Conclusion

Frequent arguments are a significant red flag that can impact relationship health and harmony. Addressing this issue is crucial for fostering a peaceful and supportive partnership. As Christians, we are called to pursue peace and resolve conflicts gently. Ephesians 4:2-3 reminds us, "Be completely humble and gentle; be patient, bearing with one another in love. Make every effort to keep the unity of the Spirit through the bond of peace." Strive to support each other in reducing conflicts and fostering peace, seeking God's guidance and strength.

92. Inability to Apologize

Understanding Inability to Apologize
Inability to apologize refers to a reluctance or refusal to admit fault and offer a sincere apology when one has hurt or wronged their partner. This behavior can hinder reconciliation and healing in the relationship. The Bible emphasizes the importance of humility and seeking forgiveness. James 5:16 says, "Therefore confess your sins to each other and pray for each other so that you may be healed. The prayer of a righteous person is powerful and effective."

Biblical Perspective on Apologizing
The Bible encourages humility, confession, and seeking forgiveness in relationships. Proverbs 28:13 advises, "Whoever conceals their sins does not prosper, but the one who confesses and renounces them finds mercy." Apologizing sincerely is essential for healing and reconciliation.

Identifying Inability to Apologize
Signs of inability to apologize in a relationship include:
- **Defensiveness:** Responding defensively when confronted about mistakes or wrongdoings.

- **Blame Shifting:** Shifting blame to others instead of taking responsibility.

- **Minimization:** Minimizing the impact of one's actions or dismissing the partner's feelings.

- **Avoidance:** Avoiding discussions about the issue and refusing to apologize.

- **Lack of Empathy:** Showing a lack of empathy and understanding for the partner's hurt feelings.

Consequences of Inability to Apologize

Inability to apologize can have several negative impacts on a relationship:

- **Resentment:** Building resentment and bitterness due to unresolved hurts.

- **Emotional Distance:** Creating emotional distance and disconnect between partners.

- **Trust Issues:** Erosion of trust and respect due to lack of accountability.

- **Communication Barriers:** Difficulty maintaining open and honest communication.

- **Decreased Relationship Satisfaction:** Overall decrease in relationship satisfaction and harmony.

Addressing Inability to Apologize

If you notice an inability to apologize in your relationship, consider these steps:

- **Communicate Clearly:** Discuss the importance of apologizing and its impact on the relationship. Proverbs 15:1 says, "A gentle answer turns away wrath, but a harsh word stirs up anger."

- **Encourage Humility:** Encourage each other to practice humility and take responsibility for mistakes.

- **Model Apologies:** Model sincere apologies and forgiveness in your own behavior.

- **Seek Forgiveness:** Make a concerted effort to seek and offer forgiveness when needed.

- **Pray for Humility:** Pray together for God's guidance in fostering humility and forgiveness. Ephesians 4:32 says, "Be kind and compassionate to one another, forgiving each other, just as in Christ God forgave you."

Reflection Questions

1. How does the inability to apologize affect your relationship and mutual trust?
2. Have you discussed the impact of this behavior on your future together?
3. What steps can you take to encourage sincere apologies and forgiveness?
4. How can you support each other in practicing humility and seeking reconciliation?

Conclusion

Inability to apologize is a significant red flag that can impact relationship health and trust. Addressing this issue is crucial for fostering a humble and forgiving partnership. As Christians, we are called to seek forgiveness and reconciliation. Colossians 3:13 reminds us, "Bear with each other and forgive one another if any of you has a grievance against someone. Forgive as the Lord forgave you." Strive to support each other in practicing humility and seeking reconciliation, seeking God's guidance and strength.

93. Holding Grudges

Understanding Holding Grudges
Holding grudges involves maintaining feelings of resentment and bitterness towards a partner for past hurts or wrongdoings. This behavior can prevent healing and reconciliation, creating a toxic environment in the relationship. The Bible emphasizes the importance of forgiveness and letting go of resentment. Ephesians 4:31-32 says, "Get rid of all bitterness, rage and anger, brawling and slander, along with every form of malice. Be kind and compassionate to one another, forgiving each other, just as in Christ God forgave you."

Biblical Perspective on Forgiveness
The Bible encourages us to forgive others and let go of resentment. Colossians 3:13 advises, "Bear with each other and forgive one another if any of you has a grievance against someone. Forgive as the Lord forgave you." Forgiveness is essential for healing and maintaining a healthy relationship.

Identifying Holding Grudges
Signs of holding grudges in a relationship include:
- **Resentment:** Feeling ongoing resentment and bitterness towards your partner.

- **Bringing Up the Past:** Frequently bringing up past hurts and wrongdoings during conflicts.

- **Avoidance:** Avoiding interactions or conversations due to unresolved resentment.

- **Emotional Distance:** Creating emotional distance and disconnect due to held grudges.

- **Refusal to Forgive:** Refusing to forgive your partner despite their apologies and efforts to make amends.

Consequences of Holding Grudges

Holding grudges can have several negative impacts on a relationship:

- **Emotional Strain:** Increased emotional stress and tension due to unresolved issues.

- **Communication Barriers:** Difficulty maintaining open and honest communication.

- **Trust Issues:** Erosion of trust and respect due to ongoing resentment.

- **Conflict:** Frequent conflicts arising from unresolved hurts and bitterness.

- **Decreased Relationship Satisfaction:** Overall decrease in relationship satisfaction and harmony.

Addressing Holding Grudges

If you notice holding grudges in your relationship, consider these steps:

- **Communicate Honestly:** Discuss the impact of holding grudges on the relationship. Proverbs 15:18 says, "A hot-tempered person stirs up conflict, but the one who is patient calms a quarrel."

- **Seek Forgiveness:** Make a concerted effort to forgive past hurts and let go of resentment.

- **Focus on Healing:** Focus on healing and reconciliation rather than dwelling on the past.

- **Practice Empathy:** Practice empathy and understanding towards your partner's perspective.

- **Pray for Forgiveness:** Pray together for God's guidance in fostering forgiveness and compassion. Matthew 6:14-15 says, "For if you forgive other people when they sin against you, your heavenly Father will also forgive you. But if you do not forgive others their sins, your Father will not forgive your sins."

Reflection Questions

1. How does holding grudges affect your relationship and emotional well-being?
2. Have you discussed the impact of this behavior on your future together?
3. What steps can you take to encourage forgiveness and reconciliation?
4. How can you support each other in letting go of resentment and focusing on healing?

Conclusion

Holding grudges is a significant red flag that can impact relationship health and harmony. Addressing this issue is crucial for fostering a forgiving and compassionate partnership. As Christians, we are called to forgive others and let go of resentment. Ephesians 4:31-32 reminds us, "Get rid of all bitterness, rage and anger, brawling and slander, along with every form of malice. Be kind and compassionate to one another, forgiving each other, just as in Christ God forgave you." Strive to support each other in practicing forgiveness and letting go of resentment, seeking God's guidance and strength.

94. Escalating Conflicts

Understanding Escalating Conflicts
Escalating conflicts refer to disputes that intensify quickly, leading to heightened emotions, harsh words, and sometimes even threats. These types of conflicts can cause significant emotional harm and strain on the relationship. The Bible encourages us to be peacemakers and to resolve conflicts calmly. Proverbs 15:1 says, "A gentle answer turns away wrath, but a harsh word stirs up anger."

Biblical Perspective on Peace and Resolution
The Bible emphasizes the importance of resolving conflicts peacefully and with a calm demeanor. Matthew 5:9 says, "Blessed are the peacemakers, for they will be called children of God." Striving to de-escalate conflicts and seek peaceful resolutions is essential for maintaining a healthy relationship.

Identifying Escalating Conflicts
Signs of escalating conflicts in a relationship include:
- **Intense Arguments:** Arguments that quickly become intense and emotionally charged.

- **Yelling and Screaming:** Raised voices and screaming during disagreements.

- **Personal Attacks:** Resorting to personal attacks and insults.

- **Threats:** Making threats or ultimatums during conflicts.

- **Physical Aggression:** Any form of physical aggression or intimidation.

Consequences of Escalating Conflicts

Escalating conflicts can have several negative impacts on a relationship:

- **Emotional Trauma:** Increased emotional trauma and stress for both partners.

- **Trust Issues:** Erosion of trust and safety within the relationship.

- **Communication Breakdown:** Difficulty maintaining positive and constructive communication.

- **Instability:** Creating an unstable and hostile relationship environment.

- **Decreased Relationship Satisfaction:** Overall decrease in relationship satisfaction and harmony.

Addressing Escalating Conflicts

If you notice escalating conflicts in your relationship, consider these steps:

- **Stay Calm:** Focus on staying calm and composed during disagreements. Proverbs 29:11 says, "Fools give full vent to their rage, but the wise bring calm in the end."

- **Set Boundaries:** Establish boundaries for conflict resolution, such as avoiding yelling and personal attacks.

- **Take Breaks:** If conflicts escalate, take breaks to cool down before continuing the discussion.

- **Seek Help:** Consider seeking help from a counselor or mediator to learn healthy conflict resolution strategies.

- **Pray for Peace:** Pray together for God's guidance in fostering peace and understanding. Philippians 4:6-7 says, "Do not be anxious about anything, but in every situation, by prayer and petition, with thanksgiving, present your requests to God. And the peace of God, which transcends all understanding, will guard your hearts and your minds in Christ Jesus."

Reflection Questions

1. How do escalating conflicts affect your relationship and emotional well-being?
2. Have you discussed the impact of these conflicts on your future together?
3. What steps can you take to de-escalate conflicts and seek peaceful resolutions?
4. How can you support each other in fostering a calm and understanding environment?

Conclusion

Escalating conflicts are a significant red flag that can impact relationship health and harmony. Addressing this issue is crucial for fostering a peaceful and supportive partnership. As Christians, we are called to be peacemakers and resolve conflicts calmly. James 1:19 reminds us, "My dear brothers and sisters, take note of this: Everyone should be quick to listen, slow to speak and slow to become angry." Strive to support each other in de-escalating conflicts and seeking peaceful resolutions, seeking God's guidance and strength.

95. Blaming You for Everything

Understanding Blaming You for Everything

Blaming you for everything involves a partner consistently shifting responsibility for problems, mistakes, or conflicts onto you. This behavior can create a toxic environment and undermine trust and respect in the relationship. The Bible encourages taking responsibility for our actions and seeking reconciliation. Galatians 6:5 says, "For each one should carry their own load."

Biblical Perspective on Responsibility

The Bible emphasizes the importance of taking personal responsibility and not blaming others for our shortcomings. Matthew 7:3-5 advises, "Why do you look at the speck of sawdust in your brother's eye and pay no attention to the plank in your own eye? How can you say to your brother, 'Let me take the speck out of your eye,' when all the time there is a plank in your own eye? You hypocrite, first take the plank out of your own eye, and then you will see clearly to remove the speck from your brother's eye."

Identifying Blaming Behavior

Signs of blaming behavior in a relationship include:

- **Consistent Blame:** Regularly being blamed for problems and conflicts.

- **Avoidance of Responsibility:** Partner avoiding taking responsibility for their actions.

- **Defensiveness:** Partner becoming defensive when confronted about their behavior.

- **Guilt Tripping:** Using guilt to manipulate and control you.

- **Unfair Criticism:** Unfairly criticizing and blaming you for things beyond your control.

Consequences of Blaming Behavior
Blaming behavior can have several negative impacts on a relationship:

- **Resentment:** Building resentment and frustration due to constant blame.

- **Emotional Strain:** Increased emotional stress and tension.

- **Trust Issues:** Erosion of trust and respect due to lack of accountability.

- **Communication Barriers:** Difficulty maintaining open and honest communication.

- **Decreased Relationship Satisfaction:** Overall decrease in relationship satisfaction and harmony.

Addressing Blaming Behavior
If you notice blaming behavior in your relationship, consider these steps:

- **Communicate Clearly:** Discuss the impact of blaming behavior on the relationship. Proverbs 12:18 says, "The words of the reckless pierce like swords, but the tongue of the wise brings healing."

- **Encourage Responsibility:** Encourage your partner to take responsibility for their actions and mistakes.

- **Set Boundaries:** Establish boundaries to prevent unfair blaming and criticism.

- **Seek Help:** Consider seeking help from a counselor to address and resolve blaming behavior.

- **Pray for Accountability:** Pray together for God's guidance in fostering accountability and responsibility. James 5:16 says, "Therefore confess your sins to each other and pray for each other so that you may be healed. The prayer of a righteous person is powerful and effective."

Reflection Questions

1. How does blaming behavior affect your relationship and mutual trust?
2. Have you discussed the impact of this behavior on your future together?
3. What steps can you take to encourage responsibility and accountability?
4. How can you support each other in practicing fair and honest communication?

Conclusion

Blaming behavior is a significant red flag that can impact relationship health and trust. Addressing this issue is crucial for fostering a responsible and supportive partnership. As Christians, we are called to take personal responsibility and seek reconciliation. Galatians 6:4-5 reminds us, "Each one should test their own actions. Then they can take pride in themselves alone, without comparing themselves to someone else, for each one should carry their own load." Strive to support each other in fostering accountability and resolving conflicts fairly, seeking God's guidance and strength.

96. Threats of Leaving
Understanding Threats of Leaving

Threats of leaving involve a partner frequently threatening to end the relationship during conflicts or disagreements. This behavior can create a sense of insecurity and instability, undermining the foundation of the relationship. The Bible encourages commitment and faithfulness in relationships. Ruth 1:16-17 says, "But Ruth replied, 'Don't urge me to leave you or to turn back from you. Where you go I will go, and where you stay I will stay. Your people will be my people and your God my God. Where you die I will die, and there I will be buried. May the Lord deal with me, be it ever so severely, if even death separates you and me.'"

Biblical Perspective on Commitment

The Bible emphasizes the importance of commitment and steadfastness in relationships. Ecclesiastes 4:9-10 advises, "Two are better than one, because they have a good return for their labor: If either of them falls down, one can help the other up. But pity anyone who falls and has no one to help them up." Committing to work through conflicts together is essential for a strong relationship.

Identifying Threats of Leaving

Signs of threats of leaving in a relationship include:

- **Frequent Threats:** Regularly threatening to end the relationship during conflicts.

- **Manipulation:** Using threats of leaving as a way to manipulate and control.

- **Insecurity:** Creating insecurity and fear about the stability of the relationship.

- **Emotional Blackmail:** Using the threat of leaving to force compliance or win arguments.

- **Instability:** Creating an unstable and unpredictable relationship environment.

Consequences of Threats of Leaving

Threats of leaving can have several negative impacts on a relationship:

- **Insecurity:** Increased insecurity and anxiety about the future of the relationship.

- **Emotional Strain:** Emotional stress and tension due to constant fear of abandonment.

- **Trust Issues:** Erosion of trust and safety within the relationship.

- **Communication Barriers:** Difficulty maintaining open and honest communication.

- **Decreased Relationship Satisfaction:** Overall decrease in relationship satisfaction and stability.

Addressing Threats of Leaving

If you notice threats of leaving in your relationship, consider these steps:

- **Communicate Clearly:** Discuss the impact of these threats on the relationship. Proverbs 15:4 says, "The soothing tongue is a tree of life, but a perverse tongue crushes the spirit."

- **Seek Commitment:** Emphasize the importance of commitment and working through conflicts together.

- **Set Boundaries:** Establish boundaries to prevent the use of threats in arguments.

- **Seek Help:** Consider seeking help from a counselor to address and resolve underlying issues.

- **Pray for Strength:** Pray together for God's guidance in fostering commitment and stability. Hebrews 13:4 says, "Marriage should be honored by all, and the marriage bed kept pure, for God will judge the adulterer and all the sexually immoral."

Reflection Questions
1. How do threats of leaving affect your relationship and emotional well-being?
2. Have you discussed the impact of this behavior on your future together?
3. What steps can you take to encourage commitment and stability?
4. How can you support each other in fostering a secure and steadfast relationship?

Conclusion
Threats of leaving are a significant red flag that can impact relationship health and stability. Addressing this issue is crucial for fostering a committed and secure partnership. As Christians, we are called to embrace commitment and work through conflicts together. 1 Corinthians 13:7 reminds us, "It always protects, always trusts, always hopes, always perseveres." Strive to support each other in fostering commitment and resolving conflicts, seeking God's guidance and strength.

97. Physical Aggression

Understanding Physical Aggression

Physical aggression refers to the use of force or violence to control, intimidate, or harm a partner. This behavior is not only destructive to the relationship but is also illegal and dangerous. The Bible condemns violence and calls for love and respect in relationships. Colossians 3:19 says, "Husbands, love your wives and do not be harsh with them."

Biblical Perspective on Violence

The Bible emphasizes the importance of treating others with love and respect, condemning any form of violence. Ephesians 4:31-32 advises, "Get rid of all bitterness, rage and anger, brawling and slander, along with every form of malice. Be kind and compassionate to one another, forgiving each other, just as in Christ God forgave you."

Identifying Physical Aggression

Signs of physical aggression in a relationship include:

- **Hitting or Slapping:** Any form of physical violence, such as hitting, slapping, or pushing.

- **Intimidation:** Using physical presence or actions to intimidate or control.

- **Destruction of Property:** Breaking or damaging property during conflicts.

- **Restraining:** Physically restraining or preventing the partner from leaving.

- **Threats of Violence:** Making threats of physical harm.

Consequences of Physical Aggression

Physical aggression can have severe negative impacts on a relationship:

- **Fear and Trauma:** Creating a climate of fear and emotional trauma.

- **Injury:** Physical harm and injury to the partner.

- **Legal Consequences:** Potential legal consequences and involvement of law enforcement.

- **Trust and Safety:** Complete erosion of trust and safety within the relationship.

- **Relationship Breakdown:** Likely leading to the breakdown of the relationship.

Addressing Physical Aggression

If you notice physical aggression in your relationship, consider these steps:

- **Seek Safety:** Prioritize your safety and seek help immediately if you are in danger. Psalm 82:4 says, "Rescue the weak and the needy; deliver them from the hand of the wicked."

- **Contact Authorities:** Contact law enforcement if physical violence occurs.

- **Seek Support:** Reach out to trusted friends, family, or support services for help and guidance.

- **Consider Counseling:** Both partners should consider seeking professional counseling to address underlying issues.

- **Pray for Protection:** Pray for God's protection and guidance in addressing the situation. Psalm 91:2 says, "I will say of the Lord, 'He is my refuge and my fortress, my God, in whom I trust.'"

Reflection Questions

1. How does physical aggression affect your safety and well-being?
2. Have you sought help and support to address this issue?
3. What steps can you take to ensure your safety and seek resolution?
4. How can you support each other in addressing and preventing physical aggression?

Conclusion

Physical aggression is a severe red flag that can impact relationship health, safety, and stability. Addressing this issue is crucial for ensuring safety and fostering a respectful partnership. As Christians, we are called to treat each other with love and respect. 1 Peter 3:7 reminds us, "Husbands, in the same way be considerate as you live with your wives, and treat them with respect as the weaker partner and as heirs with you of the gracious gift of life, so that nothing will hinder your prayers." Strive to support each other in fostering a safe and loving relationship, seeking God's guidance and strength.

98. Emotional Blackmail
Understanding Emotional Blackmail

Emotional blackmail involves manipulating a partner's emotions to control their behavior. This can include guilt-tripping, threats, and other forms of psychological manipulation. The Bible emphasizes the importance of love and honesty in relationships. 1 Corinthians 13:4-5 says, "Love is patient, love is kind. It does not envy, it does not boast, it is not proud. It does not dishonor others, it is not self-seeking, it is not easily angered, it keeps no record of wrongs."

Biblical Perspective on Manipulation

The Bible encourages honesty and love, condemning manipulation and deceit. Proverbs 24:28-29 advises, "Do not testify against your neighbor without cause — would you use your lips to mislead? Do not say, 'I'll do to them as they have done to me; I'll pay them back for what they did.'"

Identifying Emotional Blackmail

Signs of emotional blackmail in a relationship include:

- **Guilt-Tripping:** Using guilt to manipulate or control your partner's behavior.

- **Threats:** Making threats to leave or harm oneself if the partner doesn't comply.

- **Conditional Love:** Withholding love and affection to manipulate the partner.

- **Blame Shifting:** Blaming the partner for issues to manipulate their actions.

- **Emotional Withdrawal:** Withdrawing emotionally to punish or control the partner.

Consequences of Emotional Blackmail

Emotional blackmail can have several negative impacts on a relationship:

- **Emotional Strain:** Increased emotional stress and tension.

- **Erosion of Trust:** Erosion of trust and respect within the relationship.

- **Insecurity:** Creating insecurity and fear in the partner.

- **Communication Breakdown:** Difficulty maintaining open and honest communication.

- **Decreased Relationship Satisfaction:** Overall decrease in relationship satisfaction and harmony.

Addressing Emotional Blackmail

If you notice emotional blackmail in your relationship, consider these steps:

- **Communicate Clearly:** Discuss the impact of emotional blackmail on the relationship. Proverbs 27:5 says, "Better is open rebuke than hidden love."

- **Set Boundaries:** Establish clear boundaries to prevent manipulation and control.

- **Seek Counseling:** Consider seeking help from a counselor to address and resolve underlying issues.

- **Encourage Honesty:** Encourage open and honest communication without manipulation.

- **Pray for Healing:** Pray together for God's guidance in fostering honesty and love. Ephesians 4:15 says, "Instead, speaking the truth in love, we will grow to become in every respect the mature body of him who is the head, that is, Christ."

Reflection Questions

1. How does emotional blackmail affect your relationship and emotional well-being?
2. Have you discussed the impact of this behavior on your future together?
3. What steps can you take to encourage honesty and prevent manipulation?
4. How can you support each other in fostering a loving and honest relationship?

Conclusion

Emotional blackmail is a significant red flag that can impact relationship health and trust. Addressing this issue is crucial for fostering an honest and loving partnership. As Christians, we are called to treat each other with love and honesty. Colossians 3:9-10 reminds us, "Do not lie to each other, since you have taken off your old self with its practices and have put on the new self, which is being renewed in knowledge in the image of its Creator." Strive to support each other in fostering honesty and preventing manipulation, seeking God's guidance and strength.

99. Inability to Resolve Conflicts
Understanding Inability to Resolve Conflicts

Inability to resolve conflicts refers to persistent difficulties in finding solutions to disagreements and issues within the relationship. This can lead to ongoing tension and unresolved problems. The Bible encourages peacemaking and reconciliation in relationships. Matthew 5:9 says, "Blessed are the peacemakers, for they will be called children of God."

Biblical Perspective on Conflict Resolution

The Bible emphasizes the importance of resolving conflicts and seeking reconciliation. Ephesians 4:26-27 advises, "In your anger do not sin: Do not let the sun go down while you are still angry, and do not give the devil a foothold." Finding ways to resolve conflicts is essential for a healthy relationship.

Identifying Inability to Resolve Conflicts

Signs of inability to resolve conflicts in a relationship include:

- **Repetitive Issues:** Continually arguing about the same issues without resolution.

- **Avoidance:** Avoiding discussions about conflicts or problems.

- **Escalation:** Conflicts that escalate without finding solutions.

- **Stalemate:** Reaching a stalemate where neither partner is willing to compromise.

- **Emotional Distance:** Growing emotional distance due to unresolved conflicts.

Consequences of Inability to Resolve Conflicts

Inability to resolve conflicts can have several negative impacts on a relationship:

- **Ongoing Tension:** Persistent tension and stress due to unresolved issues.

- **Erosion of Trust:** Erosion of trust and respect within the relationship.

- **Communication Barriers:** Difficulty maintaining open and constructive communication.

- **Emotional Strain:** Increased emotional strain and dissatisfaction.

- **Decreased Relationship Satisfaction:** Overall decrease in relationship satisfaction and harmony.

Addressing Inability to Resolve Conflicts

If you notice an inability to resolve conflicts in your relationship, consider these steps:

- **Communicate Openly:** Discuss the importance of resolving conflicts and its impact on your relationship. Proverbs 15:1 says, "A gentle answer turns away wrath, but a harsh word stirs up anger."

- **Seek Compromise:** Focus on finding compromises and solutions that work for both partners.

- **Address Issues Promptly:** Address conflicts promptly rather than letting them fester.

- **Seek Mediation:** Consider seeking help from a mediator or counselor to facilitate resolution.

- **Pray for Wisdom:** Pray together for God's guidance in resolving conflicts and fostering peace. James 1:5 says, "If any of you lacks wisdom, you should ask God, who gives generously to all without finding fault, and it will be given to you."

Reflection Questions
1. How does the inability to resolve conflicts affect your relationship and emotional well-being?
2. Have you discussed the impact of unresolved conflicts on your future together?
3. What steps can you take to improve conflict resolution in your relationship?
4. How can you support each other in finding compromises and solutions?

Conclusion
Inability to resolve conflicts is a significant red flag that can impact relationship health and harmony. Addressing this issue is crucial for fostering a peaceful and supportive partnership. As Christians, we are called to seek reconciliation and resolve conflicts. Romans 12:18 reminds us, "If it is possible, as far as it depends on you, live at peace with everyone." Strive to support each other in resolving conflicts and fostering peace, seeking God's guidance and strength.

Conclusion

Summarizing the Importance of Red Flags
Understanding the Significance of Red Flags
Red flags are warning signs indicating potential problems in a relationship that, if left unaddressed, can lead to significant emotional, physical, and spiritual harm. Recognizing these signs early is crucial for making informed decisions about the future of the relationship. Proverbs 22:3 says, "The prudent see danger and take refuge, but the simple keep going and pay the penalty."

Biblical Perspective on Awareness
The Bible encourages vigilance and wisdom in all aspects of life, including relationships. Proverbs 27:12 reminds us, "The prudent see danger and take refuge, but the simple keep going and pay the penalty." Being aware of red flags helps protect us from harm and guides us towards healthier, more fulfilling relationships.

Key Points from Each Chapter
1. **Personality and Character Traits:** Recognizing traits like dishonesty, lack of empathy, and arrogance helps identify potential relational challenges.

2. **Communication Issues:** Addressing poor communication skills, frequent interruptions, and defensive responses is vital for maintaining healthy interactions.

3. **Financial Red Flags:** Being aware of financial irresponsibility, significant debt, and secretive behavior helps avoid future financial stress.

4. **Relationship Dynamics:** Identifying controlling behavior, lack of respect, and infidelity is crucial for establishing a respectful and trusting relationship.

5. **Lifestyle and Habits:** Understanding the impact of substance abuse, unhealthy lifestyle choices, and workaholism on the relationship's health.

6. **Family and Background:** Recognizing the influence of dysfunctional family dynamics and unresolved family issues on your partner's behavior.

7. **Emotional and Mental Health:** Addressing unaddressed mental health issues, emotional unavailability, and mood swings for emotional stability.

8. **Compatibility and Values:** Ensuring alignment in life goals, values, and religious beliefs to build a harmonious future together.

9. **Future Plans and Expectations:** Discussing and aligning future plans, commitment levels, and views on important life decisions like having children.

10. **Behavior in Conflict:** Recognizing harmful conflict behaviors like physical aggression, emotional blackmail, and inability to resolve conflicts.

Reflection on the Journey

Recognizing red flags is not about condemning your partner but about understanding potential issues and addressing them constructively. It's about making wise, informed decisions to build a relationship based on mutual respect, trust, and love.

Ephesians 5:15-17 encourages us, "Be very careful, then, how you live — not as unwise but as wise, making the most of every opportunity, because the days are evil. Therefore do not be foolish, but understand what the Lord's will is."

Encouragement for Making Wise Decisions

Seeking God's Guidance
Making wise decisions in relationships involves seeking God's guidance and wisdom. James 1:5 says, "If any of you lacks wisdom, you should ask God, who gives generously to all without finding fault, and it will be given to you." Trusting in God's plan and seeking His direction can lead to healthier and more fulfilling relationships.

Embracing Courage and Wisdom
It takes courage to address red flags and make decisions that align with your values and goals. Proverbs 3:5-6 advises, "Trust in the Lord with all your heart and lean not on your own understanding; in all your ways submit to him, and he will make your paths straight." Embrace wisdom and courage in making choices that honor God and promote your well-being.

Building a Foundation of Love and Respect
A healthy relationship is built on a foundation of love, respect, and mutual support. 1 Corinthians 13:4-7 reminds us, "Love is patient, love is kind. It does not envy, it does not boast, it is not proud. It does not dishonor others, it is not self-seeking, it is not easily angered, it keeps no record of wrongs. Love does not delight in evil but rejoices with the truth. It always protects, always trusts, always hopes, always perseveres." Strive to build relationships that reflect these values.

Encouragement for the Journey
As you navigate the complexities of relationships, remember to seek God's wisdom and surround yourself with supportive friends and mentors. Philippians 4:6-7 encourages us, "Do not be anxious about anything, but in every situation, by prayer and petition, with thanksgiving, present your requests to God.

And the peace of God, which transcends all understanding, will guard your hearts and your minds in Christ Jesus." Trust in God's plan and take steps towards building healthy, loving relationships.

Reflection Questions
1. How can you apply the lessons learned about red flags to your current or future relationships?
2. In what ways can you seek God's guidance in making relationship decisions?
3. What steps can you take to build a foundation of love and respect in your relationships?
4. How can you support your partner in addressing and overcoming red flags?

Conclusion
Recognizing and addressing red flags is a vital part of building healthy, fulfilling relationships. By seeking God's guidance, embracing wisdom and courage, and fostering love and respect, you can make wise decisions that honor God and promote your well-being. Proverbs 4:7 reminds us, "The beginning of wisdom is this: Get wisdom. Though it cost all you have, get understanding." Strive to build relationships that reflect God's love and wisdom, seeking His guidance every step of the way.

Resources for Further Support

If you need further support or guidance in navigating relationships and addressing red flags, consider reaching out to the following resources:

- **Christian Counseling Services:** Seek professional counseling from a Christian perspective to address relationship issues.

- **Support Groups:** Join support groups within your church or community to share experiences and gain support.

- **Books and Articles:** Read books and articles on Christian relationships, conflict resolution, and personal growth.

- **Pastoral Counseling:** Seek guidance and counseling from your pastor or church leaders.

- **Prayer and Bible Study:** Regular prayer and Bible study can provide wisdom and strength in navigating relationship challenges.

If you have any questions or need further support, you can always reach me, at **standardwordz@gmail.com**. I am here to support you on your journey towards building healthy, fulfilling, and God-honoring relationships.

May God bless you and guide you in all your relationships.

Questions to Ask Before Marriage

Before committing to marriage, it's important to ask and discuss key questions to ensure alignment and mutual understanding in various aspects of life.

Personal and Character

1. What are your core values and beliefs?
2. How do you handle stress and conflict?
3. What are your views on honesty and trust in a relationship?
4. How do you feel about forgiveness and moving past conflicts?

Communication

5. How do you prefer to communicate about difficult topics?
6. How do you handle disagreements and arguments?
7. What are your expectations for communication frequency and style?
8. How do you feel about discussing feelings and emotions?

Financial

9. What are your financial goals and priorities?
10. How do you handle budgeting and financial planning?
11. Do you have any debt, and how do you plan to manage it?
12. What are your views on joint vs. separate finances?

Family and Relationships

13. What is your relationship with your family like?
14. How do you handle family conflicts and dynamics?
15. What are your expectations for family involvement in our lives?
16. How do you feel about integrating our families?

Lifestyle and Habits

17. What are your views on health and wellness?
18. How do you balance work and personal life?
19. What are your hobbies and interests, and how important are they to you?
20. How do you handle household responsibilities and chores?

Emotional and Mental Health

21. How do you manage stress and emotional well-being?
22. Have you ever sought professional help for mental health issues?
23. How do you feel about supporting each other's emotional needs?
24. What are your views on mental health and seeking help?

Compatibility and Values

25. What are your long-term life goals?
26. How do you feel about religious practices and spirituality?
27. What are your views on having and raising children?
28. How do you feel about political and social issues?

Future Plans and Expectations

29. What are your career goals and aspirations?
30. How do you envision our future together?
31. What are your expectations for marriage and commitment?
32. How do you feel about planning for the future together?

Conflict Resolution

33. How do you handle conflicts and disagreements?
34. What are your views on seeking help for relationship issues?
35. How do you feel about apologies and forgiveness?
36. How do you handle unresolved issues and grudges?

By discussing these questions openly and honestly, you can gain a deeper understanding of each other and ensure you are making a wise decision about your future together.

If you need further support or guidance, you can always reach me, at **standardwordz@gmail.com.** I am here to support you on your journey towards building healthy, fulfilling, and God-honoring relationships. May God bless you and guide you in all your relationships.

About the Author

Osoria Asibor is a prolific author and a servant of God, whose influence spans across various aspects of Christian living. With over two decades of focused study and experience, Osoria is a wellspring of knowledge and wisdom, guiding individuals through the intricate pathways of faith, relationships, and personal development.

As a seasoned Christian Counselor with more than a decade of practice, Osoria's insights are invaluable to those seeking to deepen their relationship with Jesus Christ. His commitment to spiritual mentorship is evident in every facet of his diversified work and ministry.

Professionally, Osoria is an accomplished entrepreneur with a sharp acumen for data analysis. He holds an MBA in Finance, demonstrating his ability to intertwine spiritual conviction with secular expertise. His achievements in both spiritual and professional realms showcase his unique ability to balance faith and practicality.

Osoria's contributions extend to various community programs and initiatives, reflecting his dedication to promoting spiritual and personal growth across diverse demographics. He is actively involved in mentoring and supporting individuals on their journey toward holistic development.

At the heart of Osoria's endeavors are family and faith—the foundational stones that guide his work. As a devoted husband and father, he embodies the Christian virtues he espouses, serving as a testament to the transformative impact of a life anchored in faith.

Osoria Asibor is an all-encompassing spiritual mentor. His writings are more than just books; they are pathways to profound spiritual awakening. His counsel extends beyond advice, serving as a catalyst for holistic growth. His entrepreneurial ventures are not merely businesses; they are practical demonstrations of Christian principles in everyday life.

Osoria stands as a beacon of hope, illuminating the way for those yearning for a closer, more profound communion with God. His legacy is etched in his words and deeds, providing a roadmap for anyone on the pilgrimage toward the divine.

Contact Information:
- **Email: standardwordz@gmail.com**
- **Website: www.standardwords.com**

www.ingramcontent.com/pod-product-compliance
Lightning Source LLC
Chambersburg PA
CBHW051330020726
47501CB00007B/1999